New Temptations

New Temptations

Kinky Companions 2

Alex Markson

This paperback edition 2020

First published by Parignon Press 2019

ISBN: 979 8 61 850230 6

Chapter 1 – Marcus

"Seriously?"

"Yes," Sally said. "That should be enough to find exactly what we want."

After we decided to find a home together, she sat me down and showed me the full extent of her father's legacy. She'd offered several times before, but I felt it was her business, not mine. Now things were different, and what I heard, shocked me. From what I already knew, I'd guessed at a sum in the hundreds of thousands. But it proved to be in the millions, and she proposed to spend a healthy chunk on a property.

"Well, if you're sure," I finally replied, my mind still racing through the figures. "We can consider almost anything for that price."

"Exactly. Now, what are we looking for?"

"Somewhere to love."

"Yes," she replied, rolling her eyes. "Stop being obtuse. What are our must-haves?"

We spent the afternoon talking it over. It wasn't difficult, as we both liked the same things. Our existing flats were similar; set in Georgian terraces, with lots of old features and a character which was lacking in newer properties. The only difference being she owned hers and mine was rented.

We made a list of things we liked but then crossed most of them off in case being too prescriptive led us to miss a hidden gem.

"We'll know it when we see it," Sally said.

"Yes, but you know what estate agents are like. They want to pigeonhole their properties and their clients. All they'll do is send us everything they've got on their books. Particularly the stuff they can't shift."

So it proved. We searched all the property websites over the weekend, and I spent Monday calling or visiting various agents. I made a few appointments to view and told them what we were looking for. None of those initial properties grabbed us, and within a week, my mailbox was full of details of unsuitable places. We waited.

Then I got a call from the smallest agent we'd seen. She had been asked to sell a flat which had been empty for over a year; a legal dispute over a will had finally been resolved, and the heirs were now able to offload it. We arranged to view it one evening after Sally finished work. I met her outside and we waited for the agent.

"It ticks the location box," Sally said.

She was right. It was on one end of an eighteenth-century terraced crescent, overlooking a sloping green with stunning views over the city. The crescent itself was famous but putting up with the occasional group of tourists taking pictures of your house was par for the course here. As we took in our surroundings, the agent appeared and led us into the communal atrium. We looked at each other and smiled; it was grand without being over the top.

"I did warn you the place hasn't been lived in for a while, didn't I?" The agent asked.

"Yes," I replied, "and that it's a bit sad."

She opened the front door and we followed her into the apartment. She was right; it was a mess. As we wandered around, we took it all in.

"You said it's being sold by executors?" Sally asked.

"Yes, that's right."

"It looks like the same person lived here for decades. Nothing's changed."

"All these patterns," I said. "I feel like I've entered a time warp."

The décor hadn't changed in forty years. Huge floral wallpaper in every room, clashing with vivid carpets, well past their best, with large stains dotted around. But as she showed us around, we kept looking at each other, both of us starting to smile.

It covered two floors; on the ground floor, there were two huge rooms and three smaller ones. All had high ceilings with elaborate plasterwork cornices, full-height windows at front and back and large period fireplaces. Downstairs was a bit of a warren. The house had clearly been converted at some point, and these would originally have been all the service rooms for the entire house. There were eight or nine of them, some quite small. The kitchen and bathroom were antiquated and would need complete replacement.

The small garden at the back was neglected and overgrown. The final surprise was along a corridor which ran the whole length of the external wall of the building; vaulted cellars which were a peculiarity of the area. But I'd never seen any like these.

"Where are we?" I asked the agent. "I thought this was the end wall, but the vaults go beyond them."

"They go out under the raised pavement." These were another feature of the city.

She led us through a door into a large garage. At some point, these vaults had been reversed; their interior walls blocked off. She opened one of the up-and-over doors, and we walked out onto the quiet road immediately outside; a park on the other side. We wandered back into the house while the agent locked the doors behind us. Sally slipped her arm into mine.

"What do you think?" I could see the excitement in her eyes.

"Needs a lot of work; it'll cost. And take time."

"Yes; but what do you think?"

"I reckon it's damn near perfect."

"Me too. Does it feel right for you?"

"Yes; apart from the smell."

It was damp; fusty. Too long empty. It needed some caring custodians.

The surveyor's report confirmed our assumptions; it needed re-wiring and re-plumbing. Gutting and starting again. But it was structurally fine. We'd already decided we wanted it. We talked about the asking price; knowing we'd have to spend a lot renovating it. In the end, we put in an offer; it was rejected. But the agent told us she'd only shown a few people around, and so far, we were the only ones who had offered. We raised it slightly; she reminded the sellers we were cash buyers and chain free. They accepted.

Then we hit a small snag.

When we went to instruct a solicitor, we had a bit of an argument when she asked us about ownership. Sally had already refused to let me put anything into the purchase, even though Mum had left me a bit. I was therefore adamant it should be in her name; it was her money. She wanted it in joint names. The solicitor tactfully asked us to let her know, and we dropped the subject. When we got home, she was angry with me for the first time I could remember.

"Marcus, this isn't going to work if you insist on being an ass."

"Sal, if we put it in joint names, you're effectively giving me the best part of a million."

"And ...?"

She was leaning against the kitchen worktop a few feet away, her arms crossed. Her face was slightly flushed, normally something that was a huge turn on, but this time was different.

"It's difficult for me," I said. I was mumbling a bit, feeling uncomfortable under the gaze of those deep green eyes. "I've never had anything like that sort of money."

"Well, now we have," she replied, putting heavy emphasis on the 'we'. She walked over to me. "Look. I've had all this money for years. You've helped me come to terms with it; I want to share it with you. Are we really going to fall out over this?"

Eventually, I made her promise to speak to her own solicitor. I wanted her to understand the consequences of effectively giving me half the property. In the end, Sally cheated. Her solicitor helped her. I would own a share of the property, which was bad enough, but Sally was also making a new will, leaving me the rest. I wasn't comfortable, but she insisted. I gave in.

Miraculously, everything went through smoothly, and we exchanged contracts four weeks later. We could now make plans. We knew there was too much work for us to do, so we needed to find someone to manage the project for us. One of Sally's colleagues recommended a guy they had used, and we liked Clive at the first meeting. The vendors were now happy to give us access, and we showed him around. After the tour, we stood in the largest room downstairs. Long ago, it had obviously been the kitchen for the whole house. One wall was essentially a giant fireplace with the crumbling remains of a massive iron range rusting away.

"This is a wonderful place," Clive said after some thought. We looked at him. "It's not been touched in years, particularly down here. Lots of possibilities."

We told him some of the ideas we'd had, and he gave us some of his own. He went away with photos and a copy of the surveyor's report.

Over the next couple of weeks, he compiled a plan; got estimates. When he came back to us, we finally had something concrete. He assured us it wasn't as complicated as we'd feared. About two month's work to make it habitable if he could get the people he needed at the right time.

We completed at the end of the month, and after collecting the keys, we rushed around to our new home. We let ourselves in and shut the door behind us. As I moved to go through the doorway into the main room, Sally pulled me back and threw her arms around me.

"This is our home now," she squealed and gave me a long kiss. I hugged her tight. We were both grinning as we separated. Hand in hand, we wandered around the place like excited children, going into every room, imagining what it had been and what it would become.

We brought two folding chairs with us, setting them up in the largest room. We simply sat there, looking around. Talking about décor; colours, carpets, furniture. We ordered a pizza; ate it. Still excited. Eventually, all the excitement got the better of us and we enjoyed each other on the floor; oblivious to the state of the place.

The next day, we went back; taking a small table, a kettle and a few supplies. Lots of paint charts. We were both creative people; it would be easy to agree on colours and textures. But after wandering around for two hours, we agreed on only one thing.

"It's no good," Sally said. "I can't see past all these colours and patterns."

"Nor can I. It's beginning to give me a headache."

"Do you think we can get Clive to strip it all out?"

Reluctantly, we left and waited for a cleaner canvas to paint. Clive saw to it; within a week, all the carpets were gone and within two weeks, three lads had stripped all the wallpaper.

By that time, he also had people working on the electrics and the plumbing, including a new boiler to take on the size of the place. The rest would have to wait until we'd reorganised the rooms. We were buzzing; still excited; making all sorts of plans and changing them the next day. What would we keep from our own flats? What would we need to buy new?

Our relationship intensified; we spent every night together in one place or another. We talked all evening about our plans; looking at brochures, catalogues, websites. Kitchens, bathrooms, fittings, carpets. We were like kids in a sweetshop. But when we finished each night, what followed was strictly for grown-ups.

I visited the flat almost every day. Not to check on the work, but to see it taking shape. Now bare-floored and bare-walled, it was much easier to visualise the finished article; to put our ideas over the template. We soon realised we needed mostly new furniture. What we had would be far too small to do the place justice; we'd need some statement pieces to fill the space.

Shortly before the May bank holiday, the first stage was complete. Electrics and plumbing mostly sorted. Some building work had begun knocking rooms together downstairs, and the next week would see work begin on the new kitchen.

As I left, I went around making sure everything was off, and the windows and doors secure. Ending in the main room, I looked around. Bare floorboards, bare patchy walls, naked light bulb hanging from the ceiling. An idea surfaced in my head. I spoke a few random words aloud; they echoed eerily around the room. Nothing to absorb them, to soften them. The idea evolved as I drove home.

Chapter 2 – Sally

It was the Friday before a bank holiday weekend and happened to be our first anniversary. At least, that's what we called it. One year since I'd first laid over his knees and experienced the intense pleasure I got from pain. We hadn't planned anything, but we wanted to do something memorable. I think we both had some ideas but left it to see what developed.

The flat was progressing well. We were both still so excited; loved wandering around, placing imaginary furniture, and some of our prized things. We'd found a designer, Annabelle, and were working with her to sort out colours, carpets and curtains. When the next round of work was completed, we were planning to move in and do the rest afterwards. It wasn't finished, but we'd have the essentials done.

I only remembered his earlier message as I walked out through the main entrance.

[TEXT ME WHEN YOU LEAVE WORK]

I sent a quick reply.

[LEAVING NOW]

I went to the car park and found my car. Before I'd moved, he responded.

[GO TO THE FLAT]

I wound my way through the Friday night traffic, hoping we hadn't hit a snag. Finding a space a few doors away – the garages weren't useable yet – I walked to the house. The front shutters were closed, which was unusual; it made it dark inside. I crossed the communal atrium to our front door.

Opening it, I found our hall in darkness; all the doors closed. I switched the light on and saw a box on the floor, tied with a bow. I put my bag down, closed the door, and picked it up. I called out Marcus's name, but there was no reply. Slipping off the bow, I opened the box to find a folded note. Lifting it out, I saw tissue paper underneath. The note was brief.

Put these on …
Squeak once …
Wait …

A shot of adrenaline ran through me; what was he doing? I pondered the question for all of five seconds before lifting the tissue, revealing a blindfold, a gag and my squeaker. This was getting interesting. The blindfold was new. More substantial than the ones we had already used, which had a habit of slipping off. All sorts of images flashed through my mind.

The gag was new as well. We'd used a ball-gag a few times, but I found it uncomfortable after a while. This one had a padded leather bit to bite on, so I placed it between my teeth and tightened the strap to a comfortable position. The blindfold went on; soft but close-fitting.

I couldn't see anything at all. I picked up the squeaker, placing the elastic over three fingers so it was snuggly in my palm. I stood still. My heart was beating faster; brief shivers of anticipation making my muscles twitch. I loved it when he planned something like this. They were always mind-blowing experiences. His imagination seemed endless. Squeezing my hand over the squeaker, I heard the sound resonating in the enclosed space.

Nothing happened. Silence. I stood in anticipation, not knowing what to expect. I could feel the throb of my heartbeat and became aware of my shallow breathing. I tried to control it, taking slow and steady breaths to bring myself into the present. I heard the door behind me open and close. The latch was thrown. I stayed still; waiting; ready.

I could sense him moving towards me with slow steps. I swallowed, willing myself to relax. God, I loved him. I jumped as his breath caressed the back of my neck, followed by a gentle kiss. His hand touched the back of my knee, causing my leg to buckle and it slowly moved under my dress. As it reached my bum, it flowed over it from cheek to cheek, gently squeezing. My body rippled at the touch.

He withdrew his hand, and checked the blindfold and gag, tightening both to his satisfaction. He moved past me and opened a door. Taking my hand, he led me forwards, stopping after a dozen steps or so. I stood still. I could hear his footsteps on the bare floorboards, followed by the door closing again. More steps, echoing around the room; sounds of material moving. Clothes being removed? I couldn't tell, but the image stuck in my brain and made me smile.

He undid the buttons down the back of my dress, slid it off my shoulders and it fell to the floor. Another kiss on my neck and he put a hand under each arm, raising them until I was holding them out to either side. He let go, but I knew I had to keep them there.

I heard a metallic clink, as a cuff was wrapped around my left wrist, tightening as he did it up. Another attached to my right wrist, followed shortly after by one on each ankle. He lifted each foot and removed my shoes. I shuddered as he kissed one thigh; a few light touches, before shifting to the other. I widened my stance; hopeful he'd go further.

But he stopped. Bringing my hands together, he joined the cuffs and lifted them above my head. I felt his hand between my legs; it made me gasp. He pulled up slightly as if lifting me, and my body rose at the pressure. My fingers found a short bar, and I folded them over it, grabbing it as best I could. I heard a click, and knew I was now stuck; trapped. I moved my hands but couldn't go far; they were attached to the bar. It was a bit of a stretch; my arms tight above me, my feet just able to sit flat on the floor.

I couldn't work out where I was. I wasn't against a wall; I seemed to be in an open space. But what was I attached to? I gave up thinking about it; I was already giving in to the moment. I heard his steps; soft now, bare feet. My mind was still; waiting. What would happen next?

Out of nowhere, sound echoed around the room; a car, driving fast on gravel. What? I tried to make sense of it. The car stopped; footsteps, mumbling, whimpers, a struggle. More footsteps, a door slamming, a heavy thud. My mind dragged a memory from its depths. The film; the abduction film on the DVD he'd made for me months ago. Since then, I'd watched it a few times when I'd been on my own; it always worked for me. Always got me hot and I'd made the mistake of telling him.

I tried to remember the sequence; what happened next. I heard a ripping sound and jumped as a hand landed on my shoulder. A snipping sound; he was cutting my bra off. Three cuts and it was gone; my breasts released, my nipples already hard.

He grabbed my hipsters; roughly cutting each side. He grabbed the front and back, and pulled them, digging between my legs and bum as he slid them slowly backwards and forwards. Rubbing into my sex, sensations flashing through me; wet. As he pulled, I had no choice but to rise on tiptoe, using my arms to lift the weight of my body. Finally, he pulled the material roughly from between my legs, allowing me to drop again.

I was conscious of the DVD again; sounds of impact and muffled cries. One of his hands rubbed my tummy, the other grabbed my bum. I stuck it out to meet him and wobbled as the first stroke landed, followed by another. No slow build-up; he spanked me, firm and fast. Not hard, but enough to make me squirm. My moans stifled by the gag; the sounds dying in my throat. I allowed my body to move as it wanted. I was suspended, so couldn't fall. I gave in to it and let myself twist and turn under the onslaught.

He stopped and stroked my stinging cheeks. Turning me, he pushed behind me. His cock pushed between my legs as he pulled me back towards him. His hand reached around and pushed his cock firmly against my pussy. Lifting his hips, he used the shaft to rub across my entrance, the tip sliding across my clit. I moaned; I wanted him to take me. I wanted him to fuck me; suspended there, helpless.

But I knew he wouldn't. I sensed him move around in front of me and yelped as a peg bit into my breast; then another, and another. Each one biting as he placed them in a row along what overhang I had. Finally, he placed one on each nipple; burning for a few seconds before settling to a dull ache. The girl was louder now; sounds of a stronger impact on her body. A whip? I couldn't remember; wasn't sure where we were in the film. I didn't really care.

A sharp breath flew out of me as the flogger chased across my back; not hard, but I hadn't been ready of it. Now I was, as it brushed me again and again. He was teasing for now; hard enough to swing nicely, but not painful. He carried on; regular strokes across my back. He spun me around and started on my breasts and tummy. Each stroke drew a soft gasp from me, the touch of the fronds exciting me. Except for the times they hit a peg, making it move against my pinched skin, causing a brief jolt of pain. My tummy flinching as the strands dragged across it. Being turned again, and feeling it strike the back of my thighs; a little harder now, but I stuck my bum out, wanting the impact there.

It came; he moved up, changed gear. Regular, stronger strokes across both cheeks. Heavier now; making me pant; making me groan. My body eager for the intense flashes racing to my brain. He turned me again, using more powerful strokes across my front. I yelped as the occasional peg flew off, or the odd frond caught my sex. Between the strikes, I was vaguely aware of the sounds of impact bouncing off the bare walls and floors; those echoes mingling together.

Turned again, to deliver more to my back. I was twisted forward now, on tiptoe, carrying most of my weight on my hands; bent at the hip as far as my restraint would allow; spreading my legs as much as I could. Seeking the pain. Groaning as his fingers landed between my legs, invading me, his thumb pushing at my ass. He roughly fucked me as I squirmed on his hand. I pushed towards him, wanting it; wanting him to make me come; needing it.

I let out a deep moan of frustration as his hand pulled away. It was quickly replaced by a muffled cry as a wand pushed hard against me. I tried to close my legs around it; needing it. But he pushed my legs apart, and pulled an ankle back, almost making me lose my footing. I was near now; trying to breathe around the gag, my body trembling. And he removed the wand. I let my head drop and did my best to utter a plea. The only response was a deep chuckle.

The vibrations hit me again and this time the wand was going full throttle. My legs came off the floor, and I swung from my hands; he followed, keeping the contact. His hand swept across my breasts several times, ripping pegs off as it passed, causing a whole new series of shooting pains. Just short of my climax, he stopped again, and I stamped my feet back on the floor in frustration.

Behind me now, he separated my legs as far as they would go. The wand touched and pushed firmly at my entrance; I dropped as far as I could. I cried out as the flogger came down vertically on my bum; time after time. I came hard; my body convulsing. The cries still muffled in my throat. I let all my weight hang from my wrists, giving way to my pleasure. As I slipped past the peak, he stopped the strikes and lowered the wand. I let my body droop; gasping for air, made much harder by the gag. Needing to recover.

But he didn't let me. He pushed my feet forward and fumbled with my wrists, and they dropped. The muscles in my arms suddenly ached, now released from their position. He pulled me a few steps, and my shaking legs touched something. I sensed him drop behind me and move my right leg, clipping the ankle cuff to something. My legs were spread as my left leg was restrained as well. He uncoupled my wrists and bent me forward; my tummy landing on a firm surface with a soft covering.

He pulled my arms out in front of me and fastened them in place. Not tight, but I couldn't move them far. I cautiously lowered my head but didn't reach anything. Whatever I was tied down on, my head was over the edge. He walked past me, running his hand from the back of my head, all along my back, over my bum, ending by gently rubbing his fingers between my spread legs. I moaned at his touch, pushing my hips to meet him. He pulled away, and I slumped back.

In the silence, I heard the girl's voice again. Much louder now; cries at every stroke. His hand ran through my hair, and I screwed up my eyes as he slid the blindfold to my forehead. Adjusting to the light, I couldn't see him. Just me; reflected in a mirror only a few feet in front of me; along with the film playing on his iPad resting against it.

I didn't know which to look at; the film was a bit small from this distance, so I looked at myself. Flushed, breathing hard; strapped down over something I couldn't see under a blanket. A gag in my mouth, a blindfold on my forehead and my hair all over the place. And loving every minute.

I looked back at the film; one of the men was now holding a cane. An implement we hadn't yet tried. A sudden expectation ran through me. Marcus appeared and squatted in front of me. He smiled, and I did my best to smile back through the gag. He kissed my forehead and both cheeks. Reaching beneath me, he slowly raised his hand to show me what he was holding. A rattan cane. About three feet long.

He held it in front of me and raised an eyebrow; I nodded vigorously. He stood, allowing his cock to stray a few inches from my face, and laid the cane on my back. He moved to my side, and I watched in the mirror as he leaned over me and undid the gag, letting it fall to the ground. I took some deep breaths and cleared my throat. He leaned down further, placing his mouth by my ear.

"I want to hear your cries," he whispered.

The first words spoken since we'd arrived; I didn't reply but held his gaze in the mirror. He picked up the cane from my back and moved behind me. I could only see the edge of his body in the mirror; his cock protruding into view at times. A weird but beguiling image.

The tip of the cane touched my cheek; resting against it. One moment lightly tapping it, moving around; letting me know it was there. Then flatter; again, tapping against my skin; no pain, just a touch. Getting firmer; a slight sting when it hit the glow from my earlier punishment. Gradually building; still only taps, nothing strong, nothing meaningful. But building my expectation; giving me an idea of the way a cane felt. Different to anything we'd used; narrow, precise, concentrated.

He stopped; leaving the cane pressing into my bum. As he lifted it away, I held my breath in anticipation of the first real stroke; trying to see what was happening in the mirror. But he was out of sight. Bastard; he knew. Eventually, I had to breathe, and as I did, he brought it down across my bare cheeks.

I flinched at the impact. Trying to attune my mind to the sensation. Another stroke came, and another. Not hard, but enough to sting; enough to send a jolt through my body every time. I wanted to raise my legs to lessen the taut skin over my bum, but the restraints prevented me. I could hear the cane through the air each time, followed by the crack of the cane meeting my soft flesh; heard the sound almost before I felt it. Several strokes in a row; no time to relax between them. My body arching; my grunts turning into a continuous moan. A pause; a few more strokes, then a hand stroking my cheeks.

I could see him now, watching me in the mirror. I nodded my head. He stood back and I heard the cane swish in the air several times. He placed it against my skin, tapped it two or three times, and struck. But much harder this time; I cried out at the impact and hissed as the pain changed to an intense sting. I wriggled my bum, trying to get some relief. It didn't help.

He left the cane resting against me. As I settled, it came down again; pain followed by a sharp sting, spreading from a single line out across my bum. He patted the cane on my skin again. Another stroke; another cry. My head jerking from the intensity; my body struggling to escape my restraint. Another stroke. Tears welled in my eyes. Another stroke. I was whimpering now in between the cries. Then another stroke; hardest of all. My scream echoed eerily around the room.

A hand touched my bum and gently stroked it. The touch was a mix of pain and pleasure. My bum was stinging; really stinging. But it was hot; throbbing. The throbbing was spreading, and he moved between my legs. His touch made me jump; I could feel the moisture oozing from me as he fingered me. Immediately groaning as he slowly stroked my lips and clit. I was so needy; wanted to come again. He knew; he stopped.

Squatting in front of me, he kissed me. I responded as strongly as I could. He saw my tears and wiped one away with the back of a finger. When he raised a questioning eyebrow, I nodded.

"Yes," I gasped. "Oh, God. Yes."

He stood slowly; his hard cock was a few inches from my face. Bunching my hair, he pulled it, lifting my head, and I opened my mouth to let him in. My lips clamped around his shaft and I closed my eyes. He slid slowly in and out. But I'd forgotten he still had the cane in his hand. My cry as he brought it down vertically across one cheek was muffled by his cock; my body wriggled with the pain.

Before it subsided, he repeated it on the other cheek; the tears came again. I felt myself calming; the emotion draining from me as they ran down my face. I was floating to a different place. I concentrated on his cock; relishing the heat, the texture. His hands rested on my back and slid heavily along it, ending by giving me a couple of slaps on each cheek. The different feeling made me want to giggle; it came out as a gurgle. He pulled out of my mouth and squatted in front of me; kissing me. I grinned through my tears.

Standing, he undid my wrist cuffs, and moving to my rear, unclipped those on my ankles as well. I went to stand, but he stopped me. I turned my head to look at him.

"Fuck me. Please …"

"I'm going to; we're going to."

A flash of panic went through me. I looked at him in the mirror; he went out of view briefly. When he returned, he dropped something behind me. I tried to see what it was. A round cushion; low. With a big dildo sticking straight up from it. He pulled my hips, and I allowed him to slide me back. He quickly adjusted the cushion, and I slid straight over the rubber shaft, gasping as it filled me. He leaned against whatever I'd been tied to and pulled my head onto his cock again.

This time I was free, so grabbed it eagerly and moved against the dildo, trying to press my clit against the cushion. I could just rub it on the surface, and I immediately started to build. He let me control this orgasm. I looked up at him, a smile on his face; watching me fuck myself. I rocked myself on the dildo, pushing my clit backwards and forwards and closed my eyes. I sucked him voraciously and imagined the cock I was riding was real. I came; strong, hard, intense. Holding his stiffness deep in my mouth.

Still high, I was suddenly aware of movement; being turned, pushed forward, still impaled on the dildo. I was still coming down from my orgasm. He was behind me and I felt a sudden coldness between my cheeks before his cock pushed into my ass. Stretching it. I was gone; throwing my arms out on the floor in front of me. Pussy and ass full; ecstasy. I was still reeling from the first climax, and now rising above it. I heard his grunts as he drove himself deep into me; slowing to change the angle, then hard again.

His thrusting lifting me up and down on the dildo; being double-fucked. His body slamming against the cane welts on my cheeks. I let go. Screams, squeals, tears, pain, pleasure. All echoing around the room, as I went over the edge again. Almost in my special place; time seemed to slow as my body demanded time to deal with all the sensations assaulting it. I was conscious of him slowing as my orgasm receded.

He pulled out of me, and rolled me over, coming to straddle my chest. I stared as he stroked himself, finally grunting as he came heavily over me. I watched his cock as his cum shot out. I felt the warmth landing on my face, on my open lips, on my hair. I lifted my head to lick him, but he moved it away and shook his head. Staring into his eyes, I used my fingers to wipe it from my face, licking them clean. He bent to kiss me.

"I love you," we said simultaneously, and grinned. Both too breathless to say anything else.

As we lay together, I looked around. He'd been busy; using a few of the workmen's tools for our adventure. A big metal clamp above the archway between the two rooms to hold me up, and a workbench to tie me over. Would they ever guess what their equipment had been used for? Fortunately, we hadn't yet decided where to put the new bathrooms, so the old one had been re-plumbed for now. We had a quick shower and returned upstairs. I asked if he had any more plans for the evening.

"That depends how you're feeling," he grinned. I had been well and truly fucked but was still ready for more. I told him so; though I might want to concentrate on pleasure rather than any more pain tonight.

"How about we call in a takeaway; have a rest."

I liked the idea. While we waited, we examined my marks; peg marks on my breasts; redness on my back, tummy and thighs. My bum was red all over. With several darker lines and six clear welts across it; slightly raised.

"Proud of those?" I asked.

"Are you?"

"Oh, yes. Been wanting those for ages."

"Then so am I."

"Good, 'cos I'm going to want more."

I kissed him, and we hugged. Interrupted by the doorbell, Marcus had to throw his trousers and shirt on to go and answer it. As we ate, I told him how the cane had felt; tried to describe the mix of sensations. How the lighter strokes differed from the heavier ones. I couldn't find the right words, but I think he got the idea.

He told me how the idea had come to him and how he'd tried to stick closely to the film, matching the action as best as he could. Even down to copying the porn essential of coming over me; the money shot.

After we'd eaten, he rubbed some moisturiser into my bum, and we lay in each other's arms on the blanket. Quiet companionship. Only naked.

"So," I asked, nearly recovered. "What's next?"

"Well, how about you take control for the rest of the evening? Tie me up if you want. Give me a good thrashing."

I looked at him, thinking. Unsure. We hadn't done that since I'd hurt him, and we were both aware of it. He'd suggested it a couple of times; to 'exorcise the ghost', as he put it, if nothing else. And I knew what he meant. I hadn't been ready; it scared me.

But tonight? I still enjoyed taking control during sex; he loved it too. But pain had returned to being one way. He was the giver and I was the receiver; that's what got us both off. It was what had brought us together. The other way was less of an attraction for both of us. He watched me as I thought this through; smiling, stroking my arm.

"Do you want to?" he asked.

"Yes," I finally said. "I do."

By the end of the evening, he'd been tied over the workbench, spanked and flogged. Not hard, but his bum was pink. I'd got rid of that monkey, and enjoyed it; so had he. I'd used him; laid him on the floor, ridden his face; ridden his cock, both to a beautiful orgasm.

Later, he sat on the floor in front of the mirror, and I lowered myself back onto him. We rocked slowly, enjoying the small movements of him inside me, using our fingers to caress and play with each other. All the time watching ourselves in the mirror. It was incredibly erotic seeing our intimacy reflected. Gradually, we quickened the pace and came almost together. Gently, lovingly. Him holding me tight as we came down.

When he slipped out of me, I turned to kiss him.

"Happy Anniversary."

The next day my bum was tender. Whenever I sat down, I got a reminder of the punishment it had received. But it brought a smile to my face every time. The rest of the weekend was much slower. We enjoyed each other; teased and tempted.

We were both pleasantly surprised by how quickly the welts disappeared.

"I'm glad I got it right," he said, after inspecting my bum.

"Well, they've gone quicker than I thought they would. You'll need to be firmer next time."

"Mmm. Or give you more strokes."

"How about both?"

Chapter 3 – Lucy

I woke with a start. Instantly awake. And slumped back, realising what had woken me. Ailsa had been to the bathroom. I watched as she climbed back into bed.

"Good morning," she whispered.

"Hello," I murmured.

She slid over and cuddled up to me, and I put my arm around her. It was early yet, but I couldn't get back to sleep. I lay there, thinking.

Ailsa and I had only met a few weeks ago. A chance meeting; mutual attraction and into bed. It was fine, but I knew it wouldn't last. It never seemed to these days. My last few lovers had all been mismatches. With some, the sex had been great, but we'd had little else in common. They were fine for a while. But as we spent more time together, I got bored with their company.

With others, we'd had similar passions, similar interests. Spending time with them had been easy. Lots to do, lots to talk about. But they'd turned out to be hopeless lovers. I'd had my fair share of pillow princesses, too. Was it too much to ask to find both in the same person? Someone who was interesting and who was heaven in bed.

I'd found it a few times in the past. But even then, none of them had lasted more than a year or two. Why? I'd asked myself so many times but never found an answer. Was I asking too much? Would I have to lower my expectations? Perhaps it was me; was there something wrong with me?

I was thirty-seven. Most of my contemporaries had found what they wanted. Many of them were on their second or third life partner. I hadn't even found my first. Many had children, stepchildren, dogs, cats, hamsters. God, even Sally seemed to have found her soulmate. She and Marcus got on so well, and from what little Sally had said, it sounded as if the sex was great too.

I didn't need a partner to feel fulfilled; that was old-fashioned nonsense. My life was great; a career I loved, a small circle of friends. I was happy. But I wouldn't mind finding someone to share those things with, in addition to some mind-blowing sex.

I occasionally thought back to what Marcus had said to me. He couldn't help Sally with all her fantasies, as they didn't all involve men. Did that mean what I thought it meant? Had I missed something? I'd be surprised. When we'd first met all those years ago at uni, I'd made a pass at her. I made a pass at every woman I met back then, as well as a few boys before I gave them up for good. She'd politely declined. But we got on well from the start and had been best friends ever since.

I'd never considered her in any other way. True, we'd shared a few fitting rooms and hotel bedrooms, where neither of us had been shy of stripping off in front of the other. I'd glanced at her body; who wouldn't? She had a great body; sensuous, curvy, graceful. She'd appeared in my dreams more than once, but I'd never thought of it as more than fantasy.

I became aware of a low moaning. Coming out of my reverie, I realised it was Ailsa. I had my fingers between her legs and was stroking her firmly. Her leg had come back over mine, and she was enjoying my actions. Ah, well. Might as well have some fun.

After Ailsa left, I thought about what had happened. Had I started playing with Ailsa whilst fantasising about Sally? Thinking about it, there was no doubt about it. That wouldn't do at all; it could get tricky. She was happy with Marcus. I needed to find my own Marcus; only without a cock.

Sal and I met later at the gym. We'd got back into a routine, going two or three times a week and surprised ourselves by enjoying it. Over the years, we'd gone through several abortive fitness drives. But neither of us took it seriously. We'd join a gym, go a few times, then get distracted by something else, and it would peter out.

This time, we were sticking to it. Not only did it make us feel good, but we were also meeting more often because of it, spending time together like we had in the past. The gym had its attractions as well; people-watching. We used one of the university gyms, so the age range was wide, but the majority of users were students.

From the vain ones who always seemed to spend more time admiring themselves in the mirrors than working out, to the ones who avoided eye contact at all costs. We saw a few who might well appear in the odd fantasy or two. It probably wasn't appropriate for two members of staff, but it was only fantasy. I concentrated on the girls, with Sal watching the guys. We compared notes and gave a few regulars nicknames; some less flattering than others.

This particular evening, Sal had some news.

"We're getting the new library," she said almost as soon as we met, nearly dancing with joy as she told me.

"It's about time. David must be relieved." David was the Head Librarian and nominally, Sally's boss.

"He's been running around all day like a schoolboy."

"When does work start?"

"During the summer break. The site's been ready for ages and the plans are all signed off. We've been waiting for the Board to authorise the money."

"I'm surprised they've made a decision."

"I know. I'm not sure how David managed it, it's been dragging on for years."

"Will you be involved?"

"Not directly, but we've decided to do a complete audit of the whole archive before we transfer everything. Nobody can remember when it was last done."

"Sounds right up your street."

"I can't wait."

***

My sister called me later in the week. I knew there must be a problem; she never rang.

"Hi, Annie."

"Hi, Lucy. I'm afraid I've got something I need to tell you."

"What's up?"

"Dad's ill."

"What's the problem?"

"He's had a stroke."

"Bad?"

"Yes. Largely immobile and can't really speak."

This was one of my nightmares. I was estranged from my parents. They were very religious with an unbending faith and a blinkered intolerance. From an early age, I'd fought against it to no avail. I wasn't surprised when they sent me packing after I came out. But it had still hurt. I hadn't had any contact with my father since; the occasional card or brief note from my mother. I had been in touch with Annie sporadically over the years, and our contact had gradually increased in recent years.

"When did this happen?"

There was a brief pause. "Four days ago."

"And Mum didn't want me to know."

"No. But I convinced her I should tell you. She doesn't want you to visit Dad, though."

"Don't worry. I don't expect we'd even recognise each other." Silence at the other end. "Sorry, Annie. I didn't mean to sound bitter."

"It's all right. I understand what you mean. If anything changes, I promise I'll let you know."

"Thanks, Annie. How are Tim and the kids?"

"Oh, they're okay. They don't see so much of Mum and Dad nowadays, anyway."

After the call, I pondered that statement. When they surprised me by inviting me to spend last Christmas Day with them, I got the impression Annie had started freeing herself from our parents. This seemed to back it up. But she and I weren't close enough for me to ask the question.

Ailsa turned up after work. Annie's call had made me brood over things I normally tried to ignore, and I wasn't in the right mood. Ailsa didn't sense that at all, and we had our first row. It turned out to be our last as well, as she stormed out, after a few choice words from both of us.

Oh, well. I was celibate again.

Chapter 4 – Marcus

Sally was still seeing her counsellor, Jenny. From my viewpoint, she seemed to be doing well. She was able to talk freely about her father now. She sometimes mentioned her sister Charlie, and even Wendy, the painted stepmother, along with everything else she had kept hidden inside. It didn't seem to bother her, and I was confident enough to mention them without her starting the conversation.

On one of her visits, Mary had told me how pleased she was Sal was coming to terms with the past. I could tell she meant it. But I didn't know if she knew I was aware of her affair with Tony, so I had to be careful.

"How are you getting on?" I asked Sal after one of her sessions with Jenny.

"I think I'm nearly done. I've not had any bad thoughts for ages."

"Anything else you need to do?"

She looked at me, a thoughtful look on her face. She took the glass of wine I proffered and sat beside me.

"I'd like to find out more about Dad. I know next to nothing about him. I don't know where he came from or what he did. And God knows where he got his money. It used to be so painful to think about those questions. Now I'm just intrigued."

"But what if you don't like the answers?"

"Jenny and I have been talking about that."

"What does she think?"

"Oh, you know how it works. She doesn't give an opinion. But she understands my interest and asked the same question as you."

"What are you going to do?"

"I would like to look into it. But even as someone used to finding answers in old records, I'm not sure where to start. I don't have many of Dad's documents. Only his death certificate, his will, and stuff to do with the money. No birth certificate, no passport, nothing."

"Not even a wedding certificate?"

"No. I've always wondered about that. But Mary assures me they were married. She was a bridesmaid."

"Did you get anything from the solicitors who did all the work when he died?"

"Only what I've got, It's not much."

"It's a long shot, but why not contact them to ask if they've got anything else?"

"Oh, Marcus. It was nearly twenty years ago. I can't imagine them having anything. They may not even exist anymore."

"No. But if you don't ask, you'll never know. If they haven't, at least you can cross it off the list."

"What list?"

"The to-do list you've already begun for this project."

She frowned at me and laughed.

"I can't keep much from you, can I?"

"Whatever you want, I don't go sneaking. But I guessed you might want to start this search at some point."

She sighed. "Yea. I guess I knew I would too."

"Anything I can do to help; you know I will."

"I do. And I think I may need it. At least, your support. Particularly if I find he was dodgy. It's the only thing that worries me. I don't care where he came from, but if he was involved in anything horrible …"

***

"How was your day?" I asked Sally when she got home one day.

"Oh, fine. I had an interesting phone call from Bellows."

"Bellows?"

"The solicitors who took over the firm Dad used."

"Oh, yes. Sorry. Why interesting?"

"Give them their due, they seem to have had a good ferret around. They didn't come across any documents. Hardly had any record of him as a client. But they do have something."

She paused. I knew she was waiting for me to ask.

"Which is …?"

"A safety deposit box."

"What?"

"An old-fashioned safety deposit box."

"How come you weren't given it twenty years ago?"

"They aren't sure; they're going to investigate."

"Are they going to send it to you?"

"It's not that simple. I'll need to prove it should come to me."

"How?"

"They're going to look into that, as well."

"So, as usual with your father, we have more questions than answers."

"Yup. That's my Dad."

***

Three weeks later, we found ourselves driving north to collect a long-forgotten safety deposit box. Sally was quiet for most of the journey, and I understood why. Yes, she was curious about the box, but it was also the first time in years she'd returned to her hometown. The memories would be flooding back, and they wouldn't all be happy.

We'd decided we wouldn't rush, so had booked a hotel for a couple of nights. The first night, we found a little restaurant close-by and had a relaxing evening. Ready for the big day.

When we arrived at Bellows, we were ushered into an office. The box was sitting ominously on the table, in front of the solicitor Sally had been talking to. It was about two and a half feet long, a foot wide, and nine inches high. Green metal, with well-worn marks where it would have slid in and out of its slot.

"Good morning, Miss Fletcher. I'm Charles Bellow."

"Hello, Mr Bellow. This is Marcus Foxton, my partner."

We all shook hands, and he offered us a seat.

"Well, this is the article in question. It's been something of a mystery, but we do now have some answers."

"Oh, good."

"It turns out we haven't had it long; about four years. We were contacted by Nat West when they closed their deposit box facility. Obviously, your father had passed away some time before, but the alternative contact they had was our predecessor. So, they handed it over to us. I'm afraid we had no way of finding you, so it was stored in our basement."

"Oh, there's no need for an apology, Mr Bellow. I never dreamed you would need to find me."

"Quite."

"What happens now?"

"Well, the box still technically forms part of your late father's estate. Provided you can prove to me you're his heir, I can release it to you."

"I've brought a few things which I hope will help. Are you aware of the circumstances surrounding my father's death?"

"No, I'm afraid I'm not."

Sally briefly recounted the tragic event, and Mr Bellow seemed genuinely saddened. But he was a solicitor; ham-acting was part of the job.

"I have his will," Sally went on, "as well as the probate forms and several proofs of my identity because I haven't used my father's name for years. I use my mother's maiden name. But I do have my original birth certificate."

I sat silent, watching the proceedings. Mr Bellow was efficient and formal. I think he wanted to get rid of the thing. Sally also had her official face on. She was sitting forward on her chair, and I noticed her foot tapping on the floor occasionally. I knew there would be some tension building under the surface. On top of the emotion, she would be thinking what Mr Bellow and I were thinking. What's in the box?

After all the relevant documents had been copied and annotated, Mr Bellow asked Sally to sign a receipt for the box. She went to sign the form and stopped.

"Using which name?"

Mr Bellow thought for a few seconds.

"Your current name will suffice. After all, people change their names all the time. I'm satisfied you are Anthony Crowther's daughter and heir. That's enough for me."

She signed the paper and slid it back.

"It's all yours," he said, waving his hand over the box. "I'm afraid there is no key. But any competent locksmith should be able to open it."

"Yes, and will want to know why he's breaking into a safety deposit box."

I picked it up. It wasn't as heavy as it looked, but there were things inside moving about. We thanked Mr Bellow and walked back to the car. Sally was still very quiet. I hoped that innocent-looking object I put in the boot wasn't going to open any more old wounds.

"What now?" I asked. I could see she was wrestling with something.

"I want to drive around a few places," she finally said. "I want to show you where I grew up."

"Just to show me?"

She turned sharply; then shrugged.

"No. I need to see them too."

I drove, she directed me. We visited her first school; still on the same site but totally rebuilt. One or two pubs where she first went drinking; hardly recognisable. Then on to the house itself. A leafy, prosperous area. Large, detached houses on generous plots. Their gardens landscaped with the occasional tennis court or swimming pool. Two or three expensive cars on every drive.

"Slow down … there it is."

She pointed at one of the houses, and I pulled in on the other side of the road. It was largely as I had imagined it. An Edwardian townhouse probably built for a prominent local man; well back from the road. Large and imposing without being over-powering.

"Has it changed?"

"Not much. The garden's been re-designed, but the house is more or less the same. New windows and new garages, though."

I turned off the engine and waited. After several minutes, she turned towards me; her eyes damp.

"I never wanted to come back here."

She looked back at the house.
"But I needed to. Thank you."
"What for?"
"For coming with me. We can go now."
She guided me around a few more former haunts. Some were still there but others had vanished. After we left the house, she became more cheerful. Telling me stories about things she had done in the places she showed me. By the time we returned to the hotel, she was nearly her normal self.
"What shall we do tonight?"
"Let's see if someone can recommend a good restaurant."
The hotel gave us two or three recommendations, and we had a quick check online before choosing one. We showered and changed before going out. Sally teased me by slowing putting her underwear on in front of me. I hadn't noticed she'd packed anything special, but she had.
"Just so you spend all evening thinking about what I'm wearing."
"I could always rip it off now."
"Oh, Marcus. That would spoil the anticipation."
We decided to walk, as it was only a few streets away, and it was a lovely evening. The restaurant proved to be perfect. Relaxed but efficient; good food, great service. We talked about anything and nothing. Sally was still in a reminiscing mood, and we regaled each other with adventures of our youth.
When we left, we walked slowly back towards our hotel, hand in hand. One of the streets was home to several pubs and clubs. It was only about half-past nine, so still quiet, but groups were milling about and arguing about where to go. We watched them as we ambled by.
"Do they make you feel old?" Sal asked.
"Old? Positively ancient."
We reached the end of the street, and as we crossed the road, Sally pulled me to a halt.
"There's a lap-dancing club," she said, looking up a side-street.
"So I see. They're quite common, I believe."
"Ever been to one?"
"Nope."
"Me neither. Let's go in."
"Are you serious?"

She turned to look at me. I recognised the look on her face. A mixture of mischief and curiosity, with an added dash of alcohol and lust. She came right up to me and kissed me. Her face now one of innocent seduction.

"I dare you to take me in."

Chapter 5 – Marcus

I couldn't resist the challenge. We walked towards the entrance, where a large bouncer was trying to look inconspicuous.

"Good evening. Is it busy?"

He looked us quickly up and down with a professional glance.

"No, sir. Not yet. Still plenty of room."

"Can we come in, or do we need to book?"

"I think you'll be welcome." He looked briefly at Sally and whispered conspiratorially. "You do know this is a lap-dancing club?"

"Yes, thanks," I replied. "This little minx has dared me to take her in. Well, I can't ignore a dare from a lady, can I?"

His face took on an expression halfway between a grin and a leer.

"No, sir. That would never do."

He stepped to one side, pulled the door open, and ushered us inside. In truth, as we went in, neither of us knew what to expect. The entrance led to a lobby area with a coat-check window, followed by a reception desk.

"Good evening. Welcome to Kittens."

Sally stifled a giggle at the name. The welcome came from a striking girl of around twenty-five standing behind the desk. Very attractive, but with about three layers of make-up, when one would have been plenty. She was dressed in a tight black mini dress.

"Hello."

"Have you visited us before?" I guessed we stood out like a sore thumb.

"No. This is a first for both of us."

"Well, I'm sure you'll have fun. Here's a little list of the rules we give to those visiting for the first time. It makes life easier for everyone. There's an entrance fee of twenty pounds per person, but I'll let the lady in free."

I thanked her as I handed the money over, and she pointed us to a further door, again flanked by a burly guardian. He'd been watching us and swung the door open as we approached. The lobby area had been a bit subdued. Light enough for the staff to see what they were doing, but not bright. As we walked through the door into the main venue, that changed dramatically.

We stopped and looked around. The space in front of us was large and airy. Two or three steps led down to a circular area with a bar against the rear wall, small groups of seats around the edge. In the middle was a series of interlinked platforms, each with a pole. Each pole with a girl dancing around it.

Around the platforms were low stools; some occupied, some empty. All this was lit by a variety of coloured lights, predominantly blue, with some neon edges and highlights. The background to all this was music. Pervasive, but not loud. Enough to be heard, but low enough to hear conversation.

Above this area, level with us was a series of circular booths. Plush padded seating, with a low platform in the middle. Some had poles, some didn't.

We may have been a little nervous, but we needn't have worried. No-one batted an eyelid at our entrance, so I touched Sally's arm, and we walked over to the bar. We ordered drinks and decided to grab seats around the edge of the lower area. We sat quietly for a few moments to allow us to look around and take in the place. It wasn't full. There were quite a few customers, but still lots of space. The booths in the upper area were mostly empty.

The clientele seemed to be a fair mix of people. Guys on their own, a few groups of two or three lads and one larger one, probably a stag party, judging by the horns one of them was wearing. Sal wasn't the only female; there were two or three others dotted around.

Then there were the girls. Each pole on the platforms was occupied by a girl dancing around it. They all had a minimum of clothing in a variety of styles and colours. Others were walking around, mingling with the clientele. Again, wearing a variety of outfits. Some wearing short dresses, others in various styles of underwear.

I noticed Sally scanning the leaflet we'd been handed.

"Well?" I asked.

"Basically, no touching. Oh, and you're on camera everywhere you go."

"And being watched by the goon squad."

There were always two or three hefty guys ambling around; earpieces in. All squeezed into collars two or three sizes smaller than their necks. They were quietly watching everyone and everything.

"I don't know where to look," Sally said.

"I do."

"I didn't mean that. There's so much going on, I don't know what to concentrate on."

"Find someone you like the look of and watch her."

We went quiet for a while, both selecting our preferred view. I picked a blonde girl on the nearest but one pole. She was wearing a high cut blue brief, with a short frilly edge, and a matching mini bra. Of all the girls on show, she actually seemed to be enjoying what she was doing. Perhaps she was simply the best actor.

Her movements around the pole were slow and graceful. The others were jerkier and more frenetic. But she seemed to be in a world of her own, moving to the music. I watched her for a few minutes, taking in her movement and her body. Lean and tall, but curvy and supple. Certainly attractive. And she knew it.

The spectators spaced out around the platforms were concentrated on the other girls. They seemed to prefer the rapid movements and more obvious sexuality. The blonde only had a couple of admirers.

"Who are you watching?" Sally interrupted my thoughts.

"Guess."

"The blonde in blue."

I turned to her. "Yes; how did you know?"

"I know what turns you on. She's soft and sensuous. The others are too 'in your face'. Besides, she's got a fantastic bum."

"True. You got me."

"So, who was I watching?" Sally asked.

I looked over the girls again and looked back at Sally. "The same girl."

"Yup."

"For the same reasons."

"Yup."

We went back to watching.

"She looks a bit like Lucy," I said.

She turned to me slowly. "Do you think so?"

"Don't you?"

She looked back at the girl. "Possibly."

The music died; it was time for the girls to swap over. The guys around the platforms were handing money to their preferred dancer. Our girl wasn't doing so well. Sally looked at me, dipped into her bag and went over and gave her a note or two.

"I gave her something for both of us."

"Good. Another drink?"

I went back to the bar for refills. When I returned, Sally had company.

"Marcus, this is Leila."

"Hi, Leila."

"Hello."

"I've been telling Leila we're lap dancing virgins."

Leila was a short, dark-haired girl, wearing a full set of black underwear. She seemed to have been made-up by the same person who'd done the girl on reception.

"What do you think?" Leila asked. "You like it?"

"It has its attractions," Sally replied.

"You like girls as well?"

Sally paused. "Yes... Well... I'm not sure." The question had surprised her, and I could see a lovely pink flush on her face.

"Relax. No judging here. Here all about fun. You have had dance yet?"

"No, we haven't."

"You like one. We can go to a booth."

"Shall we, Marcus?"

We agreed on the price and followed Leila up the steps, where she led us to one of the booths. The place was filling up; we'd taken one of the last free ones.

The next five minutes or so was a strange experience. Leila had a great body, but it was clear her heart wasn't really in it. She danced mechanically to the music, gradually removing her bra and her briefs, but it wasn't very erotic. She'd no doubt done it hundreds of times and had perfected the routine to achieve her goal, the money, with minimum effort. At the end of the second tune, she stopped abruptly, retrieved her discarded underwear and put it back on.

"Thanks, guys. Enjoy rest of evening."

With that, she was gone. I looked at Sally, and after a second or two, we both burst out laughing. Sally leaned on my shoulder.

"Tell me. As a man. As a lover of women. Did that turn you on?"

"Umm. Not really. It was a bit … cold."

"I'm glad it wasn't just me. How can a good-looking woman, stripping in front of you, be so boring?"

"Because it's a job, I guess. Because she does it dozens of times every day. Because she's bored. But it must work for some people, otherwise these places wouldn't exist."

"Mmm."

"Do you want to go?"

"Oh, no. Not yet. I reckon we need to find the right girl."

A little later, another girl came over to us, offering her services. She performed for us. A lot better than Leila, and we both enjoyed it. But there was still something missing.

"Do you know, Marcus. I think I've got these places sussed. Perhaps I was expecting too much."

"How do you mean?"

"Well, we've all heard guys excuses for coming. Saying it's all a bit of fun; it's not about sex. I think they might be right. Look around. It is a fun place. It's like any nightclub in the land. Except there are lots of girls walking around in their underwear, happy to remove it for cash. In some ways, it's more honest than your average nightclub."

"Yea. I see what you mean."

"Unless I'm missing something, there's no extras on offer. The girls know why they're here, and so do the guys. Everybody's happy."

"But has it turned you on?"

"Yes, but not in the way I thought it might. I'm not gagging for it."

I gave her a shocked look; she punched my arm.

"But," she continued, "I am enjoying watching lots of nearly naked women, dancing and performing. I'll happily admit that. Has it turned you on?"

"Yes, but you're still the sexiest woman here."

"So, you'd turn them all down?"

"For you, yes."

"Ooh, you old charmer." She looked at me, and I saw a thought cross her face. "Okay. If you had to pick one ..."

"Our girl on the pole. You?"

She looked at me cheekily. "The same. How about a threesome?"

I leaned close to her ear. "You little slut."

"When I want to be; and you love me for it."

"Too right."

"Want another drink?"

Looking around, I could see the place was busier now. All the booths I could see were occupied, and the floor area was heaving. I spotted Sally at the bar. It was busy; two or three deep. And she was the only woman there. But somehow, the guys queuing gave way, and a passage opened to let her through. She was back much quicker than I expected.

"How did you do that?"

"What?"

"Get through the crowd?"

"Oh, you noticed?"

"Yea."

"I think they were so surprised to see a female customer at the bar, they let me through."

"Get any offers?"

"Not directly, but I heard one or two comments. Made me feel quite good."

"You'd have eaten them alive."

"Well, most of them were only about twenty."

"Wet behind the ears. They don't know how lucky they are to have escaped."

She sat by my side.

"I invited someone to join us."

"Oh, who?"

"The girl we both liked. She was finishing another stint. She's going to change."

A few minutes later, she arrived.

"Hi, guys. I'm Celine."

Celine looked even better close-up. Beautifully built, graceful, confident. Wearing red; red stockings, red suspender briefs, red bra.

"Hi, Celine. Sally, Marcus. I would offer you a drink, but I guess you don't when you're working."

Celine sat opposite us. "No, thank you. I'm fine. Thanks for the tips earlier on."

"Oh, you're welcome. We both thought you were worth it. You seem to have a different style to the others."

"You could say that. I'm not very good at shaking my booty, which most of the guys seem to prefer."

"We couldn't keep our eyes off you, could we?"

"No. Best thing we've seen all night."

"Why, thank you. Have you had a private dance?"

We talked for a while about our impressions of the place, and the two dances we'd already had. She told us a little about herself. Trained as a dancer, but not good enough to make a full-time living from it. She did this to supplement her income and loved it.

"You get your fair share of jerks, but I can handle them. And this club is the best I've worked in. I'm a bit different to most of the other girls, but I think the boss reckons I add a bit of variety. What brought you guys here for the first time?"

I gestured to Sally. "This little minx dared me to bring her in. So here we are."

"You wanted to come in?" Celine asked.

"Yes." Sally flushed. "I was curious."

"Curiosity satisfied?"

"Sort of. We were trying to work out why guys come here."

"All sorts of reasons. Fun, loneliness. Or perhaps a dare."

"You got me. Do you only work on the poles?"
"Oh, no. I'll happily dance for you."
"We'd like that, wouldn't we?"
I had to agree.
"Great," Celine replied. "We can do it here or go to one of the private cubicles. I can be a bit more personal there. It does cost more, though."
We agreed on the price for a few songs, and as we went to follow Celine, Sally paused.
"Hang on, I need to visit the girl's room."
"Don't worry, there's one upstairs."
We climbed a short flight of stairs and reached a wide corridor with a few doors leading off it. While Sally popped to the loo, Celine and I chatted in the doorway of a free room.
When Sally returned, Celine ushered us inside and closed the door, telling us to make ourselves comfortable. The cubicle was subtly lit, with no ceiling. The sound of the club drifted in but was quieter. The only furniture was a circular couch, as in the booths. We sat next to one another, and I put my arm around Sally's shoulder. In front of us was a large round padded podium with a pole in the centre.
"Same rules in here guys. You can't touch … unless I invite you. Okay?"
She went to a small panel by the door, and the music playing in the club was suddenly piped into the cubicle. Not loud, but we could now hear it clearly. It blocked out most of the background noise.
"Comfy?"
She checked the pole, and when the track changed, wrapped herself around it, caressing it. Almost made love to it. It was instantly a cut above the dances we'd seen earlier. She was erotic and sensual; seemed to be able to turn it on at will.
She slid up and down the pole, wrapping her legs around it, stretching one up to the top, achieving the splits along its height. Slowly working her way around it, so that at times, we were viewing her front, at others, taking in the curves of her legs and bum.
When the music changed, so did her movement. She constantly changed her position, winding sinuously around the bar, turning and stretching. Using her skill to display different parts of her body in

different ways. Always sultry and alluring. She left the podium and moved towards us.

Still swaying, she held out her hand to me and stood me up. Sensuously lowering herself in front of me, and lightly running her hands down my arms and legs, before working her way up again. She took my hands and moved them behind her back, leading them to her bra strap. Nodding to me, I undid the hook. She stepped forward as if to kiss me, but a few inches from my face, she laughed lightly and pushed me gently back into my seat.

Moving back to the pole, she slowly edged her bra away from her breasts, exposing one nipple, then the other, before throwing it on the couch. She hadn't stopped dancing the whole time. Now she was using her hands to stroke her own body.

A short time later, she came towards me again. This time she put one foot on the couch between Sally and me. Her groin facing me, her briefs stretched tight over her sex. In time to her movement, she undid the suspenders on one stocking. Swapping legs, she did the same for the other leg; this time, her groin facing Sally.

She slowly danced around the podium, before approaching me again. The music had now changed, and she climbed onto the couch, straddling my legs. She rubbed herself against me, placing her arms over my shoulders. Teasingly pushing her breasts towards my face; her nipples so tempting.

I glanced at Sally; she was watching, entranced. I returned my attention to Celine. But as I did so, she got off the couch again and turned around. Her bum was now swaying above my knees. My cock was getting uncomfortable now. In one movement, she dropped onto my legs, and slowly slid backwards, up my legs, until her bum hit my tummy. I could feel her weight resting on my cock. The temptation to touch was almost too much.

She slowly moved backwards and forwards, well aware of what she was doing. So was Sally.

Chapter 6 – Sally

Not two feet away, a beautiful woman, nearly naked, was grinding her bum on my fully clothed boyfriend's cock. I had no doubt it was hard, and no doubt she'd be able to feel it. But the only thing I felt was hot; incredibly hot.

I'd enjoyed the evening so far, but this was something else. My nipples were so hard, they were aching and the feeling between my legs was intense. Watching this was making me horny as hell. I found myself wishing he could fuck her, while I watched every stroke.

The track ended, and Celine slowly stood up. Turning, she leaned forward and gave Marcus a brief kiss on the cheek. As the next track began, she turned towards me. Still in time with the music, she stood in front of me and bent to give me a quick peck on the cheek as well. She turned around and bent away from me, her bum above my legs this time.

Showing great flexibility, she put her hands between her legs and opened my knees. Swiftly stepping back between them, her bum was now close to me, swaying sensually. Reaching back either side of her, she gestured for my hands, and taking them, placed them either side of her waistband. She started pushing it, and I pulled gently as she wriggled her hips. I knew what I'd been invited to do.

I slowly slipped her briefs from her hips and over her bum. She opened her legs slightly and they continued, finally peeling away from her sex and dropping to her ankles. I was sitting there, with a naked woman bent over in front of me. Close enough to take in every detail.

I stared as she continued swaying; hypnotised. She moved forward slightly and closed my legs again and repeated what she had done with Marcus. Sitting astride my legs, she slowly slid up my legs towards my hips.

But this time, it was different. I only realised it as my dress rode up with her movement. First, my stocking tops were exposed, then my thighs, until her bum pushed into me. She lowered her hands and I gasped as they briefly brushed against my naked skin.

I looked across at Marcus. His face was a mixture of amusement and lust. I knew that look; it was often a prelude to him fucking me senseless. She rose, very slowly, and stepped forward. Again, reaching back and spreading my legs. I looked down. My dress was rucked around my waist. My stocking-tops and naked thighs exposed; my knickers visible. She turned around and deliberately looked between my legs. I did nothing to prevent her. I was enjoying it; taking in her nakedness at the same time.

She moved her hand between her legs and started to play with herself. I hadn't expected that. But I wasn't complaining. I wished I could do the same. Her eyes didn't stray from my covered pussy while she played with herself. I slid forward on the couch, moving my bum nearer to the edge, so she could get a better view. My underwear tonight was sheer. She could see right through it; see how wet I was.

Turning away from me again, she backed towards me. To my surprise, she lowered herself onto the small area of the couch still available between my legs. Her bum came into contact with my bare thighs. Oh, God. She rubbed her bum between them. She did it gently, so my clit was between her cheeks, and not being rubbed. She took my right hand and placed it on her breasts. Taking my left hand, she laid it on her thigh. She gradually leaned backwards, pressing against me. Pushing me onto the couch, her weight pressing on me.

She pushed her bum into my groin more firmly and started to grind, her flesh now rubbing over my clit. I was stroking her breast and her thigh; almost daring myself to move my hand between her legs. I so wanted to, but something held me back. I have no idea how long she did this, but eventually, she lifted herself off me. I noticed moisture on her bum and realised it must have been mine. She turned around, and leaning over me, gave me a long, deep kiss on the mouth.

Returning to the podium in front of us, she laid on her back. I knew what she was going to do. She spread her legs and began to play with herself again. Marcus's hand rested on my bare thigh, and I put an arm around his shoulder. We didn't move as we watched Celine bring herself to orgasm in front of us. It wasn't faked either; a woman can fool a man, but not another woman.

After she finished, we sat there, both horny as hell and not able to do a thing about it. After a minute or two, Celine sat up, smiling.

"Wow, Celine," I said. "That was … well, mind-blowing."

She smiled. "I don't normally go quite so far, to be honest. But I enjoyed it, too. We don't get many female customers, you see."

"Ah, gay?"

"Bi, and a sexy woman always turns me on."

I turned to Marcus. "Well, darling. I don't know about you, but I think it's time to go. It's all Celine's fault. She's made me horny as fuck. How about you?"

Before he had time to answer, I grabbed his crotch; rock hard.

"Yup. I see it worked for you too."

Celine laughed. "That's why I'm here."

We excused ourselves, leaving Celine to get dressed, but with double the fee she had asked. She had been damned good. As we left the club, the bouncer outside asked if we'd had a good evening.

"Yes, thanks," I answered, before Marcus had the chance. "But it's going to get even better when we got back to the hotel."

It was only a couple of streets away, and we walked more quickly than we had earlier in the evening. Both needing what awaited us when we arrived. Marcus suddenly pulled me into an alleyway between two shops and put an arm around me.

"Do you remember our early dates?"

I thought for a moment. "Yes …" Before I had time to react, his hand shot under my dress. On one or two early dates, he had teased me. Running his hand up my thigh but leaving me frustrated. This time there was no need to be gentle. He knew the state I was in.

His fingers found my briefs and yanked them aside. I gasped as they penetrated me, sinking in as far as they could go. His thumb finding my clit and circling it. I didn't care where we were; who saw us. I needed to come. He rubbed my clit roughly with his thumb; his fingers stretching my pussy. I was nearly there.

Bastard. I should have known. He stopped. Withdrawing his hand and replacing my gusset. With my breathing still heavy and uneven, he took my hand and pulled me back onto the street. I leaned towards him and quietly called him all the names I could think of. It only made him smile; I was smiling too. Just. I needed him.

We reached the hotel and went to the lift. One of those mirrored lifts. As we went to our floor, he pulled me towards him, and his hand lifted my dress. I looked into the mirror behind him, seeing my own bum's reflection in the opposite mirror. It was reflected umpteen times.

"Enjoying the view, you bastard?"

"Yes. This would be an interesting place to have sex. Reflections everywhere. Well, it would be. If it wasn't for the camera."

I pulled back slightly and yanked my dress down. I never did work out if there was a camera. When we were safely in our room, I pinned him to the wall and put an arm on his shoulder. I spoke softly, so he had to strain to hear me.

"Do you know what I was thinking when Celine was grinding her bum into your groin?"

He was smiling. "No ..."

"When she was rubbing her ass along your cock?"

He stayed silent; his eyes holding mine. I reached for his trousers and undid his zip. Reaching in with my fingers, I squeezed his cock through his pants.

"I wasn't jealous at all. All I wanted to do was watch you fuck her. Right there in front of me." I pulled his cock clear of his underwear. "Bend her over, rip her knickers off and fuck her hard."

"As long as I could have fucked you too; bent over right beside her."

I played with that image for a few moments, slowly stroking his cock. I liked it.

"Well, you didn't get to fuck her. Will I do?"

He moved swiftly, taking me by surprise. Pulling me over to the bed, he swung me onto my hands and knees, lifting my dress over my back. I squatted slightly so my bum was over the edge. I felt him pull my knickers to my knees and gasped as his cock drove into me in one firm movement. He slowly slid in and out.

I realised he was stripping as he did so. I tried to slip my dress over my head. But it proved difficult while on my hands and knees, and it ended up caught around my neck and shoulders.

I didn't get time to sort it out. Evidently, he had managed to disrobe first, because he gripped my hips, and fucked me. Fucked me as I'd wanted to see him fuck Celine. Driving in and out of me. Deep, strong, hard.

We both knew I wouldn't last long. The time in the club, his teasing on the way home. It had all taken me so close. This time, he took me there; and more. My orgasm came hard. No gentle ripple, no delicate butterflies this time. A fierce, intense, whole-body experience. My body bucking and tensing. Curses, cries, shouts. Wanting more; needing more.

He knew. He knew what I was like when I was in this state. He didn't stop. He slowed a little during my peak, but as I relaxed, he started again. A little slower, a little gentler. But still long deep strokes. A few slaps on my ass. Fingernails running down my back.

My shoulders slumped onto the bed. My dress now covering my neck and my head. I couldn't see what was going on. I could feel it; that was enough. I was in a continual state of euphoria; knowing I was going up that hill again. I let the feeling engulf me; images filling my head. Marcus, his cock, my pussy, Celine. Him fucking her. Oh, God. It overtook me again, and this time, as it hit me, I vaguely heard his cry. Dimly aware of him pulling me deeper onto him as we both released all our pent-up tension and lust.

As we recovered, cuddled up together, we talked about our experience at the club. Mostly about Celine's performance. It had worked for both of us, and I told him again how turned on I'd been by the idea of watching him fuck her. I didn't tell him what I'd have liked to do with her, but I think he knew.

***

The week after we retrieved the safety deposit box, we decided to move into the flat. It wasn't finished, but all the necessities were there, and we wanted to start turning it into our home. Over the space of a week, we moved everything from our separate flats and discussed where things should go. The box was temporarily forgotten.

One evening when I got home from work, I spotted it in the dining room, leaning against a chest. Marcus must have put it there, but he said nothing. Every time I walked past it over the next few days, I looked at it and wondered. What does it contain? Do I want to know? It's probably nothing; a few odds and ends. But I knew I had to look.

"Okay," I said, after breakfast on Saturday morning. "How do we open it?"

"I reckon we can break into it with the right tools. The Dremel should get us in."

So, we covered the dining table with old towels and lifted the box onto it. Marcus set to work trying to cut the lock off. It wasn't a hefty lock. After all, the box would have originally been housed in an underground vault, so the boxes themselves didn't need to be too secure. After a few minutes, the front of the lock fell away. Using a screwdriver and a hammer, Marcus managed to push the rest of it back into the box, and the lid was loose. He stood back.

"All yours."

I hesitated before lifting the lid. What new surprise was waiting underneath? Did I really want to do this? Yes, I couldn't stop now. I looked inside. Nothing immediately jumped out at me. No piles of pirate treasure; no glinting gold. There were three identical leather items, which looked a bit like wash bags, and two soft cloth bags, tied together. I looked over at Marcus.

"They won't bite," he said.

"You can never be sure with my father."

"Why don't you lift it all out, and I'll get rid of the box and towels?"

We were soon sitting at one end of the table, with these innocent-looking items in front of us. Marcus was first to notice the initials. The three leather bags each had two letters embossed on them. AC, BM and PD. Encouraging me, Marcus picked the one initialled AC and handed it to me.

"Might as well start there."

I slowly opened the bag and tipped the contents onto the table. A passport, a few folded pieces of paper, credit cards, some business cards, and a small bundle of banknotes. Marcus mumbled something which I didn't catch.

"Sorry?"

"A life in a bag," he replied.

I sat still, looking at the things on the table.

"May I?" he asked.

"Mmm."

He picked up the passport and quickly leafed through it. Then the documents, unfolding each one, quickly casting an eye over it. The cards, the notes.

"I was right. Passport, birth certificate, driving license, credit cards, various membership cards and a handsome wad of cash. All in the name Anthony Crowther. A life in a bag."

"But what does it mean? Why?"

"I'm not sure, but I have a hunch now what will be in the other two bags."

We took one each and emptied them into separate piles. Marcus was right. Virtually identical contents to the first. Except in one everything was in the name of Brendan Mahoney with an Irish passport. The other in the name of Paul Doyle with a Hong Kong Territories passport.

"Curiouser and curiouser," Marcus said.

"Why would he have these? It can't be good."

"Honestly, Sal," he said softly. "What did you expect? To find he'd been working for MI6 all these years? One of the good guys?"

"I suppose not. Whatever he was doing, he assumed these other two names to do it."

"It might be a bit more complicated than that ..."

"How do you mean?"

"Well, he has complete documentation here for three different identities. How do we even know Anthony Crowther was the real one?"

That hit me like a brick. I opened my mouth to answer, and nothing came out. I turned to look at Marcus.

"Think about it," he continued. "All these documents were in a bank. We don't know when he last accessed this lot before he died. But he was living day to day without any of these items. He must surely have needed them sometimes."

He shuffled through the pile.

"Driving license, credit cards. Why are they here? Why didn't he have them with him?"

He had a point.

"Do you remember seeing a passport or driving licence when you went through your Dad's stuff?"

I tried to remember, but it was difficult. The events after the accident were a bit of a blur and I'd tried so hard over the years to forget them.

"I can't really remember."

"Even if you did, I bet they weren't the ones we have here."

I thought about my father. The man I had really begun to come to terms with over the last six months. Yet here he was goading me again.

"Do you want to carry on with this? Or put it away for now?"

"Oh, no. He can't hurt me anymore. I won't let him. I've come too far to be afraid of him now. I want to know what he was up to."

We set about examining everything. The passports were the first step. The British one was mainly used to fly to Schiphol and back, with an occasional trip to Spain. But the other two were well-travelled. All over Europe, as well as Hong Kong, Japan, America, Thailand. The list went on and on. Most visits were only for two or three days. Never very long.

By the time we had examined everything, it hadn't really helped.

"Well, we know he had three different identities. But it doesn't tell us anything about why."

"No," Marcus replied. "And I don't see how we're going to find out."

"Nor me."

After the initial shock, I began to enjoy the task. I had accepted the role my father had played in my life now. With Jenny's help, and with Marcus's support. I could look at all this new information with a certain detachment; almost like a detective story. At least, that was my hope.

After we had thought for a few moments, I had an idea. I called Mary and asked her if she was free to come over later. She happily accepted, even when I warned her what the invitation was about. I turned to Marcus.

"I'm not sure any of this will mean anything to her, but you never know."

"Do you want me to keep out of the way?"

"No. I need your help."

"What about the other two bags?"

I'd forgotten all about them. I picked them up and undid the cord holding them together. Two identical soft bags. As I held them, there was a faint clinking sound. I put one down and undid the drawstring on the one in my hand. I peered in, but couldn't see much, so turned it over, and tipped the contents out. As they trickled onto the table, Marcus let out a long whistle.

"I hate to say it, but I'm a bit disappointed I never got to meet your father."

I was shaking as I looked at the sparkling heap.

"Are they what I think they are?" I said.

"I'm no expert, but I'm guessing they're diamonds."

"Yea. Me too."

"What about the other bag?"

I undid the drawstring and emptied it onto the table. This time, not diamonds, but other stones. A variety of colours. We couldn't hope to identify them. There were now two piles of stones in front of us. Most were fairly small, but there were some larger ones, including a couple of beautiful green stones and a brilliant blue one.

"Perhaps he was a gem dealer?" he said.

"And I'm the Queen of Sheba. Marcus, I know enough about my father now to know whatever he did, it wasn't legit. A genuine dealer doesn't need three identities."

When Mary arrived, we told her the story of the solicitor and the box. She clearly had no idea of its existence. We showed her the passports and identity documents.

"Do either of these other names mean anything, Mary?"

"No, darling. I'm afraid not. I always knew him as Tony Crowther. He often mentioned travelling abroad. But he never went into detail and was evasive whenever I asked him. I gave up in the end."

"Do you remember seeing his passport or driving license and so on when we cleared out his stuff?"

Mary thought for a while.

"Well, we never found a birth certificate, because someone asked for it, and we had to tell them we didn't have one. But I think if we had found the other stuff, we would have kept it for you."

"I wouldn't have wanted it."

"Perhaps not then, but I would have put it away somewhere for the future."

I looked at her. I saw in the warmth of her smile she would have done just that.

"I know you would. Sorry."

"No apology necessary, darling. But I'm afraid I'm not much help with this lot."

"There's more ..."

I picked up the bags and emptied them onto the table again.

"We don't know what they all are yet. But we're assuming they're not artificial."

I looked at Mary and a knowing smile crossed her face before she let out a deep chuckle.

"Oh, I expect they're genuine. I don't know what they all are either. But ..."

She lifted her right hand, and on the middle finger was a beautiful ring with a dark blue stone, simply set in a claw with a line of clear stones running around the band. I'd seen it so many times over the years, I no longer noticed it. I took her hand; looked at the ring, and up at her.

"Dad?"

She glanced over at Marcus, uncertainty on her face for the first time. I squeezed her hand.

"Don't worry Mary," I said, as lightly as I could. "Marcus knows."

She sighed. "Oh, well. So much for my reputation."

I squeezed her hand again, to bring her back to the ring.

"The ring was a present from your father. I've always liked it." She paused. "Unlike a lot of the other things he bought me. Over the years, I learnt to disassociate it from the source."

"I can understand that. It is beautiful."

"It is. And valuable."

"Really?"

"Yes. I wore it every day. A few years ago, I was itemising things for insurance and wondered if it should be mentioned on my policy. I took it to a jeweller. If they were real stones, I expected it to be worth perhaps a couple of thousand."

"And?"

She paused again. "Seventy-five thousand."

Marcus let out a long whistle. I sank back into my chair, my head swimming for a few seconds.

"Seventy-five thousand? And you still wear it every day?"

"I didn't for a few weeks after they told me. But then I thought, sod it. I've been wearing it for years, and no-one has bothered about it. So why should it be any different now I know its value? Mind you, it is fully insured."

"Marcus. If this ring is worth that much, how much are these stones worth?"

"God knows."

"And I'm not sure how we find out."

"How do you mean?"

"Well, we can't march into a jeweller, throw this lot on the counter and expect them to value them without a good story about where they came from."

"I don't see why not. If you say they were part of your father's estate, it should be fine. You can prove it, after all. The box and all its contents are legally yours. But I think we'll need to find the right jewellers. Not a random shop on the High Street. Mary, where did you take yours?"

"To Gendall's. But they had to send it away somewhere else."

"Perhaps we need to find a professional?" he said. "A diamond merchant, or something?"

"Yea. We'll have to look into it."

After we had put all the stuff away, Marcus asked Mary to stay for dinner. Lucy was coming around.

"Thank you, but I can't this evening. Ken and I are going to the theatre."

"So, it's still going well?"

"Yes, Marcus. Surprisingly well." She turned to me, smiling. "After all, I have a reputation as an old tart to keep up."

Chapter 7 – Lucy

"How's your father, Luce?" Sally asked.

"About the same, apparently. They don't think he'll get any better. It was a massive stroke."

"What happens now?"

"The hospital say they can't do anything else for him as an in-patient. So, he'll have to be looked after at home."

"Did you want to see him?"

I thought for a moment. "No. Not really. We haven't spoken for over fifteen years. There's no point now."

I was having dinner with Sally and Marcus. It always cheered me up. Sally had always been good for me, and in the time I'd known him, I'd come to like Marcus. He was laid-back, funny and intelligent. Good company. And he made Sally happy. That was enough for me. He stayed quiet while Sally and I discussed Dad.

"Do you know about my family?" I asked him.

"No. Well, except Annie." He smiled wryly. "I was told not to ask."

"I'm afraid we're both from somewhat dysfunctional families."

"Sometimes, I think we all are," he replied.

"Mine's not as mysterious as Sally's. Simple really. They disowned me when I came out. I haven't spoken to my father or mother since, just an occasional note or card from my mother through Annie."

"That must have been hard."

"You get used to it. You live with it. Luckily, if you can call it luck, I was never close to them. They were – are - very religious. I never followed that path and it led to big arguments through my teens. When I went to uni and came out … well, that was the end. I never went home again."

"We'd both lost our families, and it brought us together," Sally said. "We became like sisters."

"Yea." I put my hand over Sally's. "I think it saved us both."

We looked at each other and smiled. She squeezed my fingers.

"Enough of my troubles. This place looks fabulous. Are you finished now?"

"No, but we're getting there," Sally said. "All the building work's finished, and most of the rooms are decorated. We've still got some finishing to do in a couple of them. Then we can take our time filling it with stuff."

"Stuff?"

"Yea. Bits of furniture, pictures, mementoes. We've already put out the things we can't live without. But we've got two spare rooms filled with all the other stuff we've brought from our old homes and not used yet. A lot of it will end up in a skip, I suspect. We're not going to rush. Just wait until we see things we like."

"It feels like a home already."

"It does, doesn't it." Sally turned to Marcus. "That's because it is."

When we'd finished eating, Sal showed me the whole flat. I had only been to the lower level when they'd initially shown me around and it had been a mess. But now? What a transformation.

Their bedroom was vast; built in what had been the main kitchen in Victorian times. They had converted three of the vaults behind it into a subterranean en-suite which was almost surreal. Brick walls, curved ceilings and hidden lighting. The centrepiece was a huge island bathtub; there were two sinks, a wet shower area big enough for half a rugby team and two hidden toilets.

The rest of the lower level had three further bedrooms, two bathrooms, and the whole of the rear was now a huge room looking out over the garden with floor to ceiling windows and doors. There were still two unused vaults next to the garage entrance.

"What are you going to do with those, Sal?"

"No idea, Luce. They're spare space for now. I'm sure we'll find some use for them."

The upper level hadn't changed as much. The two main reception rooms had been redecorated, and one now opened into a kitchen I could only dream of. The smallest room had been converted into another shower room.

The whole thing looked like something out of House and Home magazine. I knew I wouldn't have the imagination to transform it in the way they had.

When we returned to the dining room, we chatted about what they had left to do. After a while, I couldn't help noticing Sally was a bit fidgety.

"Can I show her?" she finally asked Marcus.

"It's not up to me, Sal."

"No, but I listen to your advice."

Marcus snorted. "When did that happen? I must have missed the one occasion one wet Sunday afternoon."

Sally went over to a cabinet and brought out two box files. From the first, she drew three leather packets and laid them on the table. I listened as she told me where they came from. It was so good to see how free she was talking about her father, after all those years of pain.

"When we finally opened the box, these were in it."

"What are they?"

"Three faces of my father."

Confused, I looked at her. She laughed.

"That was our reaction, at first."

She showed me the contents, and I was as amazed as they must have been.

"Where did they come from? What do they mean?"

"No idea, have we?"

"No," said Marcus. "We could try to dig deeper, but knowing Sal's father, we're not sure what we might find."

"So," she added, "we're going to sit on it for a while. But that's not all there was."

She opened the other box and lifted two bags out. They clinked as they hit the table.

"Put your hands out; cup them into a bowl."

She took a bag and undid it, pouring the contents out. My breathing stopped as I realised what I was looking at. It was as much as I could do not to drop them.

"Are those …?"

"We think they're diamonds. We've got to get them checked. Darling, can I borrow you?"

He held his hands out next to mine, and she poured out the contents of the other bag. More sparkle.

"We don't know what all these are, but I can guess one or two."

"Where did they come from?"

"Your guess is as good as ours. But with Mr Crowther …"

I looked at all those stones glittering in the light. I'd never seen anything like it. As we tipped them back into their respective bags, I made sure I didn't have any still sticking to me.

"What are you going to do with them?" I asked.

"No idea," Sally said. "We need to find out what they are first."

Once Sal had put the boxes away, we left the dining room, and moved to the lounge. This was the most impressive room in the flat. It was huge, and still a bit bare. Plenty of room for them to add 'stuff', but it was already warm and comforting. It hugged you.

Sally poured some more wine.

"Can I tell her?"

"What about?" Marcus replied.

"What else we did when we picked up the box?"

"Oh, that. You don't need to ask. Lucy will be getting the impression you always bow to my authority."

"Don't worry, Marcus. I know Sal. She only asks permission if she thinks she might embarrass someone."

"Besides, I don't bow to anyone's authority." I noticed a brief look pass between them. "Well, only when I want to." She turned back to me. "Marcus took me to a lap-dancing club."

I was momentarily taken aback. "What?"

"Hang on, hang on," Marcus interrupted. "Lucy, I'd like to set the record straight on this one. We walked past one, and Sal dared me to take her in."

"Oh, is that what happened?" Sal asked with exaggerated innocence.

I was curious now. "What was it like?"

They described their adventure. Sally did most of the talking, with Marcus adding the occasional detail. It was as I had imagined it would be, until she related what had happened in the private room. Sal got more animated at this point and I noticed she was flushing slightly. I wondered if telling the story was turning her on as much as hearing it was affecting me. When she finished, she sat back, slightly breathless.

"It was quite an evening, Luce. I think you'd like it. Don't you, Marcus?"

"Well, I don't know Lucy's taste. But I reckon Celine would have done it for anyone."

I looked at Sally. "Did you enjoy it?"

"Well, it was … interesting." I could see her skin had flushed. "Celine was very … good."

Marcus laughed. "Lucy, she was like a bitch on heat all night."

"Marcus!" Sal hissed.

He looked at her. "True or false?"

She stared back at him defiantly for a second or two, before dissolving into laughter. "True."

"Why is it I never have all this fun?"

"Ailsa?" Sally asked, hesitantly.

"Sacked."

"Ah. Sorry."

"Oh, I'm not bothered. She wasn't up to much; in bed or out."

Marcus snorted. "Sorry, Lucy. It was the way you said it."

"Perhaps I ought to visit a lap-dancing club."

"You two should go together."

We both looked at him, a wry smile on his face.

"Why not?" he said. "Sal's an expert now, so she can show you the ropes."

She threw a cushion at him, and as usual, he'd managed to lighten the mood. But his idea stuck in my mind, and the thoughtful look on Sally's face made me realise she was pondering the idea as well.

I needed the loo, so excused myself, and when I returned, Sally had topped up my drink. It was a good job I was staying the night, now they'd furnished a spare room.

"What are you doing for a holiday this year, Luce?" she asked.

"Haven't planned anything. No-one to go with, and with Dad and everything, I hadn't really thought about it."

"Why don't we go? Like we used to?"

Sally and I had been on many holidays together over the years. But apart from the odd weekend, we hadn't been on one for three years.

"Oh, you wouldn't want to leave Marcus ..."

"Don't worry, Lucy," he said. "It takes a long time to die of starvation. If you send red cross parcels, I might survive."

"I didn't mean that ..."

"We know," Sal said. "But Marcus is fine with it. What do you say? The term ends soon, so easier for us to get time off. How about a couple of weeks somewhere?"

"Two weeks?"

"Why not? Perhaps an active week, then chill out on a beach."

"I ... well, it does sound good."

"Great. And Luce ..."

"Yes."

"It's all on me. Let's do something special."

"Oh, Sal. I struggle with that."

"I know. But remember the weekend in London? Wasn't it good?

"Yes, it was. But ..."

Marcus broke in. "Lucy, just nod, smile and let her do it. Believe me, you won't win this particular argument."

I thought for a few moments. "Okay, Sal. You win."

Lying in bed later, I realised I needed a holiday. I hadn't been away for longer than a weekend in ages. Sal and I had gone on holiday together almost every year in our late twenties and early thirties. But it hadn't happened recently. It would be good to do it again. And with Sal paying. I was less sure about that, but I knew her.

She'd always had a generous character, and now she had come to terms with her past, she seemed determined to have fun with her father's legacy. I knew Marcus was right; if she decided she was going to pay, I wouldn't change her mind. I might as well enjoy it.

I thought back to their description of the club, and their private performance. I wasn't sure what I thought about lap-dancing clubs; they weren't exactly havens of feminism. But I would have welcomed such a display right now. The bed was warm and comfy, I'd had a fair bit to drink, and I was relaxed. I wasn't tired yet, so let my hands wander over my body. As they slid between my legs, I closed my eyes and tried to imagine someone dancing for me.

Sally popped into my head. It annoyed me. It was happening too often. But my fingers were already doing their job, so I went with it. Imagining her slowly undressing in front of me. Grinding on my lap; feeling her naked skin against mine. Imagining I could hear her begin to moan, as we caressed each other.

I stopped. I realised the sounds weren't in my imagination. I could hear a girl moaning. I lay still; it had to be Sally. Little moans and whimpers floating through the wall, a short pause, then resuming. Gentle, flowing. No rhythm to them. I tried to picture what they were doing but couldn't be certain. The sounds were increasing. I let my fingers play; stroking myself gently. There was no hurry. They might have been coming from a straight couple, but the sounds were a real turn on.

I heard a screech, followed by a giggle before the whimpers resumed, and I recognised a woman on the edge. I wasn't near enough to follow, as Sal let out a long series of groans, slowly going quiet. Ah, well. At least someone was enjoying themselves. I would too.

I was taking my time, pleasing myself. I often liked to masturbate slowly, teasing myself. It added to the build-up; increasing the eventual climax. I heard sounds again. Still Sal, I was sure. But this time, regular, rhythmical. Even I knew what that meant. They were fucking. I concentrated on the sounds; imagined what they were doing. I was building now, my legs spread. One hand stroking the lips of my pussy, the other closely circling my clit. My breathing juddered in my chest.

They speeded up, and she was louder now. I heard occasional harder noises, which I couldn't work out at first. I realised he was slapping her bum. She'd hinted a few times it was part of their sex lives.

Three loud cries signalled her orgasm. And brought mine. A long, slow release. Warm, fizzy, sending warm shivers through my body. I lay still; let my breathing calm. I closed my legs on my hand, leaving it between my thighs. Pulling the duvet closer around me, I snuggled into it. I could sleep now.

But not yet. A few minutes later, the sounds came again. I had to laugh. How long could she keep going? How long could he? The sounds were quieter but still had a regular rhythm. Slower, gentler. I listened as she had her third orgasm in about twenty minutes. Go, girl. Then another sound. Several deep cries a few seconds apart. Marcus, I guessed. I didn't even know men made much noise when they came. Come to think of it, why would I?

There was a gentle tap on the door, and Sal came in with a mug.

"Morning Luce. Tea?"

"Oh, yes, please. Morning ..."

"Did you sleep well?"

"Yes, thanks."

"I'm up, Marcus is getting up. No hurry. Breakfast whenever you feel like it."

"Okay."

I'd intended to leave early, but Sal and I talked about where to go on holiday. We agreed early on we didn't want two weeks lying on a beach. We'd be bored. But a few days lying in the sun would be good. So, a week somewhere interesting, followed by a lazy week by the sea. We told Marcus about some of the trips we'd taken in the past and wondered if we might return to any of the scenes of our past indiscretions. We grew excited about the possibilities. After lots of googling, dozens of places were suggested and discarded. We finally settled on Italy.

"I haven't been for years," I said, "and my Italian's going to be rusty."

"How about Rome? I've never been."

"Sounds wonderful. I visited a few times when I lived in Italy."

"When was that, Lucy?" Marcus asked.

"I spent a year in Florence as part of my PhD."

"Must have been heaven."

"It was. I had access to lots of things normally behind barriers or hidden behind crowds and some of the people I studied with were wonderful. I loved the whole experience."

"I seem to remember tales of interesting lovers too," Sal said.

"One or two." Memories came flooding back. "I was young, and I learnt a lot."

After a few moments, I realised they were both watching me, amused by my reverie. I felt myself blush slightly.

"Right," I said. "So, a week in Rome."

"Yep. I'll have my own private guide."

"Well, I'll do my best, Sal."

"And on to a resort somewhere?"

"Yes. Somewhere chic and sophisticated."

"Like where?"

"I don't know. I can't normally afford chic and sophisticated."

"Well, this time we can."

Chapter 8 – Sally

As we descended towards Leonardo da Vinci Airport, we were already in a holiday mood. Exactly as we were years before; two girls looking for a good time. Except we were no longer girls, and our definition of a good time had changed, too. We'd grown up. Ten years ago, we still visited museums and historical sites. We were both culture vultures, after all. But we would also have been thinking about nights out; drinking, talking about the future. Teasing the guys; well, girls in Lucy's case.

Now, it was more relaxed. But we were still excited. Two weeks, with no responsibilities, and lots to see. The money made a difference. Earlier holidays were always carefully budgeted. Cheap hotels, public transport, and restaurants which sometimes left a lot to be desired. Things had eased as our careers progressed, but this time it was different.

We could indulge ourselves. Lucy was still uncomfortable with it, but if I couldn't spend my money enjoying life with my oldest friend, what was the point in having it?

After collecting our bags, we took the train into central Rome and a taxi to our hotel. We'd chosen it on the back of a lot of positive reviews, and they proved correct. It was a boutique hotel in the centre, with an old-world charm, impeccable service, and a wonderful atmosphere. It also proved to have a cocktail bar famous throughout the city.

We settled into our room and ordered a leisurely afternoon tea in the sumptuous courtyard garden. The first decision we made was we weren't going out for the rest of the day. It was four in the afternoon; we'd been travelling since early morning. So, dinner in the hotel, and plan for tomorrow.

We both had a list of places to go, and we were planning to visit two a day, choosing one each. Whether this ambitious target would be achievable remained to be seen.

The next morning, we did the most touristy thing we could think of. We bought tickets for the open-top hop-on, hop-off bus tour of the city to get our bearings. It proved the easiest way to see the layout of the centre, and where most of the places we wanted to visit were in relation to each other. The weather was perfect, sunny and warm but not too hot.

We stayed on the bus for the whole circuit, and when we got off, looked for somewhere to have lunch. We found a trattoria on a small square, with some free tables outside. As we ate, we watched the world go by.

"Have you noticed anything?"

"What's that?" Lucy replied.

"You can always tell the Roman women from the tourists."

"They have a certain style, don't they? It was the same in Florence years ago. Even the old matrons dressed up when they went out."

"Makes me feel distinctly dowdy. Fancy a change of plan?"

"How do you mean?"

"Let's go shopping."

We spent a few minutes googling the best shopping areas. Heading off on foot, we soon found what we were looking for. A few streets full of enticing boutiques and quirky shops, as well as some big names too. One or two would be expensive even for me.

We spent the rest of the afternoon staring in windows and popping into places that took our fancy. Trying things on, talking to the assistants. This was different from shopping at home. Here, you got personal service. The assistants were always friendly, always helpful, and knew their stuff. They were happy to spend time with you, giving honest opinions and make recommendations. There was no rush; it was all very relaxed. It also helped that Lucy spoke pretty good Italian. It seemed to ease the way.

The first time we bought anything, we had a brief stand-off about me paying. I was used to it now and understood. Lucy was strong-willed and valued her independence. But I insisted; she shrugged. After that, she didn't argue. We tried on loads of things and bought a few. After a couple of hours, we needed a break, so stopped for coffee.

"I think we've bought enough," Lucy said. "Rather, you've bought me enough."

"Luce, I know you don't like me paying, but please let me. I don't want to go through the whole holiday having this debate."

"It feels odd, Sal. We always used to pay our own way."

"I know. But I wasn't using the money then, was I?"

"No, true."

"But now I am. God knows it's taken me long enough. I want to share it with the people who helped me get here. That means you and Marcus."

"I didn't manage to help in fifteen years. It's Marcus who's knocked you into shape."

She spoke lightly, but I detected a hint of regret in her voice. I laid a hand on her arm.

"Luce, you know that's not true. If Marcus has finally pushed me into sorting it out, fine. But it's you who got me through those fifteen years. I wouldn't be where I am without you."

She looked at me, and we shared one of those moments. Two friends acknowledging how important they've been to each other over the years. She finally laid her other hand on mine and squeezed it.

"Okay. I've wiped a few tears away at times. As you have for me. I'm not used to it, I suppose. Having someone pick up the tab all the time." She looked at me and smiled. "I could get used to it, though."

"Good. So, at least for the next two weeks, I'm paying. Agreed?"

She scowled mockingly at me for a second or two before her face lightened. "Okay. Agreed."

The subject was put to bed, and we resumed our shopping expedition. By about five o'clock, we each had several bags.

"Well, my feet are getting sore. Shall we head back?"

"Yes," I had to agree. "I'm not sure I can carry much more. We could get a taxi."

"I think the hotel's only about three streets away. Let's keep walking. We can crash out when we get back."

I followed Lucy; she seemed to know where she was going. I'd lost track of where we were. As we turned the second corner, I stopped. Lucy turned and followed my gaze. A lingerie shop. The window was beautifully dressed. Simple, elegant.

"I've got to go in."

She laughed. "Okay."

We were the only customers. The assistant was an elegant lady, possibly ten years older than us. She looked each of us up and down carefully before welcoming us. Everything in the shop was beautiful. Well-made, classy, and designed to make you feel special. We didn't know what we wanted. We soon found out her appraisal of us when we entered wasn't disdain. She'd worked out our sizes by eye, and she was spot on. She was spot on about something else, too.

"You love wearing beautiful lingerie, yes?" she asked me, smiling.

"Yes."

"And your man loves it too, I think."

"Yes …" I was amazed. She turned to Lucy.

"You prefer more practical underwear, I think."

"Well, yes. I suppose so."

"That is a shame. A woman with your figure should wrap it in beautiful things."

I noticed Lucy blush and saw she was lost for words.

"Now," the assistant continued. "Let me see what I can tempt you both with."

Lucy soon recovered, and we spent an hour looking at some beautiful items. I was spoiled for choice. I ended up with half a dozen items I fell in love with; I was certain Marcus would too. Lucy eventually selected a few things as well. We thanked the assistant and resumed our walk back to the hotel.

"Do you wear underwear like this because of Marcus?" Lucy asked.

"No, I wear it for me. It makes me feel good and gives me confidence. Mind you, it works for him as well."

"I'll bet it does. I just look for comfort."

"No reason it can't be sexy and comfortable."

"No. I suppose not."

When we got back to the hotel, we dumped our bags on the floor and threw ourselves onto the bed.

"It's a shame there isn't a spa here. I could really use a massage now."

"That would be heaven," Lucy answered.

"Try reception. See if there's anywhere we could get one."

As usual, I couldn't follow the conversation. Partway through she looked at her watch. I waited for her to finish.

"We're in luck. They do have a masseuse. She'll come to the room in an hour. Let's have a shower."

Refreshed and relaxed, we waited on the bed, and the masseuse arrived right on time. She was short; not much over five feet, and brusque. She wheeled in a folding massage table and set it up by the bed.

Lucy went first. She took off her robe and stretched out. I watched as her almost naked body was oiled and kneaded. I tried not to look but couldn't help it. Then it was my turn. Each massage lasted about half an hour. She may have lacked personal skills, but the masseuse knew her job.

By the time she left, our aches and pain had drained away. Replaced by a warm, comfortable peace.

"Where are we going for dinner?" I asked.

"I don't know. Let's wander and pick somewhere."

"Okay. But we're dressing up. New clothes; new underwear."

"Really?"

"Really."

We spent half an hour getting ready. Starting with underwear. I watched as Lucy tried to decide, eventually choosing for her.

"Well?" she asked when she'd put it on. She was standing in front of me in a pair of delicately patterned boy-shorts and a matching bra. She was a bit curvier than me with bigger breasts. Years ago, I'd been jealous of those.

"How does it feel?"

"Good." She was looking in the mirror. "It does fit well."

"You look fabulous." She did, too.

The choice of dress proved easier, and ten minutes later, we walked out of the hotel to begin our hunt for dinner.

The next morning after breakfast, we headed for the Vatican. It was going to be a full day, there was so much to see. As we passed reception, Lucy held out her hand to stop me.

"Shall we book another massage for when we get back? We'll be on our feet all day, and now I'm happy to spend your money ..."

Having arranged it for six o'clock, we set off. It was a fascinating day. First, to the Sistine Chapel and St Peter's Basilica. We wandered as slowly as we could through the crowds. Most seemingly on route marches, following guides.

It was wonderful, as always, to visit such a place with an art historian. Lucy was never patronising; she knew me well. Pointing out elements I might have missed and filling me in on context and history. Far better than any tourist guide. We took a leisurely lunch at one of the restaurants.

"This is one of those places that depresses me," Lucy said, as we were relaxing after our meal.

I looked at her, puzzled.

"Oh, not the place itself. It's fabulous. But look at the visitors. How many of them are really interested in what they're seeing? Most of them are rushing from A to B. They don't see anything; they don't understand anything. They're just ticking it off their list."

"I know what you mean. You see it everywhere though, don't you? It's Instagram fodder."

"Oh, I think it's more than that. People did it long before social media. I've seen it ever since I started studying art. I'd go to the National Gallery and sit in front of one painting for an hour. I'd see people almost running through the rooms. I wondered why they bothered."

"But that's why you do what you do. I guess if these people remember one object, one painting from today, it's something. And perhaps you are generalising a bit?"

"Could be. But it makes me sad. They'll be off to 'do' the Pantheon next, or the Colosseum. No context, no understanding, no appreciation."

We sat quietly for a few minutes.

"Right," I said finally. "Enough about the others. Time for you to give this tourist her next lesson."

"Okay, sorry. I got a bit melancholy there."

We returned to our sightseeing; ignoring the streaming crowds as best we could. The afternoon took us to the Vatican Museum and the Library. And what a library. I was awestruck. Yes, I'd seen pictures. No, they didn't tell half the story. It was like walking into a painting. Colour everywhere. Too much, in truth. Your senses are overwhelmed. Well, mine were, anyway.

By the time we got back to the hotel, we were aching again, and looking forward to our massage. But it wasn't to be. As we crossed the lobby, the receptionist called us across and explained the masseuse was unwell, and not working today. She apologised and gave us the number of a spa nearby, who might be able to fit us in. But we were out of luck there too. When we rang them, they couldn't help.

"Well, that's that," I said, lying on the bed, rubbing my tired feet. "Let's rest for an hour and think about dinner."

"Mmm," was the only reply I got. Within minutes, we were both asleep.

We woke at the same time.

"What time is it?" I asked. "I feel like I've slept for hours."

"It's only ten to seven."

"Baggsy first shower."

I got off the bed and winced as my back twinged. The shower refreshed me, and I pulled a robe on and went back into the room.

"All yours."

"Thanks. I was thinking. We used to give each other massages. Fancy trying?"

"I haven't done that for years, but I'll give it a go."

"I'll have a quick shower. Have we got any oil?"

"I've got some baby oil. It'll have to do."

I slipped on a pair of briefs and laid a towel on the bed. While I waited, I looked at what I might wear for dinner. After ten minutes, Lucy came out of the bathroom, drying her hair with a towel.

"I'll do you first if you like. I'm still damp, so my skin will be sticky."

I slipped off my robe and laid face-down on the towel. I was still sleepy and could have easily nodded off. She started on my feet, her oiled hands raising one at a time, and rubbing them gently but firmly.

The heels, soles and each toe. I jumped, as her fingers tickled a sensitive area. She worked along my legs; ankles, calves, the backs of my knees.

I relaxed under her touch. Her hands moved to my thighs, pressing into my muscles. I opened my legs slightly to let her reach between them. I followed the route of her fingers to the edge of my briefs, as she concentrated on my thighs. Not as good as the masseuse, but worth it, nonetheless. My mind was relaxing too. I was enjoying this holiday. I missed Marcus, but he was going to be there when I got back. I'd forgotten work, forgotten my father. A real break.

My consciousness returned sharply, as Lucy's hands slid up my thighs. She was close; very close. Her fingers running along the edge of my briefs between my legs. Staying there for a few moments, then moving away. I dismissed the thought. She moved on the bed and straddled my thighs.

Before I had time to analyse any further, her hands landed on my shoulders, and she began to press on them. Slowly moving along each arm. Returning to my back, she worked her way down until she reached my briefs. She lifted the sides, and placed them between my cheeks, exposing my bum, which she proceeded to massage.

Lifting the material, she pulled it gently to expose more of me. But at the same time, it pulled across my pussy. Several times. Was she playing with me? Or was I mistaken?

Her hands continued to massage my bum. With each movement, I could feel my pussy stretching. My mind was racing. What was happening? Was my own curiosity making me imagine things which weren't real?

I felt a gentle slap on my right cheek, and her weight lifted off my thighs.

"Right, turn over."

I rolled over and settled on my back. I was surprised to see she was completely naked. I couldn't help looking. She was kneeling beside me; smiling.

"Is this working?"

"Yes. You're good. I mean … it feels good."

I was not so relaxed any more. My brain was busy trying to work out what was happening, while my heartbeat was experimenting with different rhythms. I also recognised the signs of anticipation. I realised

I was turned on. Oh, God. What now? Do I carry on, and ignore it? What if …? I watched as she put more oil on her hands and turn away from me to work on my shins.

She was now kneeling in a position where I could take in her bare bum. I looked; I wanted to. Her beautiful curves raised slightly above her ankles. Her thighs. I allowed my eyes to wander over them all. I'd seen Lucy naked hundreds of times over the years. But never like this. Never with these thoughts in my head. Her hands were on the front of my thighs and reached my briefs … and moved down again. Several times.

She shifted up the bed slightly and settled on her knees by my tummy. Oiling her hands again, she took each of my hands in turn and stroked the fingers. She was concentrating on what she was doing; not looking at me. In one movement, she straddled my hips. My eyes were drawn to her pussy. Open above mine. But hers was exposed; I could see its enticing contours.

She placed her hands on my shoulders and worked on them and my neck. I laid my head back on the bed and closed my eyes. My mind came to a decision. I decided to go with it. If I was imagining all this, it would be fine. If I wasn't? Well, I didn't know what would happen. So many fantasies; so many dreams. Perhaps I'd satisfy some of them.

Her hands were now on my breasts. I wasn't a big girl. Lying on my back, they weren't very prominent. But I could feel my nipples standing up; hard. They are sensitive; very sensitive. Marcus loved teasing them. Marcus. God; would I have some explaining to do if …

I stopped thinking. Lucy was gently rubbing my nipples between her fingers. I couldn't prevent a gentle moan. Her hands moved to my tummy, circling. Gradually getting nearer and nearer to my briefs.

Then they went under; I flinched slightly. Knowing now, I was not imagining this. Her fingers slowly circled under my briefs working their way closer and closer. They reached my hairline, and moved towards …

Her weight shifted and I sensed a presence. Opening my eyes, I saw her face hovering above mine. A faint smile on her lips.

"Want me to stop?" she asked.

I swallowed hard, closed my eyes and took a deep breath. Made my decision. I opened my eyes.

"No."

"Sure?"

"Yes."

She slowly lowered her lips onto mine and kissed me. Kissed me for the first time as a lover would. I hesitated for a moment, conscious of the significance of this moment. But my body had already overruled any reservations building in my mind. I relaxed and began to respond. I responded even more when she let her fingers run over my clit until they rested on my pussy. My wet pussy. She pulled up slightly and withdrew her hand. I must have looked disappointed.

"Don't worry," she said, twanging the waist of my briefs. "I just think this would be easier without these."

She lifted off me, and I raised my bum as she slipped them down my legs. She stretched out beside me, laying half over me, easing a leg between mine. I felt warm moisture as her sex brushed my thigh. She stroked my hair and kissed me again.

"I … I'm not sure what to …"

She put a finger to my lips.

"Ssh. You relax and leave this to me."

She dropped and took one of my nipples between her lips. I moaned. She let a hand crawl between my legs again. Reaching my pussy, she let her fingers explore. Gently spreading it. I opened my legs wider, and she ran a finger over its length. I let out a deep sigh. I placed an arm around her, stroking her, enjoying the feel of her skin under my fingers.

She turned to the other nipple, teasing it with her lips, and nibbling it with her teeth. My mind was a blank; giving in to the situation. Her finger circling my clit, moving nearer to it. She teased the hood, stretching it, and my body rose to her touch unaided. Moving her fingers smoothly, she eased a couple into me and pressed them upwards, making me gasp. I groaned as she placed her thumb on my clit and steadily rubbed her fingers and thumb in tandem.

It seemed I was floating; it all seemed so unreal, like a dream. Like one of my fantasies. But this was real. I knew I was going to come. I grabbed her hair and pulled her head towards me. She placed her lips on mine, and I kissed her hard. She lifted her head away slightly. My orgasm overtook me as my hips rose under her fingers, and an intense heat filled my groin.

Through the whole thing, we stared into each other's eyes. At that moment, we were closer than we had ever been. No words, but so much passed between us. She slowed and reduced the pressure. Eventually easing her fingers out, and laying her hand on my tummy, slowly stroking it. She lowered her lips onto mine and gave me several light kisses.

As my breathing slowed, she laid her head on my breast, and I pulled her close. I don't know how long we lay there.

"Luce," I finally said, softly.

"Mmm."

"Why now?"

She raised her head.

"How do you mean?"

"After fifteen years. Why have we done this now?"

"Regret it?"

"Oh, God. No. We haven't finished yet. I'm curious, that's all."

She looked thoughtful for a moment.

"You love Marcus, don't you?"

"Yes, with my very soul." I didn't understand where she was going.

"And you trust him?"

"Implicitly."

"Well …"

She told me about the conversation with Marcus several months ago when he gave her a hint. Hearing that, I decided to tell her everything. How I'd had increasing fantasies about women, and how he'd encouraged me to find a way to explore them. Lucy got it.

"So, he knew you wouldn't do anything about it," she said. "You wouldn't, would you?"

"Honestly? Probably not."

"And he set me up to seduce you."

"I think he let you know the possibilities."

"I must remember to thank him." She was grinning. "Does he really not mind?"

"He's always encouraged me to explore. No; we encourage each other. But I guess I'll find out when I tell him."

"I think you might have found a keeper there."

"He's something else. And here am I being unfaithful."

"I didn't think of it like that. But you're right. How does it feel?"
I sat up.
"I'll tell you in a day or two. Now, hand me the oil, and lie down."

I spent the next half hour exploring Lucy's body. It wasn't much of a massage, to be honest. It was strange; daring. To be running my hands over a woman's body in a way I'd never done before. To be touching another woman in such an intimate way. I was looking at her in a different way.

We'd seen each other naked or nearly naked often enough. But now I was looking at her in a blatantly sexual way. Letting my eyes feast on her skin, her curves, her breasts and her sex. Letting my hands caress her legs, her bum, her nipples. Moving between her thighs and feeling a pussy other than my own for the first time. My fingers caressing her wetness, my senses keen to her response as I invaded her.

I had no plan; wasn't sure what she needed. That would come later; hopefully. But I repeated what she'd done to me. And she responded in the way I had, coming under the touch of my fingers.

Chapter 9 – Lucy

I knew I'd taken a risk. A hell of a risk. Ever since Marcus had dropped the hint, I'd been thinking about it. Had he been encouraging me? Giving me permission? I didn't know. But it did tell me something I hadn't known; Sal fantasised about women. I'd finally decided I needed to do something about that. And while she slept earlier on, I came up with a way to do it.

Now as we lay intertwined naked on the bed, having enjoyed each other, I was glad I'd taken the risk. I think she was too. I hoped so. She kept running her hands over my body, exploring it. Her touch was gentle and my response to it surprised me. She seemed to know how to play me; perhaps we had similar needs. We had time to find out.

"What about dinner?" I asked.

She gave me a big kiss.

"How about skipping dinner tonight? Let's order room service."

"Fine by me. We can relax."

"I wasn't thinking of relaxing. I was thinking of all the other things we can do."

"Such as?"

"Whatever you want. Corrupt me."

I set about doing exactly that.

The rest of our time in Rome was magical. All the famous places singing out to us across the centuries. But it was often the smaller things that appealed more. Walking along a street and realising the wall of a house was two thousand years old. The house built around it, centuries later. Finding a curved street which followed the shape of an ancient theatre. Those were the things which struck. So much to see, and we had to be ruthless. We realised we could have easily filled the whole two weeks, and still not seen half of it.

"Never mind," Sal said. "We'll have to come back."

Somehow, I believed we would. We went somewhere different for dinner every evening. As always in Italy, slow, relaxed and friendly. If you avoid the tourist traps, which we did with the help of the concierge at our hotel. He seemed to know everyone and everything. I guess that was his job. But he steered us to some good restaurants, where the focus was the food, not fleecing gullible visitors.

Then back to the hotel, and, well, sex. Sal wasn't shy. After her initial hesitation, she didn't hold back. I had known her a long time, and I knew sex had always been important to her; she'd always been open about that. But her appetite and curiosity still surprised me.

From the first night, she wanted to try everything. Asking me what I liked, asking me to show her. She was willing to try anything and everything. She seemed to enjoy it all. As for her appetite; well. I was more a long slow build girl, gradually coming to orgasm. That made me happy. I usually struggled to come again. But Sal was almost the opposite. When she was in the mood, she seemed able to come again and again … and again.

We didn't have any toys with us. Neither of us had thought it a good look to use a vibrator while sharing a hotel room with a friend. But we did find a shop where we managed to get one, and it added to the fun. After something of a marathon session, where she had given me a second powerful orgasm, we were lying stretched out on the bed.

"Have you always come so much, Sal?"

"Yes and no."

"That's not an answer."

"I know. I mean, yes, I've always been able to give myself multiple orgasms. Sometimes, I need to. But I've not generally had them with partners. It's Marcus who's really brought it out."

"Lots of stamina, eh?"

She chuckled. "Not really. That's why he's so good."

I turned my head towards her; I must have looked puzzled.

"You know his health isn't brilliant, and he says he was never able to keep it up for hours."

We looked at each other, both mouthing 'Brian' at the same time, and collapsed into giggles.

"But he's developed other skills. And he has patience; the patience of Job. He's happy to concentrate on me for as long as we want." I noticed her smiling. "Sometimes too long."

"Eh?"

"When he teases."

"Oh. How?"

She looked at me, a pensive expression on her face.

"Tie and tease. You know; that sort of thing."

I rolled onto my elbow, looking at her.

"What sort of thing? Out with it, girl."

"Well, he'll tie me to the bed, and use a wand or something. He can keep me on the verge for ages. So close for so long, until I'm … well, desperate. Begging. The things I've offered him to let me come."

"And he doesn't take them?"

"Oh, he does … eventually. After making me come until I sometimes have to beg him to stop."

"Sounds wonderful."

"Yup. He's given me the most awesome orgasms I've ever had. Mind you, he gets a few in return."

"I'll bet he does. Did you do all this before Marcus?"

"Not really. It was one of the things that brought us together. Things we both wanted to do but hadn't had the opportunity."

"More than a bit of tying up?"

"Mmm."

"Such as?"

"Not telling."

"Spoilsport."

"I'd be happy to tell you. But I think I ought to ask Marcus first."

"Yea. Fair enough."

"After all, I wouldn't tell him what we've done without you agreeing. Not in detail, anyway."

"I wouldn't mind. Don't straight men dream about girls together? You could use it as foreplay."

The week in Rome came to an end. We were heading to Positano on the Amalfi coast for a week of relaxation after the pace of city life. We took the train to Sorrento, with the intention of getting a taxi to the resort. As we were leaving the station, we passed a car hire desk.

"Let's hire a car," Sal said.

"Will we need one?"

"Well, we've got to get to Positano. And are we going to be happy lying on the beach for a week?"

We looked at one another and walked towards the desk. The available choice was limited, so we settled on a Fiat 500. Well, when in Italy ...

Sal wanted me to drive. I hadn't driven in Italy in years, and I remembered it as something of a wild ride. But at least I wouldn't be driving around a big city. We set off towards Positano, only a few miles away. We found our hotel easily, managed to park, and checked in.

"Right, we're here, settled in, and it's only lunchtime. Shall we find somewhere to eat?"

"Yup. And wander around for the afternoon."

"Sounds like a plan."

Positano was positively stunning; famously so. It was a bit packed. It was also very hilly. Everything seemed to be uphill or downhill. Nothing you wanted was ever on the level you happened to be. We found ourselves thankful for the car.

We walked down the hill to the seafront and picked the first café with a spare table. We stayed for a couple of hours, watching the world go by. Looking at the colourful buildings climbing their way up the steep hills, and watching people messing about in the azure water.

The afternoon was equally relaxing; if a little more tiring. Wandering around, taking in the sun and all the colour. Feeling the sea breeze on our skin. Totally different to Rome. We passed a shop selling a huge range of gelato. Well, we had to go in. Sal took ages to choose, and I had to promise her we'd come here every day. Which we did, bar one. We walked back up the hill to our hotel, and by the time we arrived, we were exhausted.

"Lie down before dinner?"

"Yes, please."

We slept for an hour or so and decided we'd have dinner in the hotel that night. Plenty of time to explore the nightlife in the coming days. We showered, dressed and went to the restaurant. Tables on a terrace overlooking the bay, a leisurely meal, beautiful fresh fish, good wine.

After we got back to our room, Sal excused herself, saying she'd forgotten something and went back out again. I shrugged and sat on the balcony. I heard her come back, and shortly after she appeared at the doorway from the room; naked. Beckoning me with her finger. I smiled and did as I was told. Three or four towels were laid out on the floor, and she was standing by them holding something covered with a small cloth.

"Clothes off," she said.

I knew by now not to argue with that request; why would I? I quickly removed everything.

"Lie on your back."

Ideas ran through my head as to what was under the cloth. When I was comfortable, she stood by my feet looking at my body. With a flourish, she removed the cloth and I could see what she was holding. A huge bowl of gelato.

"You're joking!"

"Nope. I'm going to smear this all over you … and lick it all off. Any objections?"

None that I could think of. None at all. She opened my legs and knelt between them. Putting the bowl on the floor beside us, she dug out a large spoonful and dropped its contents on my breasts. I gasped at the cold. She used the spoon to spread it around. I shivered as my flesh reacted to the cold. It was a strange feeling; first, a little shock, followed by a cooling from the heat in the air and a few tickles as it slid around.

She placed another spoonful on my tummy, then another above my groin. Watching me, her fingers landed on that last spoonful and moved it slowly over my pussy. I braced for the shock of cold, but it didn't come. Just a cool feeling, as it slid over my clit, and melted over my sex. She massaged the area slowly, rubbing the gelato into my folds.

A crazy mix of sensations was running through me. Heat from my sex, mixed with cool flashes as the coldness reached new places. Topped by the pressure of her fingers tracing over my delicate flesh.

She leaned over me to give me a kiss, and I knew what I had to do. I couldn't resist. I nudged her knees and pulled her arms simultaneously. With a shriek, she collapsed on top of me, sandwiching the gelato between us. We both dissolved in a fit of giggles. Bringing my legs over hers, I rolled us over, so I was on top of her. She was still giggling.

"You're mad."

And I kissed her fiercely. She instantly responded, and our hands mauled anything they could reach. Arms, legs, bums. We were now well-covered in rapidly melting gelato. I split her legs, and pushed my pussy onto hers, rubbing them together. Her hands pushed my bum, asking for more. After a few humps, I stopped.

"Who's licking who?" I asked.

She reached for the bowl. It was still over half full.

"I think there's enough for both of us, don't you?"

There was. More than enough. You can only take so much melting gelato. And we did have to lick it out of some interesting places.

A lot later, after we'd showered together and made sure we'd got all the bits out and washed all the stickiness away, we lay on the bed.

"Whatever made you think of that?" I asked.

"Marcus and I tried it once." She turned to me. "You don't mind me talking about me and Marcus, do you?"

"Hell, no. The other day, you wouldn't tell me enough."

She grinned.

"Only we tried it with fruit and cream. It didn't really work. They weren't the right consistency. The cream melted instantly, and the fruit was too big. We ended up laughing too much to do anything. We had to shower and ended up with a fruit salad in the shower tray." She was giggling now. "But when we were eating the gelato this afternoon, it occurred to me it might be worth a try."

"It worked. But I'm not sure I'll be in a hurry to try it again. It's a bit messy."

Sal gasped and sat up.

"What?"

She looked at me. "What are we going to do about those towels?"

I looked at the floor. Lying there were the towels, in a crumpled heap. All soaked in melted gelato, with some odd stains, and tiny bits of fruit and who knew what dotted here and there. They were a mess. I turned to her, and we both got the giggles again.

"Well," I said. "We could try washing them out …"

"But the bits might block the drain."

"Or leave them in the bathroom. I'm sure the staff see plenty of worse things."

"Mmm."

We sat pondering the question for a while. We both knew we should at least wash the worst of it out. But we couldn't summon up the energy. In the end, we quickly held them under the shower, trying to catch the bits before they disappeared down the plughole. We hung them to dry on the balcony, before replacing them in the bathroom. God alone knows what the staff thought the next morning.

We spent the next day on the beach; well, part of the day. The beach at Positano was a typical Italian beach. Rows and rows of loungers and parasols. All in regimented lines. We slapped sunscreen on, took plenty of water with us. We each had our Kindles. We took dips in the sea. We spent some time watching our neighbours, agreeing scores. There were some beautiful people, and some … not so beautiful. And we had a moment of déjà vu.

A group of women passed us. They weren't much younger than us, but they looked good. Very good. Two in one-piece suits, the rest in bikinis. Much more stylish than ours. I turned to Sal; she was watching them too. We caught each other's gaze.

"Are you thinking what I'm thinking?" she asked.

"Another shopping trip?"

There were a variety of shops in the town selling beachwear. As I expected, Sal chose the one that looked most expensive. But as usual, she was right. The assistant spent an hour patiently guiding us, and we came away with a bikini and a one-piece each.

Sal was more daring than me. Her bikini was tight and quite revealing. I liked something a little fuller, particularly on the top. But we were confident we could compete with the best now. Well, not the youngsters, but anyone nearer our own age.

We decided we weren't going to sit on the beach all the time but go somewhere every day. Then return to the beach for a couple of hours before dinner. That proved a good decision, and the car proved its worth.

One day we went to Pompeii. I'd visited many years before, but more of it was accessible now. Another day, we followed the coast road east towards Salerno. Every turn, every corner revealed ever more stunning views. The colours of the sea and the sky were almost unreal; as if the work of a great artist.

There were lots of small towns along the way to visit. We only got about halfway, so went back the next day to finish the journey. We crossed over to Capri for a day, just catching the last ferry back.

Every day, the colours, the light, the views were spectacular, and we enjoyed it all. We enjoyed every night too. I don't think I'd ever had sex so often. Nor had it been so consistently good. I'd had one or two lovers in the past where I'd been their first experience with a woman. They had been hesitant, a bit shy; freaked out on one memorable occasion. But always slow to accept their new-found pleasure. Not Sal. She seemed comfortable with it from the outset. Revelled in it; as did I.

As the week drew to a close, we spent the final day relaxing in Positano. Some time on the beach and strolling around the town. A rest at the hotel, and a final few hours back at the beach. We had noticed our new beachwear attracted a bit more attention. We loved it.

As the air slowly cooled towards evening, we chilled out. Lying on loungers under parasols, looking out to sea. We were flying home the following afternoon and had to travel to Naples to get our flight. It would be an early start.

I'd been looking forward to this holiday. Two weeks away from everything, with an old friend. But I hadn't been expecting what had happened. It had been in the back of my mind, perhaps. But only as a dream; a fantasy. But here we were. We'd had two fabulous weeks, doing things we both loved, visiting places that filled us with positive energy. That would have been more than enough.

But during those two weeks, we'd been lovers as well. Sally and me. Two people who had been friends for over fifteen years. Best friends. Known each other's secrets. Known each other's lovers; and quite a bit about some of them.

Yet, I never imagined this. Yes, I'd hit on her when we first met. She'd not been offended, and we became friends. I'd never thought of her that way since. Now, here we were. Sharing a bed in the carnal sense. Definitely in the carnal sense.

A variety of thoughts floated through my head as I lay in the shadow of my parasol. Could this have happened before? Had I been missing this for years? I decided not. By her account, she'd only developed these fantasies in the last few years. And it was clear it was her relationship with Marcus which was giving her the confidence to explore. Well, I owed him for that.

That brought me to the big question. What happened now? What happened when we got home? I looked over at Sal, seemingly asleep. Lying there, in her new brief bikini. I let my eyes flow over her. Over a body which had responded so well under my touch the last ten days and given me so much pleasure too.

If this had been a holiday romance, we'd be saying our goodbyes tomorrow, and store it in our pleasant memories file. But it wasn't; it wasn't like that at all. If Sal were single, it would have been easy. From my point of view, anyway. But she wasn't. She loved Marcus; really loved him. That was obvious. I didn't want to hurt either of them. But I wanted her.

The more I thought about it, the more complicated it appeared. How could it possibly continue when we got home? It wouldn't work. Yes, Marcus had encouraged her; had encouraged me. But would he be happy now it had happened? Surely no man would accept the situation. Had he thought it through this far?

What did Sally think? Was she asking the same questions I was? Was she as confused as me? I lay there wondering what to do. Should I leave it until we got home? Everything would return to normal. Sally would be back with Marcus, and she and I just friends again. It might be for the best. But something deep inside me bridled at that. If she had enjoyed this as much as I had, wouldn't she want to continue as well?

Chapter 10 – Marcus

The last two weeks had been strange. It had been the longest Sally and I had been apart. We sent the occasional message. She sent me some pictures and short videos. Before she left, she had suggested Face Timing every couple of days, but I said no. She was on holiday. Enjoy it.

I missed her but had done a lot of writing, I'd found what I thought was the right place to have her stones valued, and I had one or two ideas about the spare vaults downstairs. Plenty to tell on both sides when she got home later that day.

I spent the morning tidying the house and doing a few odd jobs. Their flight arrived at about three in the afternoon, and it would take them another two hours to get home. I planned dinner and chilled out. I knew Sal would have lots to tell me, and I knew she'd tell me in one animated session. Better get some wine ready too.

I heard the key in the lock and a suitcase roll over the wooden floor in the hall. A few moments later, Sally appeared in the doorway. She was wearing a gorgeous summer dress I hadn't seen before. Mid-thigh and loose, it hung beautifully on her. She looked a million dollars.

"Hello, you," I said.

"Hi."

Her reply was slightly hollow. It put me on my guard.

"You okay?"

She walked towards me, a guarded expression on her face. Serious, slightly nervous.

"Yes. I need a word with you."

She got straight up on the sofa and sat astride me, her dress displaying a lot of her thighs. I looked down to enjoy the view.

"Marcus. Look at me, please."

I did. She took a deep breath. I noticed her look now had a hint of defiance.

"Did you, or did you not, talk to Lucy about my fantasies involving women?"

Things began to click into place. I made a play of wracking my memory.

"I think it might have cropped up in passing."

"In passing? What did you say?"

I realised she was a mixture of nerves and playfulness. I guessed why.

"She said you'd told her we were helping each other act out our fantasies. I told her I couldn't help you with all of them. Something may have been mentioned about why."

"And why would you do that?"

I saw now she was playing. She knew I knew where she was going.

"Oh, just small talk."

She suppressed a smile.

"Small talk? Telling my gay friend I fancied women?"

"Harmless enough, don't you think?"

She took another deep breath.

"Marcus."

"Yes, Sal."

"This is serious."

"Sorry. Do go on."

She was trying to conceal her smile, and I was struggling to maintain a serious expression.

"I've got a confession."

I kept silent.

"Lucy and I … Well …"

She was flushed now. More flushed than she had been for a long time. It was hidden slightly by her new tan, but I could see it. I stayed silent.

"...slept together."

"Good idea. Cheaper that way."

She whacked my arm and let out an exasperated sigh.

"I don't mean that."

"Well, spit it out."

She scowled at me.

"We had sex. We fucked. Okay?"

"Ah."

"Is that all you're going to say? 'Ah'? Nothing else?"

I wasn't hiding my smile now.

"Did you enjoy it?"

Her face cracked now, and her body relaxed. She looked away, trying to hide her grin. After a few moments, she turned back to me.

"Yes. Yes, I did. You bastard."

"Me?"

"Yes, you. Bastard. You beautiful bastard."

She threw her arms around my neck and collapsed onto my shoulders. I put my arms around her. We stayed still for a while, holding each other. Finally, she spoke softly into my ear.

"You really don't mind?"

"Come on, Sal. You both know now I nudged you."

"That's what Luce said."

"Would I have done that if I wasn't happy for it to happen?"

"She said that too."

"Then perhaps you should listen to your other lover."

She laughed. Naturally, lightly this time. Pulling away, she looked at me again.

"It doesn't change anything? You still trust me?"

"Yes, Sal. You could have kept quiet and said nothing."

"I couldn't."

"I know. That's why I trust you."

She laid her head by my shoulder again, and we sat there. Still.

"I love you," she whispered. "So much."

"I know. And I love you." I replied softly.

"So, what happens now?"

"What do you think?"

"Luce and I talked about it last night."

"And?"

"Can we talk about it later?"

"Of course. You must be tired."

"It's not that."

"Oh?"

She bent forward and kissed me. I realised it was the first time since she'd come through the door.

"No. It's just that after ten days with a woman, I fancy a man."

"Do you?"

"Yes." She placed her hand on my crotch. "This man, to be precise."

"I don't know. Can you fit me in? Your schedule seems quite full."

She swiped my arm again, put her feet back on the floor and stood up. In one movement, she pulled her dress over her head. I immediately noticed her underwear. Silk, tiny floral print. A delicate bra, and high cut shorts. It fitted beautifully. She saw me looking and did a twirl.

"Like it?"

"It's gorgeous."

"It's lovely to wear. I bought a few pieces."

"It looks fabulous."

"Almost a shame to take it off."

"Not really."

Grinning, she removed the bra, before sliding the shorts off. I stood and shed my clothes. She came towards me, and our naked bodies touched. Our arms encircling each other, kissing gently. She pushed me back onto the sofa, climbed over me, and sat across my lap. Her pussy pressing my rigid cock against my tummy. Slowly rubbing, her head hanging over my shoulder.

"God, I want you," she whispered.

"You can have me."

She sat up, raising her hips. Staring into my eyes. Those glorious green eyes burning right through me. Now suffused with a gentle lust. Her hand gripped my cock and guided the head to its target. I groaned with pleasure as she lowered herself down its full length. She grunted as she reached the base. With a wicked smile, she moved forward to kiss me and rocked her hips.

Half an hour later, we were lying on the sofa. She was curled into me and enjoying my hand stroking her. Nothing had been said since we reached an almost simultaneous orgasm. She finally stirred.

"I need the loo."

She slowly stood up and wandered off. By the time she returned, I'd put some clothes back on.

"Are you hungry?" I asked.

"I am now."

"Dinner in thirty minutes."

"Right. I'll take my case downstairs and have a quick shower. I'll unpack later."

Over dinner, she told me what happened between her and Lucy. Unembarrassed now she was comfortable with my reaction. No details, but I didn't expect them. She was clearly still coming to terms with it herself, so I listened, without asking questions. I let her get it all out. I knew she wanted to tell me. Eventually, she came to an end.

"Sorry, I've been doing all the talking."

"That's all right. A lot to tell. And a lot to think about."

She looked at me. "Yes."

"Take your time. Up to now, it's all been fantasy. Reality is a bit more ... well ... real."

"Any thoughts?"

"Yes. But you're not getting them now. It sounds unhelpful, but you need to think about this for a while and work out what you want to do."

"I know."

"Talk to Lucy again. What about talking to Jenny as well?"

"God, I'm not sure about that."

"She's a counsellor, Sal. This will be a piece of cake compared to some of the things she's heard."

"Oh, I'm sure she wouldn't bat an eyelid. I'm just not sure I could tell her. But I will speak to Luce again. The first step was telling you."

"Did you really think it would be a problem?"

"Not really. Lucy blamed you anyway for setting her up to seduce me. She says thanks by the way. She told me you'd be fine with it. I thought so too. But as you said, reality is different from fantasy. I was so mixed up on the journey home. Part of me was scared stiff. Part of me felt liberated. And a lot of me was confused. Now, I've only got the confusing bit left."

"It'll sort itself out. Let's wait and see. Want to drop it for tonight?"

"Yes. I think that's a good idea. But you're happy for me to discuss it with you when I want to?"

"Anytime."

She reached for my hand, and raising it to her lips, kissed it. "Thank you."

"Right. Are you going to tell me about your holiday? The few bits which happened outside the bedroom, that is."

It seemed they had left their room occasionally. She'd taken some pictures, and a video or two. But it was her commentary that was so appealing. Telling me where they went, what they saw and how she reacted. Like me, history was one of her passions and that animated her descriptions. Not only of the places they'd visited but of the people they'd met. About their shopping trips, and the reasons for them. Promising to show me the things she'd bought; hinting I'd like them.

It was clear she and Lucy had shared their enthusiasm. Sal often dropped in Lucy's comments about places and events. Describing their discussions; their differences of opinion; their giggles. I don't think I said a word. I loved seeing her so enthused. By the time she came to the end, she was clearly tired. We went to bed but didn't get to sleep before reacquainting ourselves with each other's bodies.

Sally didn't surface until nearly lunchtime the next day. She appeared in the living room in another new summer dress.

"Like it?"

"Sure do; it's beautiful."

"I'm wearing new underwear too. Wanna see?"

She lifted the dress to her shoulders. Underneath, a bandeau bra and briefs. Silk again, in pale pink, with slightly darker flowers.

"Very nice. Do I get to feel?"

She let her dress glide down her body again. "Maybe later. I'm hungry."

I put some brunch together, and we sat at the dining table, taking our time to pick at it.

"What did you get up to while I was away?"

"I got a fair bit of writing done; over forty thousand."

"Wow. Was it the peace and quiet?"

"I'm not sure. I just carried on until I came to a natural break."

"You can do that anytime. You don't have to stop when I get home."

"I know. But I want to. Besides, I'm not sure I could do that on a regular basis. My gut's playing up."

"Bad?"

"Not yet. I've got a gastro appointment on Thursday."

"Did it start while I was away?"

"No, it had begun to grumble before."

"You didn't tell me."

"I'm so used to it; I didn't think to mention it."

"You should. I like to know. Please."

"Okay, I will."

"Anything else?"

"Yes, as it happens. Don't book anything for next Saturday."

"Ooh, what are we doing?"

"We're going to talk to a man about some funny coloured stones."

She stopped nibbling an olive. "Really?"

"Yup. Midday."

"Where?"

"Hatton Garden. I had a chat with the guy and explained what we needed. I hope you don't mind."

"Not at all. I needed the nudge; I was letting it fester again. What did you tell him?"

"Not much. You'd inherited some stones from your late father, and we wanted to get them checked out. Nothing more. How much you tell him, is up to you."

"Shall we make a weekend of it? Stay Friday and Saturday?"

"If you like."

"Can you book something?"

"Will do."

"Anything else?"

"Just one. About the empty vaults."

She was still picking at the olives and nibbles; her fingers covered in olive oil, butter and various dressings.

"What about them?"

"Have you had enough?"

The hand holding a piece of artichoke paused in front of her lips. She poked her tongue out at me and popped the sliver into her mouth.

"For now." Picking up some tissues, she wiped her fingers. "Let's go."

The corridor that had run the length of the house had been split during the renovations. The half at the front had been incorporated into our bedroom between the main space and the bathroom built into the vaults behind it. A door now closed off the rest of the corridor. It led eventually to a door into the garden room beyond the entrance to the underground garage.

But between there and the door to our bedroom, the corridor opened out into two large arched vaults. It was the only unfinished area in the flat. I explained my idea. She listened and agreed on the spot.

Chapter 11 – Sally

As we walked to Hatton Garden, the butterflies started. We'd discussed what to tell the gem dealer. After all, small stones can be valuable items. We guessed dealers were presented with stolen items on a regular basis, and they had their reputations to maintain. If any of the stones were valuable, they would want to know where they came from.

The story of how I'd acquired them sounded so far-fetched, we had thought of simplifying it. But in the end, we agreed to tell the whole tale. I had the documents to prove I was legally entitled to the contents of the box.

The shop was reassuringly old-fashioned. Mahogany counters with glass panels laid into them. Wooden cabinets with rows of small drawers. But we were shown straight into a small office with a heavy old wooden desk. Clear except for an inlaid black area. Behind the desk, a middle-aged man with half-glasses. He rose to greet us.

"Miss Fletcher? Mr Foxton? I'm Frank Wynne. I believe you have some stones you'd like assessed?"

"Yes," I replied, as we took the seats he offered. We'd agreed I'd do the talking. "I hope we're not wasting your time."

"Oh, we are asked to examine things all the time. A lot of them turn out to be of little value, but it's always worth getting an expert opinion. May I ask how you came by them?"

I took a deep breath and told him the whole story. I tried to stay calm and factual. He sat very still, listening. I showed him the will, and the documents giving me title to the box and its contents. When I'd finished, he thought for a moment.

"A fascinating story. And one I think wasn't easy for you to tell." I nodded. "It does mean, I suppose, you have no idea where your father acquired the stones?"

"None at all, I'm afraid. I … I suspect their origin may not be entirely legitimate."

"I think I may have to agree with you. However, as far as I am concerned, the documentation makes you the legal owner. May I see the items in question?"

Marcus had been carrying the two bags in a small rucksack. Taking them out, he put them on the table. I picked up the first, undid the drawstring, and carefully poured the contents onto the desk. I did the same with the other bag next to the first.

I looked across the desk to Mr Wynne, who was looking at the two piles. He slowly raised his head, looking first at me, then at Marcus, before returning his gaze to me.

"Well, Miss Fletcher. I think we may be here some time."

He reached over, and brought a lamp across the desk, switching it on, and angling it over the first pile. He prodded about with his finger, moving stones. Spreading them out over the desk before doing the same with the second pile. Finally, he leaned forward. For the first time, I saw a keen interest in his eyes. Again, he looked slowly at Marcus and then me.

"I am at a loss for words. I've been in this business for forty years. I have rarely had a member of the public come in with such a treasure trove."

"You mean they're all real? Knowing my father, I half expected them all to be fake."

"Oh, no. I think perhaps you should have more faith in your late father's discrimination. I will need to properly assess each item. But from an initial glance, I can tell you these are all very real. Some quite beautiful, in fact. You don't live in London?"

"No."

"Are you returning home today?"

"No, we came up for a couple of nights; we're going home tomorrow."

"Ah. Good."

He cast his eye over the stones glittering under the lamp on his desk.

"I will need three or four hours to assess these. You are welcome to stay or return later. I can stay open until any time convenient for you."

I looked at Marcus. We had discussed this possibility. It seemed a little strange to leave them with someone we didn't know, but we exchanged silent agreement. I looked at my watch; twelve-thirty.

"What if we come back at four-thirty? Will that be enough time?"

"More than adequate, thank you."

He showed us out to the door of the shop. We now had a few hours to kill, but I sensed Marcus wasn't feeling brilliant. He'd seen his consultant during the week and been put back on steroids, which he hated. He was due to have some tests the following week. We returned to our hotel, chosen for its proximity to our destination.

He kept apologising. I told him to shut up, but I was worried about him. He was used to this, but it was the first flare he'd had since we'd been together. I didn't know what to do; how to help.

When we returned, the shop was closed. We rang the bell, and Mr Wynne himself came to the door and ushered us inside. He led us back to the office. On the table where there had been two jumbled piles, there were now several groups of small clear bags.

"Please, sit." He took his seat on the other side of the desk. "Well, what a delightful afternoon, I must say. Did your father travel much?"

"We think he did. There were a couple of old passports in the box as well, and they seem to have gone around the world a few times."

"These come from all around the world. I wonder if he picked them up on his travels?"

"Your guess is as good as ours, Mr Wynne."

"Anyway. Let's deal with the more mundane first …"

He proceeded to pick up one bag at a time and describe its contents. The stones in what we'd called the clear bag all proved to be diamonds.

"The uncut stones are all reasonable quality but, in truth, not of great value. They will sell easily enough, but the value of the rest is in their cut."

He had graded the remaining diamonds; a few in each bag.

"There are two values on each bag. The higher is my estimate of the full market value; the lower is the price a dealer would give you."

I looked at these figures and showed a couple to Marcus. He kept his face neutral. As Mr Wynne continued, the stones grew in size and value. Finally, there were six diamonds left in a row on the table.

"These are the best of the diamonds. All beautiful stones. If your father chose these, he had a good eye. It's difficult to be sure, but I think these were all cut in the nineteen seventies or eighties. The cuts are slightly old-fashioned for today's taste, but they would still be highly desirable."

He lifted each in turn and named their market value. My heart began to race, and I didn't even try to conceal my amazement. The amounts were stunning, though perhaps not surprising; this was all to do with my father, after all. Then he turned to the contents of the other bag.

"A wonderful variety of stones here. All precious; a few quite unusual. I had to ask a colleague to confirm the identity of one, it is so rare."

Again, he went through the collection. Some I'd never heard of. As before, he had left a few out of their bags. As before the prices were astonishing. The isolated stones went even further. Finally, only three were left.

"Now to the real gems; if you'll forgive the pun."

He picked up the blue stone. I was now sure I knew what it was.

"This is a perfect sapphire. Absolutely beautiful. So clear, such a deep colour. Again, a slightly old-fashioned cut, but it wouldn't matter. Anyone would pay you fifty thousand for it."

I stared at him, hardly believing my ears.

"Seriously?"

"Oh, yes. More on a good day."

I looked at Marcus; he still had his poker face on.

"Now these ..."

He had put the sapphire down and picked up what I knew would be emeralds; one in each hand.

"I see emeralds of this quality perhaps once a year. But to have two? Of this size? I've not seen a pair like this in years. Whoever cut them was highly skilled. To the naked eye, they are identical. Beautiful. I know several jewellers who would kill for these. What a pair of earrings they would make."

"That's what Marcus suggested."

"Quite right," Mr Wynne replied. "They would match your eyes perfectly."

I felt myself blush. Marcus laughed, and I looked at him.

"You said that too."

"As for their value ... it's difficult. I think the market would be competitive. On their own, I'd say about a hundred thousand each."

My chest tightened at this news. It was surreal; like a dream.

"But together ... as a pair? Nearer three hundred thousand."

A silence fell on the room. I didn't know what to say. Marcus broke the tension by laughing. I turned to him.

"What?"

"Your father never ceases to amaze."

"Even from beyond the grave."

"Are you considering selling any of this collection?" Mr Wynne asked as he put the few loose stones into their bags.

"We've no idea, to be honest. We'll take them home and think about it."

"Well, if you want to dispose of any of them, there's not a stone here I wouldn't buy from you. For the right price, obviously."

"Obviously."

Marcus leaned forward. "Mr Wynne; are you in a position to recommend any good jewellers or jewellery designers in case Sally needs one?"

"We deal with many of the best. I've made some notes of all the stones I've examined today and given each bag a number. I'll put all the descriptions and values in writing and send it to you. I'll enclose a list of jewellers I can recommend. But you'd need to find the one which best matched your style."

"That would be most kind. Thank you."

We gathered everything together, and Mr Wynne showed us to the door again.

"I hope to see you again soon, Miss Fletcher."

"I suspect you will, Mr Wynne. I can't possibly turn all of it into jewellery."

As we walked back to the hotel, we talked about what we'd learnt.

"Did you get a feel for how much it was all worth in total?" I asked Marcus.

"Not really. I didn't see all the bags. But even if you're only talking about the best stones he singled out, the total was not far short of half a million."

"What are we going to do with them?"

"That's up to you."

"You're not being very helpful again."

"I know. But you need to think about it first."

"What would you do?"

"No. No clues. Have a think, and we'll talk about it."

I scowled at him, then gave him a kiss. I could tell from his face he was struggling. He'd been taking pain killers all day and looked exhausted. When we got back to the hotel, he insisted he was well enough to go out to dinner. But he didn't eat much; his gut didn't want food. When we got back, he took more pain killers and went to bed. I felt helpless.

The following week, he had an MRI scan and a colonoscopy. At least I could help him with this. We could afford to go privately to speed things up, and I could drive him to and from the hospital and keep him company. The colonoscopy was fairly clear, but the MRI showed a severe narrowing in a section of his bowel and an unusual mass around it. He'd need to see his consultant again.

Marcus was used to all this; I wasn't. He thought he'd need surgery again, and the thought worried me. But he reassured me.

"I've had surgery for this three times now. It's pretty routine. And I've always been much better afterwards. Nothing to worry about."

Chapter 12 – Lucy

The week after the holiday was a bit of a daze. Getting back to work was the easy part. It was summer break. No students to see; no lectures, no tutorials. Just time in my office getting to grips with everything else. I set about revising some of the lectures for the coming year and made some notes for a book I'd agreed to collaborate on.

But spending most of the day alone also gave me time to think. Far too much time. I wasted hours thinking about what had happened. Trying to get my head around it and rationalise it.

There were no regrets. None at all. The holiday had been fabulous. We hadn't been away together for two whole weeks for years. We weren't identical characters, but we shared a lot of interests and had similar outlooks. We'd known each other so long, we were completely comfortable in each other's company. We were sensitive to each other's moods and feelings. Spending two weeks together was a blast. Add in what had happened, and it took it to a whole new level.

Coming home had been something of a reality check. On our last night, we'd had a long discussion about what we'd done, and what we wanted to do when we got home. We were both unsure. After going around in circles for a while, we agreed we needed to think about it in our home environment. We'd revert to our old routine and have the discussion again.

Key to the whole thing was Marcus. I soon realised Sally was carrying more than a little guilt. I could understand that. Marcus was her partner; her lover. I had seen the effect he'd had on her over the last year or so.

Given her back her confidence; helped her face her father's shadow. Their sex life sounded interesting, as well. She was happy, really happy, for the first time in a long time.

I didn't want to jeopardize that. She was my friend, first and foremost. But I also spent time thinking about Marcus. When I first met him, I'd liked him, but he'd seemed almost too good to be true. Laid back, supportive, calm. He appeared a little lifeless until you got to know him. Intelligent, perceptive, funny and a verbal match for anyone when he wanted to be, I came to see the attraction he held for Sally.

She'd had more than her fair share of misfits over the years. Not that I ever told her in those terms. One or two alphas who used her; or rather misused her. Perhaps a match for her sexual side, but oblivious to her emotional and intellectual needs. One or two who appeared staid, and unfortunately turned out to be even duller than they looked. They may have matched her intelligence but didn't understand her physical needs. It appeared Marcus ticked both boxes.

He was no idiot. I was sure he had deliberately told me about Sally's gay fantasies. When she finally told me he'd encouraged her to do something about them, I knew I was right. He'd understood she wouldn't feel right about taking the initiative; with me or anyone else.

He was also a thinker. Surely, he would have thought through the consequences of his actions? Sally had been nervous on the plane home, rehearsing what she was going to say. I laughed a couple of times, which didn't go down too well. In the end, I convinced her to play it by ear. I had a suspicion he knew exactly what she was going to say when she got home.

The day after our return, I got a text saying everything was fine. We met for lunch three days later.

"He was okay?" I asked.

"Yes. He played me."

"How?"

"You were right. He knew what I was going to say. At least, he half expected it. But he played the innocent, making me spell it out."

She recounted the conversation and I had to laugh. She ended up giggling too.

"He's right, you know," I said at the end.

"What about?"

"You should listen to me sometimes."

"Always have, Luce. Always will."

Sally was worried about Marcus; he wasn't well. She told me about his symptoms and the tests he'd been having. I knew he had a chronic condition, but this was the first time I'd heard the details. It sounded like he'd need surgery.

"Well, time for revenge," I said.

She looked at me, puzzled.

"Remember when you had your appendix out? How he looked after you?"

A grin spread across her face.

"Yes. If he has an op, I'll be able to set the rules this time."

***

After one of our gym sessions the following week, Sally paused as we reached the car park.

"Luce?"

"Mmm."

"Are you ready to talk?"

I thought about it.

"Yes. I think so."

"Me too. We're booked for the gym after work on Friday. How about we talk after that?"

"Where shall we go?" Sal asked.

We'd showered after the gym and were walking to the car park.

"Are you happy to come to my place? Or do you want somewhere neutral?"

"Oh, yours will be fine."

"Let's pick up a takeaway en route."

When we got home, I opened a bottle of wine, and we attacked the food first. As we got to the fork-poking stage, it went a bit quiet. I looked at her; she was looking thoughtful. Perhaps a little nervous. Was that a bad sign?

"So …?" I asked.

She took a deep breath.

"Okay. Who's going first?"

"I think you should. Your situation is the complicated one."

"True, but if you aren't interested, there's no complication."

"All right," I said. "My position is simple. What happened was incredible. The best sex I've had in years with someone who already means something to me. Of course I'd like to carry on, but I don't want to hurt you or Marcus. I've never even imagined being in a situation like this before, and I am struggling to see a way it would work. What would we do? Rush home at lunchtime for a quickie? Snatch an hour or two here and there? It all sounds a bit desperate."

"Yes, the way you portray it is a bit tacky."

"Have you got a better idea?"

"Yes, as it happens."

"Go on."

"Luce, I know I'm being greedy, but I want it to continue as well. Perhaps I'm being selfish. And I want to be clear my primary commitment is to Marcus."

"I understand that."

"But I want to explore this side of me; find out where it leads, what it means. The opportunity to do this with someone I trust and who means something to me as well is perfect. I had a few ideas about how it could work, but it was talking to Marcus that clarified it."

"Why am I not surprised?" Sometimes I wondered if he was our puppet master.

"Well, they were ideas I'd dismissed because I didn't think he'd be happy with them."

"Such as …?"

"How about we spend the odd night together or the occasional weekend away? Or both?"

It was better than I'd dared hope.

"Really?"

"Yes. But would you be happy with that?"

"God, yes. My last few lovers never lived with me. I was happy to see them once or twice a week. I've grown accustomed to more personal space as I get older."

"I had noticed. It's one of the reasons I thought of it. Look, I don't know if this is going to work. It might all go pear-shaped. But isn't it worth a try?"

My heart was racing. The prospect of having a friend and lover in this one person was exhilarating. I'd thought of little else since we'd got home.

"Yes. I think it is."

Sal reached her hands across the table and I clasped them.

"So," she said, "we have a plan?"

"Marcus is happy?"

"He seems to like pimping me."

"Aren't pimps supposed to make money out of it?"

"Good point. I'll tell him he's doing it wrong."

"No, keep quiet. Otherwise, it'll cost me a fortune. I don't think I could afford you."

We carried the remains of the food back into the kitchen, and Sal watched while I tidied up. I needed to ask a question.

"How often would this happen? I mean, are we going to plan these things, or go with the flow."

"I was all for formalising it. But Marcus pointed out we might want to keep it flexible, so it didn't become too rigid. He suggested a night every week or so and a weekend away every so often. But I'm open to suggestions."

We chatted about the possibilities, both relieved to have got the worst part over. I suspect we both feared the other might have decided not to continue. Now it was about the details. After we'd agreed a rough plan, Sal went to the bathroom.

I sat there; my heartbeat now stable. I realised how important this had been to me. I'd been so tense in the lead up to this meeting. Not sure whether I was facing disappointment or happiness but expecting the worst. I closed the curtains and put some lights on. When Sal returned, she came over to me and pushed my back to the wall.

"Are we good, then?"

"Yea. We're good."

She put her lips on mine, and kissed me slowly, putting her hands on the wall behind me. My body woke surprisingly quickly. I responded, my arms around her back.

"This plan …" I asked.
"Mmm."
"When does it start?"
She kissed my neck.
"Well. When I left Marcus this morning …"
Another kiss.
"… I said, 'see you tonight'."
And another.
"Do you know what he said?"
My skin tingled as her lips kept brushing my skin.
"No …"
"He said, 'see you in the morning'."
Another kiss.
"Which means I'm homeless for the night."
"I might be able to help you there."

Her lips glided across my cheek, finally reaching mine again, and kissing me hard. I responded, but as I did so, she pulled away slightly and unbuttoned my dress. Occasionally teasing me by leaning in towards me again; withdrawing her lips as I bent to meet them. Sliding her hands under the material, she slid the dress off my shoulders, and I leaned away from the wall to allow it to fall to the floor.

I'm not sure if she'd noticed I hadn't put my bra back on after the shower at the gym, but she smiled as she looked at my breasts. She leaned in again and kissed me, but before I could respond, she moved to my neck and kept going. Reaching my breasts, she placed kisses all around my nipples.

I gasped as she took a nipple between her teeth and squeezed. I hadn't been expecting it. She chuckled, her hand cupping my breast, bringing the nipple to her mouth again. I let the wall support me, as she sucked it hard, occasionally flicking it with her tongue. I placed my hand on the back of her head and pulled her towards me. Her face met the softness of my breast, and she just had time to open her mouth wide, enclosing the whole aureole.

I pulled until she was squashed against me, held her there, before letting her go. She moved across to play with the other breast. As she did so, one hand moved around my back. I arched it away from the wall, and she ran her fingers up and down my spine. After a few tingling passes, her hand carried on over my bum. Stroking one cheek, then the other.

I saw her head drop, as she crouched in front of me. She didn't lose contact with my skin. Her mouth continued to kiss my tummy as she went; both hands now on my bum. As her kisses got closer to my briefs, her fingers slipped into the waist, and slowly eased them over my hips, and let them fall to the ground. Her hands returning to my naked bum, gently squeezing, and pulling me towards her. I tensed in anticipation as her kisses got closer and closer to my sex. Waiting for that first intimate touch.

And she stopped. My body relaxed; the anticipation thwarted. She stood slowly, a kiss on each breast as she did so. Finally, a kiss on the lips.

"You're a tease, Miss Fletcher."

"Fun isn't it?" She was undoing the straps on her own dress. "Marcus taught me. He's a master."

She let the dress fall to the ground; she was braless as well.

"Remember, two can play at that game," I said.

"I hope so. That's what makes it fun."

She slipped her shorts off and leaned against me.

"Now you. Let's find somewhere comfortable, and I'll finish what I started."

I didn't need to be told twice. I led her through to the bedroom and when we reached the bed, I turned towards her intending to kiss her. But with a gleam in her eye, she pushed me, and I fell back onto the bed. I looked at her naked body standing over me. I could see the moisture glistening between her legs.

My bum was near the edge of the bed, my feet still on the floor. She opened my knees with hers and knelt between them. Her hands stretched up and flowed over my breasts, running over my tummy. Somewhere, it tickled slightly, and I flinched. I heard a soft laugh and gasped as her lips sealed themselves over my clit, and she sucked hard, pulling me into her mouth. The suction eased a little, and her tongue flicked over my bud; then pressed into it several times. Hard and firm, sending little spikes of intense pleasure through my groin.

Her hands moved under my thighs and came over on top of my hips, and she raised my legs slightly. Taking the hint, I lifted them and placed them over her shoulders, trapping her between my legs. She seemed happy with that. I'd long given up the idea of trying to watch. I relaxed my head, feeling the sensations between my legs.

Her lips had released my clit and were moving over my pussy. Her tongue was lapping at my lips and the roughness on my soft flesh was exquisite. I realised if she continued much longer, she would bring me to orgasm. The speed surprised me, but I wanted it. Her fingers were now spreading my lips as her tongue licked around my entrance.

I hissed through my teeth as her tongue continued lower, leaving my pussy, and reaching that beautiful spot. It continued, and I lifted my hips. She could just reach my ass in this position, and I felt her tongue playing along one side, making me groan. She had quickly discovered how sensitive it was. Her fingers were gently stroking my lips, occasionally continuing up to circle my clit. I was near now.

She knew it. Leaving my ass, she concentrated on my pussy with her mouth, moving her fingers to my clit. I needed her mouth on it, so I put my hand on her head, and she let me guide it. I moaned as her mouth went over the hood and went to work. It was enough. Still pushing her head onto me, I was on the verge of orgasm. My hips rose as my bum tensed; I subconsciously took a deep breath and held it. She carried on, applying more pressure until it happened.

A long deep groan pulled the air from my lungs. My body letting all its tension flow away. My hips tensing and relaxing several times; Sal gamely following their movement. As I slowly relaxed, she released me from her mouth. She knew how sensitive I was after orgasm. Too damn sensitive; it took me a while to recover. She slowly lowered my legs until my feet found the floor.

She was stroking my tummy; letting me come down. I eventually lifted my head to find her looking at me; her head resting on my thigh. Holding my eyes, she teasingly tugged a couple of hairs with her teeth until I flinched. Smiling, she rose and leaned over me. She could just reach far enough to kiss me, and I put my arms around her. I could taste myself on her lips. We stayed like that for a few minutes.

"It's no good, Sal, my legs are going to sleep."

She got up, holding out her hand. I sat on the bed, then stood up. I took her arm, and guided her onto the bed, leading her to the middle. Laying her on her back, I lay on my side next to her. My turn to play. I had come to realise why Marcus loved her eyes so much. They were such a brilliant, deep green. But when she was turned on, they were bright, erotic, full of the most lustful promise. Almost a way into her very soul.

But it wasn't her soul I was interested in right now. My hand was already gliding over her body. From her neck, over her breasts, her tummy, her thighs. I'd again seen how wet she was. I knew she needed some attention. Leaning over her, I kissed her; simply, gently. When she responded, I let my fingers wander between her legs.

Her response was immediate; a gasp, a deep groan. Her legs spreading wide. I continued to kiss her, not taking my lips off hers. My fingers now roughly rubbing her clit. She was breathing hard; not only from the approaching orgasm but also from my continuous kiss covering her mouth. That kiss was hard now too, my lips covering hers. My tongue invading her mouth.

Her body suddenly arched; holding itself in a rigid position for a few moments, before collapsing on the bed. Her cries muffled in our joined mouths. She finally had to break away, gasping furiously, as she tried to fill her lungs with oxygen. I stopped my assault on her sex and stroked her thigh. Watching as she recovered. Her neck, face and breastbone heavily flushed.

I moved to lay over her side. She put an arm under me, pulling me into her. I lay one leg between hers, and my head on her breast. Both of us recovering; both coming down from our pleasure. Eventually, I needed the loo, and the movement brought us both back to life. She went after me, and we ended up back on the bed, in a sprawling cuddle. Comfortably relaxed, gently stroking each other.

Chapter 13 – Sally

Lying there, skin to skin with Lucy, the unbridled happiness returned. Since the holiday my mind had been in a constant state of confusion. I'd satisfied myself Marcus's acceptance of the situation was sincere. I'd known him long enough now to know that if he'd had any concerns, he would have voiced them. Particularly when it concerned our relationship.

But I still had doubts. Just because he was happy with it, did it make it fair on him? Was I being too selfish? That was the question I had been battling. There were others, but that had been the main one. In the end, I'd taken a leaf out of his book. Play it by ear. Go with it and see what happened. And it had led here, to Lucy's bed; the two of us resting after sex, with the whole night ahead of us.

I knew by now her body had different needs to my own. I could keep going once I was in the mood. She needed breaks; time to recover. So, we lay there, wrapped around each other. Warm and comfortable. I was relaxed but ready for more.

After half an hour or so, Lucy stirred.

"Fancy some more wine?"

"Mmm."

I took in her body as she got off the bed and walked out to the living room. Then again, as she returned with the bottle and our two glasses. Topping them up, she handed one to me and re-joined me on the bed. After a few leisurely sips, she put her glass down.

She leaned over and gave me a kiss, before sliding off the bed, and going over to a chest of drawers. Opening one, she took something out. When she turned around, I saw she was holding a strapless strap-on. Bright pink, almost neon. She walked slowly back to the bed and offered it to me. I took it, and ran my fingers over it, bending it. Feeling its surface and gauging its flexibility. She leaned over and kissed me.

"Want to fuck me?"

I kissed her back.

"Only after you're fucked me. Shown me how."

"I don't think you'll need much instruction, Sal."

She got off the bed and retrieved some lube from the bedside cabinet. She placed one foot on the bed, exposing her sex. Taking a little lube, she rubbed it on the shorter end and eased it in, moving her hips to let it slip in smoothly. With a final wiggle, it settled in place, and she put her leg back on the floor. It was a beguiling sight. I'd seen them on porn films, but never in the flesh. This gorgeous woman, standing there with a big neon cock protruding from her. All I could think about was her fucking me with it. I wanted it.

She picked up the lube and gave me a questioning look. I shook my head. We both knew I wouldn't need it. Climbing onto the bed, she leaned over me and kissed me. I wrapped my fingers around the dildo and moved it.

"Slow and gentle," she whispered. "The other end's in a sensitive place."

She moved her legs one at a time between mine. Her fingers glided over my pussy, gently spreading my lips. The tip of the dildo eased into me. She dropped her hips steadily, knowing I was more than ready for it. Continuing until she was lying on me, the whole thing buried in me. We put our arms around each other, and she lay there; still.

"How does it feel?" she asked.

"Wow. Just wow."

"Does it feel different?"

I thought about it; wriggled my hips slightly to get a better feel from it.

"Yes. It's cool. A cock is … well, hot. And the texture's different. There's another difference, too."

"What's that?"

I shifted slightly.

"I can't normally feel another clit rubbing on mine."

"One of the joys of girls together."

She rolled her whole body backwards and forwards. I could feel the dildo moving inside me, but more noticeably, I could feel her clit playing with mine. I closed my eyes as the movement sent little shivers through me and my body started its climb to orgasm.

She stopped and kissed me.

"Not yet, you don't."

She lifted her upper body enough to separate our groins and began to thrust in and out. I wrapped my legs around hers, as she took longer strokes. I was mesmerized by the sight before me. I could feel a cock fucking me, but I was looking at a pair of breasts swaying above me. I reached around her and put my hands on her bum. Definitely a woman's bum.

My breathing was beginning to increase, as my orgasm neared. Lucy dropped again, our skin now rubbing each other's bud. But she kept up the deep strokes. The action of her skin on my clit, and the dildo sliding in and out brought me to orgasm. I wrapped my arms around her back, and as I came, I pulled her towards me hard. My shaking transferring to her body. Our heads side by side.

She stopped her movement as I came down, lifted her head and kissed me. I responded as best I could while I recovered my breath.

"Well?"

"That was fucking amazing."

"As good?"

I must have frowned because she laughed.

"Don't worry, you don't need to answer that. I guess not."

"You'll have to do it more to try and convince me."

"Try and stop me."

I was stroking her back and bum.

"Does the other end do anything for you?"

"Oh, yes. It hits the right spot."

"Right. Let's change over. I want a go."

She lifted herself off me and eased the dildo out. Then the fun started. I took it and spreading my own legs, I slid the end into me. When I moved towards Lucy again, it fell out. I replaced it, trying to secure it in a slightly different position. But when I knelt over her, about to guide it in, it slid out again.

We tried two or three more times, both of us beginning to laugh. By the time it had fallen out for about the fifth time, we were both in stitches. Hardly able to say a word or catch our breath. We collapsed in a fit of giggles. It took us a few minutes to recover.

"You're too wet," Lucy finally managed to say.

"Seems so." I'd looked forward to using it on her. She sensed my disappointment.

"Don't worry. I know what we need."

She got off the bed, kissing me on the way, and returned to her drawer. After rummaging about, she turned around holding what I thought at first was an ordinary double-ended dildo. But it had straps, and I soon saw what it was.

A traditional strap-on, but with two heads. Bringing it over she motioned me to sit on my haunches. She squatted behind me and brought the dildo between my legs, gently easing it in. When it was comfortable, she tied the strap around my waist and one around each thigh.

"There," she said softly by my ear. "That won't come out."

She put one hand over my breasts and caressed them, while she used the other to stroke my purple cock. Occasionally letting her hand come back to flick over my clit.

"Now you can fuck me."

She released me and moved back further up the bed. I turned around to look at her. But I was distracted by my purple cock. Marcus and I regularly used dildos and vibrators on me. I also used them on him. We didn't have a strap-on and I made a mental note to get one. I liked the idea of using one to fuck him. I looked down and stroked the dildo. As I moved it, the other end moved inside me, bringing a smile to my face. Almost as if it really was a part of me.

"Hey," Lucy broke into my thoughts. "Are you going to fuck me, or just have a wank?"

I grinned.

"Oh, I'm going to fuck you. But I want you on your knees."

"Ooh. Yes, ma'am."

She turned over and pushed her bum back towards me. Fleeting thoughts went through my head. I could see the attraction of this position. I loved it when Marcus fucked me like this; so did he. I could now see it from his viewpoint. I didn't know if it was the cock between my legs, but I had a feeling of dominance. In front of me were a pussy and ass inviting my penetration; waiting for me to take it.

I knew Lucy didn't get as wet as me, so I reached over for some lube, and rubbed it over the dildo. I shimmied up behind her and put my fingers between her legs. She shivered as they found their mark. Easing the tip of the dildo into her, I gently slid it all the way in. She leaned back to meet it.

I put my hands on her hips and slowly slid in and out. That was when I was reminded this dildo was double-ended. She gave a tiny moan every time I sank deep into her, but it was having a similar effect on me. At the end of every thrust, the part in me had its effect. I speeded up; fucking her. Gripping her waist to pull her into me as I did so. Without thinking, I brought my hand down hard on her bum a couple of times; she gave a shriek, followed by a giggle.

"Sorry." I stopped.

"No," she said in an amused tone. "I'm okay if you want to."

I did want to. As I fucked her, I gave her the occasional slap on her bum, which was reddening nicely. But I realised I was going to come soon. The whole picture was too much. Seeing her from this angle; watching my dildo invading her, slapping her bum. The dildo in me. I hardly had time to whisper 'sorry', before I came. Quite hard. Hard enough I had to stop and give in to it. Hard enough that I had to slip out of Lucy and drop to my haunches as my body took over. I saw her curl round, resting on her side looking at me; a smile on her face. She waited for me to recover.

"You seemed to enjoy yourself," she said.

"Sorry. I couldn't help it."

"Don't be sorry. It's not a competition."

She knelt towards me, kissing me.

"You lie down. I want to take control."

I wasn't going to argue. I laid on my back, and she swiftly straddled me. Spreading herself, she slid onto the dildo and bent over me. A wicked look on her face.

"Right, Miss Multiple Orgasm. I'm going to ride you. I'm going to ride you until I come. And if you come fifteen times while I'm doing it, so be it. But I'm not stopping."

She gave me a passionate kiss and sat back up. Her hands on my tummy, she started to rock. Sometimes fully impaled, sometimes along the dildo. Changing direction, changing pace. After a few minutes, I could see she was starting her long build. She concentrated on herself. She was enjoying this.

So was I. I could feel another orgasm coming. I let it happen; my hips bucking, adding to her movements. She was moaning now; grinding on the dildo. The harder she ground herself, the more the end in me had an effect. She gripped my waist; I saw the look on her face. She looked right through me, and after a few final deep strokes, she froze momentarily, and let out a long cry, as her orgasm flowed through her. Sinking onto the dildo, her body arched backwards, her head flopping back. I laid my hands on her quivering thighs and lay still.

After a few minutes, she came back. Slowly sitting up and looking at me. She leaned over me, her lips lowering onto mine. Kissing gently, just touching each time. With a big sigh, she allowed herself to flop onto me, her head resting to one side of mine. We lay like that for a few minutes, until I realised the dildo in me was becoming uncomfortable. It must have been pressing in the wrong place. I tried to move slightly to relieve it without her noticing.

"Need to take it out?"

"Yes, it's a bit uncomfortable now."

She lifted her head, kissed me, and lifted herself off the dildo. I went to sit up, but she gently pushed me down. She undid the straps, and I opened my legs allowing her to slip the dildo out.

"Better?"

"Mmm. Now come here."

She lay half over me, and I put my arms around her. And we both fell asleep.

I slept like a log, and we enjoyed each other again in the morning. If this was what our nights together were going to be like, we'd made a good decision.

***

As soon as I entered our flat, I knew something was wrong. It was eleven o'clock in the morning, and all the curtains were still drawn. Relax Sally. Marcus isn't feeling well; perhaps he's stayed in bed. It wasn't like him, though. I almost ran down the stairs. Called his name. No reply.

Pushing the bedroom door open, even in the darkness of the room, I could see he wasn't in bed. Where was he? The light was on in the bathroom. I walked around the partition, into one of the concealed sections, and saw him. Prostrate and lifeless on the floor in front of the toilet. Blood covering his bum and legs. And on the floor. And the toilet.

I rushed over and touched him. Warm. I reached for his wrist, laying two fingers on it; searching for his pulse. It was there; slow, weak, but it was there. Instinct took over. I grabbed my phone from my bag and called an ambulance.

At the hospital, I sat in a daze while people did things to Marcus. I'd been able to tell the paramedics about his Crohn's and about his current flare. So, when we got to the hospital, they had a starting point. They had his recent scans and tests.

I sat in the cubicle while they attached lines and monitors. A drip and a blood transfusion. He looked so pale. His blood pressure was very low. He was drifting in and out of consciousness. The doctors asked me one or two questions; couldn't tell me much at this stage.

I don't know how long I sat there. I tried to think if there was anything I needed to do, but there wasn't. I would stay right here for as long as it took. I kept telling myself he'd be okay. That they'd sort him out. But the blood? Where had it all come from? I knew he passed small amounts of blood at times. But not this. What had happened? What could they do?

I was going around in circles, and I realised I was getting emotional which wouldn't help. I asked a nurse what was happening. She told me they thought he was now stable, and they were waiting for a consultant to review him. It would be in an hour or so. He wasn't in danger at the moment.

I went out to the corridor and rang Mary. I needed to talk to someone. She was her usual self. Concerned, but calming. She listened while I unloaded. After fifteen minutes I'd regained some control. She told me to ring her any time I needed her. I sent Lucy a short text telling her where we were. I recognised a twinge of guilt in me about last night. The fun I'd had compared to what he must have been through. It brought me crashing down to earth and I burst into tears.

When I recovered, I went back to Marcus and sat by his bed. The Consultant finally came to see him. After reviewing the notes, he spoke to me. He couldn't tell exactly what had happened, but there'd obviously been a massive bleed. He was currently stable but would almost certainly need surgery. The plan was to try and do another MRI to see what was going on. Then decide the next step.

Soon after he left, I was wondering what to do, when Lucy arrived. I was glad to see someone I knew and threw my arms around her.

"You didn't need to come."

"I thought you might want some company. How is he?"

I told her what had happened, and what the consultant had said.

"Is he conscious?"

"He's drifting in and out. They think he'll come around as the fluid and blood goes in."

"What are you going to do?"

"Wait. Wait until I've had a chance to speak to him and see if they'll do the MRI today."

"Right. I'll stay too."

"You don't have – "

"I'm staying."

"Thanks."

A little later, Marcus stirred. I moved towards him and laid my hand on his.

"Marcus?"

A little murmur.

"Can you hear me?"

"Mmm."

"How do you feel?" I knew it was a stupid question before I'd even finished asking it.

He gave a deflated sigh in response.

"You're in hospital. You've had a bleed. They're going to do an MRI."

"Mmm."

"You're going to be all right." I was trying to convince myself more than him.

"Mmm."

"I love you."

This time I got a little smile. We sat there, no more to be said. Lucy sitting on a chair at the end of the bed. An hour later, they took him for an MRI and Lucy took me to get something to eat. I wasn't hungry, but she forced half a sandwich into me. When we returned, he was being wheeled back into the cubicle. He was conscious now, but largely asleep. I didn't try and talk to him.

A little later, the consultant returned. The scan had shown a probable bleed from the site of the strange mass which had shown on the earlier one. They were going to send him to a high dependency ward, keep him stable, and let the surgeon decide the next step on Monday. At least we had a plan.

By the time he had moved to the ward, he was more with it. He looked at me now and said a few words. Each one took visible effort. I told him what had happened, what the plan was. He understood.

A little later, Lucy took me aside.

"You need to get some rest, Sal. I know you want to stay, but what for? He's stable and in safe hands. You've been here for what? Eight hours? He's going to need you when things settle."

I knew she was right but hated the idea of leaving him. I wavered. In the end, Lucy made the decision. She went over to Marcus. I followed her.

"Marcus?"

"Luce ..." His voice was barely audible.

"Sally wants to stay, but I think she needs to get some rest."

His finger beckoned me; I went to the edge of the bed. He looked wearily up at me.

"Bugger off."

His face broke into a grin.

"I'll come back later."

"Tomorrow."

"No, tonight ..."

He scowled as much as his energy allowed.

"Tomorrow."

Lucy took me home, settled me in, and left. Neither of us had mentioned the night before. It seemed strange in the flat on my own, knowing Marcus was in hospital. I rang in the evening, and they told me he had been awake, but they'd increased his painkillers and he was now asleep again.

I thought about visiting, but Lucy was right; it would worry me, and tire him. Tomorrow would be fine. Lying in bed that night, I had a lot on my mind. The bed seemed empty without him. Without his arms around me. I still felt guilty about being away when it had happened. And worried about what would happen next.

Chapter 14 – Marcus

I woke with a start and tried to sit up. A searing pain in my abdomen forced me to give up that idea. I was groggy, spaced out and in pain. I took in my surroundings, and it slowly all made sense. Hospital. I was in hospital, of course. Operation. Yes, that was it. I'd had an operation. Was this the recovery room? I looked around again. Yup. No mistaking it; a few other people looking how I felt. Well, I was still alive.

"Hello, Marcus. How are you feeling?"

A nurse.

"Wonderful. Can I go home now?"

She smiled.

"Not yet, but it sounds like you're ready to go to the ward."

When I got there, I fell asleep again, until the pain woke me. They upped the morphine, but I knew from experience the quicker you could get off it, the better. The next thing I was aware of was Sally coming through the door, her face suffused with anxiety. She saw me, almost ran over, and looked down, trying to work out how she could hug me. I had a drip in one arm, the morphine pump in the other. In the end, she bent awkwardly, put her arm around my neck, and rested her head on my shoulder.

"I love you," she whispered.

"I know."

She was crying.

"Thank you," I said softly.

"What for?"

"For saving my life."

She let out two or three heavy sobs, staying on my shoulder.

"I never want to see you like that again."

I wanted to hug her, but I was hurting, and the drips made moving my arms difficult. But it was true; she had saved my life. I'd had a bleed years ago, but I'd been in hospital. This time, I wouldn't have made it if she hadn't found me. Tears welled in my eyes.

Finally, she sniffed, stood up, and wiped her tears away.

"How are you feeling?"

"Not bad. The morphine's helping, but it makes you loopy."

"How will I tell?"

"Ha, ha."

"Have they told you anything yet?"

"No. I think the surgeon will come around soon. They said about sixish."

She unpacked the things she'd brought and collected a few items to take home.

"Anything you want?"

"Well, I won't be able to eat for a few more days yet. Oh, you could bring my kindle, iPad and phone."

"No."

I looked at her. She smiled; a hint of defiance on her face.

"Remember after my op? You gave the orders. Well, now it's my turn."

"But – "

"I'll bring the kindle. And I've got an old iPod somewhere. I'll load some music onto it. But no phone and no iPad. You need to rest."

"But – "

"No buts. Just accept it."

I did; I didn't have the energy to argue.

The surgeon eventually appeared at my bed.

"Well, Mr Foxton. You're a lucky man."

"I am?"

"Yes. The lump on the first MRI turned out to be a mass of inflamed tissue surrounding an artery. Luckily, it ruptured into your gut and came through. If it had burst into your abdomen … Well."

"And now?"

"Oh, you should be fine now. I've taken out the mass and the constricted section of gut. Put it all back together. Home in ten days. A few weeks recovery and you'll be back to normal."

"Thank you."

"I'll see you again over the next few days."

He nodded to Sally and moved on.

"There," I said. "Nearly back to normal."

"Yes, but until then, you're going to do as you're told."

Sally wasn't joking. When I got home, I wasn't allowed to do anything. I'd already decided I needed to sleep on my own for a week or two, and she understood that from her operation. You needed the whole bed to turn over, and an accidental kick from a partner in the night didn't bear thinking about.

But from the moment I got up to the moment I went to my separate bed, she wouldn't let me do anything. Mary and Lucy both popped in to see me a few times, as well.

One evening, after I'd been home a few days, Sally was curled up beside me on the sofa. I asked her how her discussions with Lucy had gone. I'd asked her about it in hospital, but she'd refused to discuss it until I got home.

"Okay."

"Come on, what's wrong?"

"We agreed with what you and I discussed. We were both happy with it."

"But …?"

She let out a heavy sigh.

"I can't get out of my head that we went on to … well, I stayed the night, while you were so ill."

I laughed. She scowled at me.

"Sal, forget it. You weren't to know. It could have happened at any time. While you were at work. It wouldn't have stopped you going back to work, would it?"

"No."

"So, forget it. Did you spend some time with her while I was in hospital?"

She almost spat her reply. "No, of course not."

I realised the question had been wrong. I held up my hand.

"Sorry, I wasn't thinking. What have you agreed?"

She told me briefly what they'd decided and asked me again if I was still happy.

"What's the plan?"

"I don't know; it's a bit on hold at the moment."

"Because of me?"

She looked at me as if she was talking to an idiot, which at that moment was possibly true.

"Okay, okay. But please, just do it."

"I can't while you still need me."

"Sal, I'm gaining strength every day, and the wound is healing well. I can cope without you for a night."

I could see she was in two minds.

"Besides," I continued. "We all know your appetite, and you aren't going to get anything from me for a while. You must be gagging for it."

She pouted, picked up a cushion to hit me with, had second thoughts, and put it down. Then burst out laughing.

"You are getting better, aren't you?"

"Yup. But seriously, if you leave it too long, you'll both find it more difficult to start again."

She gave one of her wicked smiles.

"Oh, I don't think there's any danger of that."

She told me more about her evening with Lucy; what they'd agreed. She was about to go into detail about what happened next but stopped herself.

"Sorry, better not talk about sex when you're incapacitated."

For once, I agreed. I was off the steroids since the operation, and my libido was returning. But the scar would prevent any activity for several weeks. Sal had had keyhole surgery for her appendix, but sex had been too painful for two or three weeks. My scar was eighteen inches long across my belly. I could only guess when I'd be able to enjoy her again.

***

After I'd been home for a couple of weeks, Sally haltingly suggested she might spend the next Friday night with Lucy. When she returned on Saturday morning, she let slip that Lucy had suggested a shopping trip, but she'd declined in order to come home. I made her ring Lucy and arrange to meet her for lunch and an afternoon of retail therapy, then bring her back for dinner.

They got home in the late afternoon, with several bags.

"Hi, Marcus," Lucy said. "How are you?"

"Much better thanks. Feeling stronger every day."

"Strong enough for a hug?"

She came over, gave me a kiss on the cheek, and put her arms around me. She didn't pull away.

"I wanted to say a proper thank you."

"What for?"

"For pimping your girlfriend to me. And for agreeing to this … arrangement."

She pulled away, and I saw she was blushing slightly.

"It's fine, Lucy," I said. "Mind you …"

I looked over at Sally standing nearby, watching us. Lucy followed my gaze, still leaning on my shoulder.

"I hope she knows what she's let herself in for."

"Why?" Sally asked warily.

"Well, stands to reason. You've got two lovers to keep you happy. But it means you'll need to work twice as hard to keep us both happy."

Lucy laughed as Sally broke into that wicked grin of hers.

"I think I might enjoy the challenge, don't you?"

She walked through towards the kitchen. Lucy leaned towards me.

"She will, won't she?"

"Yup."

I had to admit, even I was surprised about how easily we all accepted the situation. Dinner was relaxed; the same as it had always been. We didn't try to avoid the subject; didn't try to deny Sally was lover to both of us. It was simply accepted as fact. The conversation flowed as normal.

"Have you got any further with solving the mystery around your father, Sal?"

"Not yet, but we've got a genealogist visiting next week to see if he thinks it's worth investigating. I'm not sure anyone could work out where to start."

"You think it might all be fake?"

"It could be. Hopefully, he might be able to tell. But I have decided what to do with the stones." She looked over to me, knowing this was news to me, too.

"Oh?"

"Yup. I'm selling some of the ordinary stuff, and I'm going to have some jewellery made from the best of the rest." She turned to me now. "You know those jewellers Mr Wynne recommended?"

"Yes."

"I've spoken to the one whose designs we liked the best. Remember?"

"Yes, I think so."

"When I sent her a few photos of the stones, she was intrigued. She's coming here on Tuesday evening."

"It'll be expensive to commission jewellery, won't it? Are the stones worth it?"

Sal and I shared a look. Obviously, she hadn't told Lucy. She raised an eyebrow, and I nodded.

"The whole lot are worth something over three-quarters of a million."

Lucy froze, a shocked look on her face.

"What? Really?"

"Whatever Sal's father was, Luce, he apparently had impeccable taste."

We all sat quietly for a few minutes; thinking. Finally, Lucy spoke.

"Why did he have them in a bank?"

"Safe place, I suppose. You have a theory, don't you darling?"

"Well," I said, "it's only a guess. But suppose your work was a bit dodgy. Wouldn't you put something small and valuable somewhere safe in case you needed to disappear for a while?"

"An escape fund?"

"Exactly. He could have picked them up – and his various identities – and run. He could sell those stones anywhere in the world. No bank accounts, no worries about exchanging currencies. Untraceable."

"Sounds plausible."

"It's plausible," Sal said. "But we don't know. I'm not sure we ever will."

***

Stephanie, the jeweller, proved to be a reader of people as much as a designer. When she arrived, I noticed her observing Sally closely as she was talking. She asked Sal to show her the jewellery she already had. We then laid out the stones we thought might make good pieces. Stephanie looked at them all closely.

"All these stones are beautiful. I can hardly wait to do something with them. There are a few that will be perfect for you."

She moved the two emeralds clear of the others.

"These two are fabulous. I know it's greedy, but it's a shame there aren't three. I could have designed a pair of earrings, and something around your neck. But they will match your eyes."

"We thought about earrings, but are they a bit big?"

"They're large, but you have a long neck. With the right setting, they'll be stunning."

She picked out one or two other pieces and suggested possible uses for them. She also examined most of the smaller stones, suggesting ones which might be useful as groups, or for using in the settings of the larger ones. She brought out a folder of jewellery pictures, and went through them with Sally, asking her to pick out those she liked. At the end, she asked if she could take a few photos of Sally; head, head and shoulders and waist-up. Plus, some photos of the larger stones. She left us, promising to come up with some potential designs to show us.

The following evening, it was the turn of the genealogist. Martin was recommended by one of Sally's colleagues. He had traced their family history quickly and efficiently. But he was honest about Sally's father, once she had told him everything we knew.

"Being objective is difficult when you're close to the subject, Sally. From what you've told me, it's not clear we even know his real name. The only starting point would be the name you know. But I have to say, it might lead nowhere. I might come to a dead-end very quickly."

"I know it's a tough ask, Martin. But are you prepared to at least do some basic research?"

"Yes, of course. If someone employs me, I do my best to answer their questions."

We agreed Martin would make his usual inquiries. See if he found anything. We'd decide where to go from there.

Our third visitor of the week was even more interesting. Matt; the dungeon builder. I'd suggested to Sally we turn the remaining two vaults into a playroom, and she'd loved the idea. I'd found Matt after trawling the internet. When I spoke to him, he'd impressed me with his calmness and candour. He'd also been the only person I'd found who not only supplied equipment but was also able to do any building or alteration work required. When he arrived, he had a woman with him.

"This is Yasmin; we work together. I hope that's okay?"

I couldn't help noticing Yasmin was wearing a choker. It might have been jewellery; who knew? We passed a few pleasantries and led them to the vaults in question. When we arrived, Matt let out a long whistle.

"My word. It's ready-made for it, isn't it?"

"It does seem appropriate. But it'll need a lot of work."

He turned to his partner. "What do you think, Yas?"

She had been looking around, a faint smile on her face.

"If we get it right, it'll be perfect."

"So, let's get it right."

Matt and Yasmin asked us how we wanted the room to look. We'd talked about that. We wanted it 'Gothic lite', if there was such a thing. Not too oppressive, but warm, cosy and rich. They seemed to understand. We talked about the walls; leave the bare brick, or cover it? What about the ceiling? The flooring? Lighting? Furniture? All this was before we even discussed what equipment we wanted.

We returned upstairs for this, and Matt suggested we split up to discuss our needs. It struck me as strange, but as Yasmin took Sally to the dining room, and Matt and I talked in the living room, it made sense.

"If I do a job for a couple or a group, I like to talk to each separately if possible. Firstly, if you'll forgive me, to make sure all parties are okay with it. In the early days, I did a job for a guy who turned out to be less than genuine. He ended up serving time for assault and domestic abuse. I don't want that again.

"But I also want to get a feel for your individual interests so I can recommend the best equipment for you. I know it means I may ask a few personal questions, but the more we understand your needs, the more we can help you get your room right."

It made sense; it was a bit strange though. I'd never discussed this side of our lives with anyone but Sally. I don't think she'd discussed it with anyone else either; except perhaps Lucy. I found myself telling Matt things which had been private until then. But he wasn't prurient; he didn't pry. He showed me a list of activities and asked me to rate them. A shortened BDSM checklist, basically. When Yasmin and Sally re-joined us, I noticed Sally was slightly flushed.

After another brief discussion, Matt offered to go away and come up with a design for the space. Enough to complete it as a room, incorporating any fixed items. He'd also provide a list of suggested equipment, although we had plenty of ideas of our own. We'd have to wait to see what he came up with.

It was five weeks since my operation and I was feeling much better. The wound was essentially healed. Still very red, but it didn't interfere with life too much; just gave me the occasional reminder it was there. I'd had another MRI, which had given me a clean bill of health; no more stricture, no unexplained mass. And no more steroids.

For all my complaining, Sally had been wonderful. After enjoying her initial dictatorship, she became sensitive to my mood. Judging when I needed help, and when I didn't. I was so grateful for her presence and love; it certainly speeded my recovery.

I'd moved back to our bed after a couple of weeks, but it had been another week before we'd tried anything. Even then, as after Sal's operation, it had been watching each other masturbate. A week later, we'd done it for each other.

Finally, we'd been able to make love. Gently, carefully. Sal riding me slowly, as we enjoyed each other for the first time in many weeks. It had been worth the wait, even though my tummy had complained. Pain and pleasure may have been our thing, but that was the wrong sort of pain.

Chapter 15 – Sally

Everything seemed to be settling down at last. Marcus had given me a scare, but he was recovering quicker than I'd dared hope. He was his old self, but still struggling with the pain from the wound, and building his strength. His love had never dimmed, but now his libido was almost back to its old level, and he was frustrated the wound was still preventing him from doing what he wanted to do. What we wanted to do.

I was spending a night with Lucy every so often. It seemed to naturally happen every ten days or so and we were both happy with that. We met for lunch at least once a week and visited the gym regularly. We knew we should go more often, but somehow never got around to it.

I'd had a second meeting with Stephanie and was blown away with some of the designs she had come up with. I'd immediately commissioned some pieces and given her the necessary stones. I'd also asked her to do a few items I hadn't told anyone about. One had made her raise an eyebrow, but she'd willingly accepted the commission. We'd agreed prices. Lucy had been right; it was expensive.

Stephanie didn't make the items herself. She contracted that to a few craftsmen who worked incredibly quickly. They were ready two weeks later, and I visited Stephanie to try them on, and see if we were both satisfied with the final products. They were exquisite; everything I imagined them to be. Just in time for Marcus's birthday.

He wasn't one for celebrations. Dinner with friends suited him perfectly, so I booked us a table at the same club we had visited for his birthday the previous year. It had been new then. Jazz-themed, it was opulent without being kitsch, and the food and music were excellent. It had become a popular destination, and we had visited several times. I booked for the night before his birthday; I wanted him all to myself on the day. I invited Lucy and Mary as well.

As we got ready, I debated whether to wear some of the new jewellery. I hadn't told Marcus I'd got it yet. I wanted to surprise him, but I didn't want to make the evening about me; it was his birthday, after all. But I decided I would. After all, I wouldn't get many chances to wear it.

After he finished dressing and went upstairs to wait for me, I opened the largest jewellery box. Two drop earrings with those large emeralds; the most valuable items. But the centrepiece was the necklace. Stephanie had surpassed herself. I'd described what I wanted as best as I could, and she'd made it real.

A platinum mesh choker, about an inch and a half deep, with a large green garnet in the centre. Hanging from the front, the mesh continued downwards slowly narrowing, forming a flowing triangle. Along the edges, more tiny green garnets. These started pale at the choker, gradually getting darker, until reaching a slightly larger one the same colour as the one on my neck. They matched the emeralds. Putting it on, it was soft and pliable, following the contours of my skin. Resting in place as if it was a part of me. There were also two bracelets to match.

I pulled on the dress I had chosen. It was green and tight-fitting. But I felt good in it, and I knew Marcus loved it. Quickly finishing off my hair, I picked up three small boxes and went upstairs.

When Marcus saw me, he gasped.

"Wow. Come here; let me see."

I went over to him, and he looked from one piece to the other. Carefully putting his hand behind an earring, running a finger over the necklace. He hadn't spotted the bracelets.

"They are fabulous. You look a million dollars, Sal."

I kissed him.

"They are lovely, aren't they?" I held up my hands. "Bracelets too."

"Well," he said, attempting a Sean Connery accent. "A girl should always have matching collar and cuffs." The accent was a definite fail.

"Not too much?"

"No."

He stood looking at me, a wonderful smile on his face, for so long I began to feel a tinge of shyness.

"What?"

"We were right. Those emeralds and your eyes."

I'd spent ages doing my eye make-up; I didn't normally wear much. But I'd tried to make them more prominent tonight. I'd come to understand how much I could turn Marcus on with my eyes. He could read them better than I could myself. See doubt, happiness, love; and lust. He loved seeing that lust, and tonight, that's exactly what I wanted him to see.

I'd booked a taxi to take us to the club. We couldn't drive because I didn't want Marcus going into the garage. I'd hidden one of his presents there. He'd see it in the morning. When we arrived, Lucy was waiting for us. As we were greeting her, Mary got out of a taxi.

It was an unwritten convention between us, that these special occasions gave us girls the license to dress up, and they'd both seized the opportunity. Mary always looked good; she was stylish, in an understated way. I think I had subconsciously inherited a lot of my style from her over the years.

Tonight, she'd reverted to the black dress; not so little now, she was conscious of the perils of mutton and lamb. But she looked good. Lucy looked fantastic. A red dress; simple, elegant and just tight enough. Our new relationship meant I now happily looked at her in a different way. She looked hot.

Once we were seated in our booth, we ordered drinks and perused the menu. It was busy already, and the air was filled with murmured conversations, and the occasional chink of glasses or crockery being placed on tables. But the room went up forever, to a high vaulted ceiling, so the sound dissipated quickly. We'd often mused about the difficulty of the space for the musicians, but it always sounded good.

"Sal, they're gorgeous."

Lucy's voice brought me back from contemplation.

"Your earrings. Are you pleased?"

"Yes, I don't think Steph could have done any better."

Mary was watching me, a faint smile on her face.

"They are beautiful, darling. But the necklace is even better. It's subtle and showy at the same time. If that's possible."

"I know what you mean. It's so light and comfortable, I hardly know I'm wearing it."

"Did I see a bracelet, too?" Lucy asked.

I held up both wrists.

"Wow, two."

"Yes, I only asked her to do one, but she suggested a matching pair. Well, almost. She told me she's put some subtle differences in, but I haven't found them yet."

"They look stunning. It's quite a set."

"I don't know how often I'm going to wear it, though. It's not exactly work gear."

"Don't worry about that, dear," Mary said. "Good jewellery will outlive all of us. You'll find occasions to wear it. It will feel even more special when you do."

I hadn't thought about it that way but realised she was right.

We ambled our way through the meal slowly, chatting amiably. Mary entertained us with some updates on her relationship with Ken. I was pleased for her; he seemed to be making her happy. By her account, he'd led a bit of a sheltered life. He'd been married to his wife for over thirty years, and for the last ten, he'd been her carer.

After she died, he and Mary had met at a bridge club, and she had spent the time since then showing him slices of life he'd missed. There seemed to be quite a few of them.

"He'd never even been to London before I took him. Can you imagine that? But what I like about him is his innocent excitement. He doesn't shy away from things. He's always up for the challenge."

"Why is it so many people lose that?"

"It's knocked out of us, I think. We're told we have to be serious all the time. We lose the sense of wonder and curiosity we have as children. It's such a shame. I'm grateful I never got it knocked out of me."

"Were Gran and Grandad good like that, Mary?"

She sniffed, before giving me a cunning grin.

"No, darling. They were not. They were very prudish, really."

"How did you keep your spirit, then?"

"They were naive. They never even dreamed of most of the things I got up to."

Marcus laughed.

"You know, Mary. I hope someone publishes your diaries one day; I suspect they'd make fascinating reading."

"Never kept one, Marcus. Only dull girls keep diaries."

"Did Mum keep one?"

Mary's face fell for an instant.

"I'm sorry darling, humour got the better of me there. I – "

I put my hand on her arm, smiling.

"Mary, it's okay. I didn't take it that way." She looked relieved. "But did she?"

She paused; for effect, I think.

"Yes."

I laughed, and the others joined me; possibly relieved the tension had eased. In truth, I didn't mind what Mary had said at all. The counselling had given me a more realistic view of my mother. It was Mary who had made me the woman I was today; not my mother. It was Mary who'd given me my love of learning; not my mother. Mary who'd freed my spirit; not my mother. I think Mary knew all this but never sought acknowledgement for it. I had a lot to thank her for.

After we'd finished dessert, we ordered more drinks. The headliner tonight was due on stage in twenty minutes or so, and that left me time for my surprise.

"Darling," I whispered. "Can I have those boxes?"

I'd asked him to put them in his pocket as I only had a small clutch bag. He handed them to me, and I kissed him on the cheek.

"I'm sorry to hijack your occasion for a few minutes, but I want to say something."

They were all listening now.

"You all know I've been dealing with some issues over the last year. Well, for far longer, but the last year is when I've tackled them. And I couldn't have done it without each of you. I wanted to tell you I've had my last counselling session. Jenny and I thought the time was right. I'm done. I can't hope to repay you, but I wanted to say a little thank you. With a little help from my father who caused most of the trouble in the first place."

Checking the boxes, I placed one in front of Mary, one in front of Lucy, and one in front of Marcus. They were bemused; deep inside, I was pleased about that. They looked at me; then each other. Mary was the first to speak.

"Shall we take it in turns? Lucy?"

Lucy picked the box up, and slowly slid the lid off. She gasped.

"Oh, Sal."

She stared at it for a few moments, before tilting it to show Mary and Marcus. I'd had a pair of drop earrings made from two rubies that had been in the collection. I knew she loved red. Her blonde hair suited the colour. Her dress tonight showed that.

"They're … beautiful."

She took one out and held it between her fingers. When she looked at me, I could see so much in her gaze. The years of mutual friendship and support now supplemented by a dash of lust.

"Thank you."

Marcus held his hand towards Mary.

"Mary? After you."

Mary picked her box up and looked at me with a strange look. The look you give an errant child. The look that says, 'what have you done now?'. I'd seen it many times over the years. When the top came off, she looked down and broke into a broad smile.

"Oh, darling. They're beautiful."

She again tilted it, to show the others. For Mary, I'd had another pair of earrings made. This time studs, with two small sapphires. To match the ring my father had given her so long ago. She took one out and put the box down before placing it next to the ring on her other hand. She gave me a shrewd look. A thought passed between us; unsaid, because Lucy didn't know the story behind the ring.

"They match perfectly," was all she said. "Thank you."

Just Marcus left. He picked the box up and looked at it; then at me.

"I'll need to get my ears pierced …"

I shook my head. He opened the box and chuckled softly. He lifted out a ring. I'd chosen it carefully. He didn't wear jewellery, although I knew he had previously worn a wedding ring and an eternity ring. I'd managed to find one to get the right size. He wasn't one for bling.

I'd had Steph design a ring from dark tungsten and embed two diamonds close together. But on the inside, flush with the surface. Nobody would know they were there except us. He took it out and turned it over in his hand, noticing the diamonds.

"Two diamonds," I said. "You and me."

He slid it onto his finger and turned it around. Leaning across, he kissed me.

"Thank you," he whispered.

"Right," I said. "That's it."

"Can I put mine on?" Lucy asked.

"They're yours. Of course you can."

She reached up and took her own out. Then carefully put the new ones in. As the last one slipped in, she turned to Mary.

"Aren't you going to put yours on, Mary?"

"At my age, Lucy, I need a big mirror and a bright light to change earrings."

"I'll do them."

Lucy slid closer, removed Mary's studs, and carefully put the new ones in.

"There. Perfect."

She looked around. I could see what she was looking for.

"It's no good. I want to see them. I could do with a comfort break, anyway. Coming?"

Mary joined Lucy on a trip to the ladies. Marcus leaned towards me.

"That was a lovely gesture."

"You like it?"

"Yes. But I was talking about Lucy and Mary."

"Well, you all deserve it. You know me, I love to share."

He kissed me slowly and I opened my eyes wide as he did so. I heard a little moan of appreciation as he saw it.

"Temptress."

"But are you tempted?"

"You wait until we get home."

"I can show you what I'm wearing under this dress."

"Ooh, don't."

I knew his mind would be wandering through my underwear; trying to guess what I had on. I saw Lucy and Mary coming back to the table.

Quickly leaning over to kiss him, I put my mouth by his ear, and whispered slowly, drawing out each word.

"Absolutely nothing."

Pulling away, I relished the look on his face, as the other two took their seats again.

"They're beautiful, Sal," Lucy said. "Thank you. They go so well with this dress, too."

They did; the happy coincidence made her look even hotter.

"They do," Marcus added, a sly grin on his face. "Anyone would think you were the scarlet woman."

Lucy and I grinned, but I kicked Marcus's shin. Had Mary not been there, we would have been able to enjoy that comment more than we did. I looked at Lucy; we were both trying to suppress our giggles.

"Well," she managed. "I have my moments."

"We all do, Lucy," Mary added, hopefully oblivious to the undercurrent. I'd always been open with Mary but wasn't ready to explain the current set-up to her. I wasn't sure I ever would be.

The headliner for the evening opened her performance. We'd seen her before. Silky and sultry, she had a soulful voice and a slightly eccentric style. Her band worked as one with her. So good, you hardly noticed them. I could listen to her all night. I leaned against Marcus and put my head on his shoulder.

After a while, I realised his hand was slowly inching its way between the bench and my back until it rested against my hip. I slowly lifted my bum half-off the seat, and he slid his hand under it before I lowered it again. For the next hour, I sat on his hand. Every so often, he would gradually squeeze the cheek. Quite firmly at times; his little finger nestling near my ass before slowly releasing his grip again.

At first, it was wonderful. As time went on, it was too wonderful. And I didn't have any underwear on. He knew it. Did I regret telling him? Hell, no.

By the time the music finished, we were all very relaxed. We'd all drunk too much. Well, all except Marcus, who never drank a lot. It was time to go, and as we got outside to look for taxis, we said our goodbyes. As usual, Mary and Lucy were sharing one as they lived quite close. Mary hugged me and thanked me for the earrings. She hugged Marcus and wished him a happy birthday for the following day. After Lucy did the same, she hugged me.

"Thank you, thank you, thank you."

I put my hand on her bum and gave it a good squeeze. Mary wasn't looking our way, but Marcus was. I winked at him and he smiled. We waited to see them safely in a cab before looking for one ourselves. It was busy, and there were more customers than taxis, so we opted to walk towards the theatre. There might be some waiting there.

I slipped my arm around his waist, and he put his around my shoulder. We strolled along. There were plenty of people around; some in a worse state than others. We avoided a couple staggering along, holding each other up. His hand went to my bum and rested there. I looked behind; plenty of people around. I moved it back to my shoulder. He lowered it again.

"Behave," I whispered. "I'm a respectable woman."

He let out an exaggerated laugh and a few people looked towards us.

"Well, fairly respectable."

He stopped and turned to face me. Holding my hands by our sides, he kissed me. His face hovered in front of mine. His eyes burning into mine. He spoke softly.

"Maybe you are, and I love you for it. You're also walking around in a tight dress with nothing underneath it, and I love you for that as well. When we get home, I'm going to find out exactly how respectable you are."

I kissed him back and replied equally quietly.

"Oh, I always leave my respectable cloak at the front door."

It was late by the time we got home.

"Let's go straight downstairs," I suggested. "No need to do anything here."

Once we got to the bedroom, I went to take my jewellery off; he stopped me.

"Leave it on. I've never made love to a woman wearing half a million in jewels."

"All of it?"

He looked me up and down slowly; almost licking his lips.

"Yes," he replied. "But the dress can go … slowly."

I went over to him and undressed him. He let me. When he was naked, I looked greedily at his erect cock and pushed him backwards onto the bed. He got comfortable, watching me all the time. I was drunk; not seriously, but enough to remove any trace of shyness. Completely relaxed and at ease with myself and my lover watching me. I was going to have some fun.

I put some music on and stood in front of the bed. Brushing my hands over my body, ruffling my hair, turning, twisting, bending, swaying. Raising the hem of my dress and lowering it just before I exposed anything. Sometimes, we would be so worked up, we'd jump each other at this stage. But tonight, we were both patient; both prepared to wait for the moment. I was pleased; it meant he'd be happy for me to lead. I knew exactly what I was going to do.

I was getting into it now, feeling downright sexy. I was no dancer; it didn't matter. I knew what turned my lover on and went for it. Moving with the music, I moved around the bed, reaching out to run a hand over his skin, the other caressing me. Turning away from him, and bending forward, sliding my dress up to reveal myself briefly, before rolling it back again.

I stood at the end of the bed and put one foot on it. Ensuring the angle was right. Or wrong; for him. He could see plenty, but not quite enough. I kicked off my shoes and climbed onto the bed. Standing at his feet, slowly dancing over him a foot on each side. Looking down at that inviting cock.

I carried on until I was dancing above his head. The lights were on, but I guessed he was only getting fleeting glimpses of me. Time to show him everything. I slowly squatted over his chest and bent to kiss him. He went to put his hands on my legs, and I brushed them away.

"Ah, ah. I'm in charge here."

He laid his arms back on the bed. Standing, I slowly gathered the hem of my dress and slid it up my thighs. He was watching closely. I eased it over my bum and hips and pulled it over my head. It proved a little too tight to do this smoothly, but neither of us cared. I squatted to kiss him again and moved back until I felt his cock between my legs.

In one movement, I grabbed it with my hand, placed my pussy over it, and slid right down onto it. This brought groans from both of us. I paused, letting us feel the warmth, the pleasure, the closeness. I laid my head by his, and he put his arms around my back. I allowed him; just this once.

"Now," I said softly. "Do you want respectable or …?"

"Or what?"

"Or harlot?"

He feigned a thoughtful look for a moment.

"Full-on harlot, I think."

"Good." I raised my head and kissed him. "Because that's how I feel right now."

I kissed him again.

"First I'm going to ride you …"

"Mmm."

"… then I'm going to ride you again."

"And then?"

"Wait and see."

I sat up, my hands going to the pillows by his head, my hair falling short of his face, and started to grind. I was using him, and he knew it. I needed to come. That first orgasm, just to ease the need. We watched each other. I knew I would be colouring slightly; my giveaway. I knew he loved it.

I ground harder as my orgasm came; his hands reached for my bum, against the rules. But I was too far gone to argue. I forced my clit onto him as my climax ripped through my body. My breathing irregular, my skin going from hot to cold and back again. I let my hips slump, and my back drooped. I smiled at him as I swallowed deep gulps of air. Finally, I laid carefully on him and basked in his embrace.

Chapter 16 – Marcus

Sally had done several dances and stripteases for me. She got better each time, and more confident. To the point where it turned her on as well. Tonight's had been one of the best. It helped she'd had a few drinks. It removed the last bit of shyness. As she lay on me, my cock still deep inside her, I could feel her heartbeat against my chest. Slowing after her orgasm.

"Harlot," I said. "I quite like that."

"It just came to me. Seemed the right word."

"Worked for me."

"Well, it hasn't yet." She wriggled on my cock. "Do you need to?"

"Not yet."

"Good. Because I seem to remember saying I was going to ride you again."

She started slowly rocking again. Gently back and forth, rubbing herself on my pubic bone. This time with no urgency, kissing me, her head hovering above me. Her eyes alive. I loved them; she knew it. Used them; I wanted her to. If you could have bottled the eroticism in her eyes …

She moved her head to pull her hair across my face, laughing as I tried to blow strands out of my mouth. Teasing me. The woman I adored was naked above me, using me for her enjoyment. That alone was glorious.

But combined with the physical sensations; her heat sliding on my cock, her hair falling on my face. Her breasts hanging above me, the nipples swollen and proud. My hands gliding over her body, feeling its warmth, its contours, its softness. The combination was pure joy. My mind was empty of anything but the moment. Is that what ecstasy is? If it was, I was there.

She was building again. I could hear her breathing getting louder. Little noises with each rocking movement. Those movements becoming firmer; more urgent. She stopped the teasing and stared at me. I let myself swim into those green pools. I saw the pupils expand as her body slowly tensed, and her moans grew louder. She was staring into me now, almost through me. She cried out and her pussy gripped me, trying to pull me in further and spasmed several times, as her body did the same.

I rested my hands on her thighs, as she relaxed. Her head hanging; her eyes no longer visible. Her breath coming in gasps. It was a few minutes before either of us moved. Her chuckle started it, coming from behind her hair. She slowly raised her head. Her face was flushed; those eyes sparkling. She bent to kiss me, and we laid there, peaceful and loved.

She stirred slightly.

"What now, my little harlot?"

Her mouth close to my ear and she spoke so quietly, I could hardly hear her.

"Now it's your turn. Relax and enjoy."

She eased her hips forward, just enough for my cock to slip out of her and spring free. She twitched as it brushed a sensitive area. Moving slowly down my body, she kissed my skin as she went. I knew what she was going to do. I'd thought this evening couldn't get any better. She was about to prove me wrong.

Down and down, until she was lying on her front between my legs, her head over my groin. I could just see the curve of her bum over her head. She grinned and moved her position slightly, so I had a better view. She took my cock gently in her hand, and using the tip of her tongue, licked her own juices from it. Almost immediately, she frowned.

"It's no good," she said, reaching around to the back of her neck. "I'm going to have to take this off. It's getting in the way."

She unclasped the necklace and placed it on the bed beside us, before returning to her task. I pulled another pillow under my head and shuffled them so I could see her clearly without straining.

"Comfy?" she asked.

"Yes, thank you."

"Good."

Neither of us spoke again for some time. Although I made a lot of noise, particularly towards the end. Her oral skills were unbelievable; except I could believe them, I'd experienced them so often. They gave me feelings and sensations I'd never had before. Her lips, her tongue and her teeth all played a part. And she maintained eye contact the whole time. The only exceptions were when I had to close my eyes or stare at the ceiling wondering if I could take any more pleasure.

The answer was always yes. The final ingredient was her enjoyment. She loved doing it. She loved teasing me. Concentrating on one spot with her tongue until it was almost unbearable. But moving just in time. Repeating the process. Again, and again. I hadn't dared to mention it, but I suspected she could have kept me going until it drove me insane. My balls were now aching; needing relief from the pressure.

She changed the intensity. I knew she was going to release that pressure. Her tongue was pressing a little bit harder. She slipped her lips over the head and clamped them behind it. The suction in her mouth now that bit stronger. I knew she was going to suck me dry. Her hands reached up over my belly, sliding up and down the sides, steering well clear of my still-red scar. Her mouth now shrink-wrapped over my cock.

And it happened. I cried out as my first ejaculation shot into her mouth. Her nails clawing at my sides making me squirm. Her lips still gripping me; her eyes drilling into me. My cock jerked again and again, as I came hard. Crying out at each spasm. My balls throbbing as they were shaken by each one.

She didn't move. As I subsided, her lips slid further along my cock, taking in most of its length. Sliding up and down. The sensations were almost too much now. She knew, and slowly pulled off. Holding my cock with one hand. Licking it, sticking her tongue into the end. Squeezing it, the last vestiges of my cum appearing for her to lick off.

I was coming down, my cock deflating. She laid it between my legs and crawled up my body. Kissing me when she reached my mouth. Passionately. I could taste my cum on her lips; in her mouth.

"Was that good, my darling?"

I looked at her; I didn't know what to say.

"I've no words. I never do."

"You don't need to. I've never known a man's body express itself as much as yours."

She kissed me again and we lay still for a few minutes before she stirred.

"Do I qualify as a harlot, then?"

"I'm not sure. There are grades, you know."

She looked at me with a playful smile.

"Grades?"

"Mmm. One through ten."

"So, where am I?"

"Everybody has to start at one."

"Only one?"

"Yes, each grade involves extensive tests, but I think we might fast-track you through a few. I think you might pass all of them in, ooh, let's see … a year or two?"

She thought for a moment.

"If I'm grade one now, could you cope with me when I reach grade ten?"

"I doubt it. But I'm prepared to have a damned good go."

As we lay in bed a little later, cuddled together, few words were spoken. We'd shared one of those special experiences. Where everything had gelled. But what was even better was it seemed to happen so often.

Opening my eyes the next morning, I looked out over an empty bed. My ears heard sounds. Sally was in the bathroom. I needed it too. When I returned, she was sitting on the bed naked, holding a small box tied with a bow.

"Happy birthday, darling."

I gave her a soft kiss.

"Thank you."

"A little something to start the day right."

She handed me the present and I sat beside her. She leaned into me and put her hand and head on my shoulder. I pulled the ribbon and the bow fell away. Undoing the paper, a brown box was revealed. Opening it, I was confronted by a black pom-pom. About four inches in diameter, fluffy and soft. I stroked it, mystified.

"Pick it up," she said.

It was attached to a butt plug.

"It's a bunny tail. Want to put it in me?"

I kissed her.

"Yes."

She reached behind her and handed me a bottle of lube before standing up. Turning away from me, she bent forward revealing a gorgeous view. I was so tempted by the sight but decided it could wait. I put a little lube on a finger and placed it on her ass. She tensed at the cold. I gently rubbed it around her hole and slowly pushed a little inside. She giggled. I picked up the plug and eased it in. It wasn't a big plug, and it quickly slipped into place. I gave her bum a slap, and she stood and wiggled her hips. I laughed as the bunny tail shook from side to side.

"Like it?"

"It's great."

"I want to see."

She went over to the large mirror covering part of the wall. Turned sideways to see how the tail looked. She picked up a smaller mirror and looked over her shoulder at her own reflection. Wiggling her bum again.

"I like that. What do you think?"

"Love it. A mix of cuteness and sin."

"So, I keep it in?"

"Yea, definitely."

"Right. You go back to bed. I've got things to do."

As I swung back under the duvet, she disappeared through the door. Naked but for a fluffy tail, which she waggled at me as she went.

Ten minutes later, I heard her coming back downstairs. She came into the bedroom carrying a tray. Putting it on the side table, she disappeared again. Shortly returning with a few more presents.

"I hope you haven't overdone it this year?"

"No. I think we both went a bit mad last year. We won't top that, so I haven't tried."

She handed me a glass of champagne.

"No bottle?" I asked.

We both grinned.

"Yes. But I left it upstairs."

We both remembered what had happened in the shower on my last birthday with the remaining Champagne. She held her glass out and I tapped it with mine.

"Happy birthday."

After we had sipped it, she brought the tray over and rested it on one side of the bed. Strawberries, cream, little chocolate croissants.

"Just an appetiser. I'll make you something special when we get up."

She came around to my side of the bed and climbed on next to me. She was about to sit, but I put my hand on her bum. She stuck it out for me. I ran my hand across her cheeks several times. It was a wonderful feeling. Soft cheek, fluffy tail, soft cheek, fluffy tail. I gripped the tail, and wobbled it; she twitched, and let out a positive gasp.

"Good?"

"I could get used to it."

Finally sitting beside me, she put one arm around me and proceeded to feed me with the other. I watched as she picked a strawberry from the plate, dipped it in the cream and brought it to my mouth. Picking one for herself, she brought it to her lips and teasingly licked the cream off, before biting aggressively through the strawberry. She raised an eyebrow when I winced.

We finished everything she'd prepared. In between, she handed me a few small presents to unwrap. All silly little things; a tacky little model of the colosseum she'd picked up in Rome, edible body paint. And some chocolate breasts. I could see this becoming a ritual. She'd give me chocolate breasts; I'd give her chocolate willies. Both were terrible chocolate, but it didn't matter.

"There are no plans today," she said. "I thought we'd see what happens."

"Fine by me."

"I've got a few ideas, though."

She was grinning.

"I bet you have."

"I thought I'd start off by giving you a shower. If you want me to, that is?"

"No champagne this time."

"No. It was a bit cold. And I think I might need to remove my tail. It'll get a bit soggy."

"I don't know, I might enjoy watching you shake it dry."

"We'd be here all day."

We stood up, and she leaned over the bed, looking at me. I didn't need a further invitation and gently pulled the tail from her ass. Taking my hand, she led me through to the shower. It had been one of our luxuries. An area big enough for about five people, with waterfalls, side sprays, the lot. We loved it. I walked in and she was about to follow me when I stopped her.

"Go and get the waterproof vibe."

"It's supposed to be your birthday."

"It is. So, I get to choose what we do."

A couple of minutes later, we were both in the shower, under cascading warm water. Lathering each other and massaging every nook and cranny long after they were clean. An occasional buzzing noise rising above the sound of the water.

Chapter 17 – Marcus

It was mid-morning by the time we dressed and got upstairs. We decided to skip breakfast and have an early lunch. As we went into the dining room, I saw quite a few presents on the table.

"Sal …"

"I couldn't help it. I love buying you things."

I frowned at her, although it was a bit of an act now. I was getting used to her generosity, but I was still uncomfortable with it at times. She knew and did her best to reassure me. She made her customary response by putting on a pout and acting innocent.

"You can spank me later."

We both grinned, and the moment passed. It was getting easier, and I hoped I could learn to accept the situation.

We already had a tradition for birthdays and Christmas of opening presents slowly through the day, not all at once. I let Sally give them to me when she wanted to. Looking at the pile, she hadn't gone as mad as the previous year, when it had taken me half the day to open them. It had been worse then because, at the time, I was unaware I was involved with a wealthy woman.

"There are presents from Mary and Lucy. Want to open them now?"

She brought two parcels over and handed me the first.

"This is from Mary."

Mary had good taste. Every present she'd given me to date had been perfect. This one was no exception. A Roman oil lamp, with a generous number of phalluses as decoration.

"It's wonderful."

"She did ask me if it would be all right. She found it in a place in London. I've got the address from her. I think it might be worth a visit."

It was always an incredible feeling to hold something so old. To imagine its history. Who made it? Who used it? Where had it been for the last two thousand years? I had two or three objects from antiquity, and they were probably my most treasured possessions. Now I had another to add to the collection.

"This one's from Lucy."

A narrow parcel about three feet tall and two feet wide. I knew it was a picture and wondered what she'd given me this time. We already had some of her work. Some she'd given us, and the portrait of Sally I'd commissioned, even though she refused payment for it. She was a talented artist.

I carefully unwrapped the frame and cleared the paper away. I found myself looking at the back. I turned it around and smiled. She obviously knew more about my taste now; from Sal, I assumed. It was a pen and wash work. Two naked women, but only from shoulders to knees. Standing or lying, I couldn't work out which, slightly overlapping each other. A hand resting lightly on each other's hips. The work was fully finished in the centre; their bums beautifully rendered. Gradually reducing until by the edge, it was no more than a line drawing.

"Do you like it?"

I was still taking it in. Then it struck me.

"This is you and Lucy?"

"Yes."

She came and sat beside me.

"It's beautiful."

I looked at it for a while. The bum on the right was slightly larger than the other. I guessed that was Lucy. I pointed to the left-hand figure.

"This is you?"

"I told Luce you'd know. She didn't think you would."

"She's slightly larger than you."

She leaned over and kissed me.

"Mmm. She is, but nice and firm."

I raised my eyebrows at her, and she blew me a kiss. I sent Lucy a quick text.

"Thanking her?"

"Not yet."

She gave me a querying look.

"I told her I love her bum."

Sally playfully whacked my arm.

"Keep off; it's mine."

Lucy texted back, and I thanked her. It was a beautiful picture, and we decided it was going in our bedroom. I sent Mary a text as well.

"Lucy's picture has made me think of something," I said.

"What's that?"

"Why don't we ask her to do some pictures for the playroom?"

"Ooh, great idea."

"Let's face it, she's not afraid to do explicit. We could let her imagination run riot. Nobody's going to see them."

"Shall I speak to her?"

"Have you told her about the room?"

"Not yet."

"Why don't we wait until it's finished."

She thought for a moment.

"Good idea."

I stood the picture against the coffee table and we sat looking at it.

"Which is the best bum?" she eventually asked, a cheeky grin on her face. I turned to her, smiling.

"I'm not answering that question. You're both beautiful and those are two gorgeous bums. End of."

She kissed me.

"Good answer, darling."

I put the picture against a wall to keep it safe and Sal cleared up all the paper lying around. I noticed she seemed to be struggling to sit still. Did she have something planned? I'd have to wait and see.

She made us a light lunch and it was warm enough to have it outside; well, nearly. We'd had the garden cleared, but not done anything with it yet. It was bare earth. The renovations had created a large room in the lower level overlooking the garden. We hadn't done much with that, either. The external wall had been replaced with full-length doors and windows. We opened all the doors and sat on a couple of cheap garden chairs we'd bought. It was lovely and after eating, we sat enjoying the late summer sun. Finally, Sally revealed her hand.

"Right you. I can't wait any longer. I've got another present for you."

She stood and held out her hand. I took it and let her lead me. But instead of heading for the stairs, she went towards the door leading to the garage. As she unlocked it, she saw my puzzlement.

"I couldn't get this one up the stairs."

She led me through two doors into the garage and switched the lights on. I stood dumbstruck; I now saw why she had been nervous. She came up behind me and put her arms around my tummy, resting her chin on my shoulder.

"Happy birthday."

I was speechless. Truly speechless. In front of us was a Range Rover Evoque. Deep blue, with a huge red bow on the bonnet. We stood in silence for what seemed like minutes.

"Well?"

"Sal, I …"

"Before you say anything, I want to say something."

She came around to face me and laid her arms over my shoulders.

"I know you still feel bad sometimes about me buying you things and paying for stuff. True?"

"Yes."

"And I understand why. It's one of the reasons I love you."

"I'm getting better."

She kissed me.

"Yes, you are, and I know you've always fancied a Range Rover."

I wasn't sure how to reply. I had mixed feelings. She saw my uncertainty.

"I've made it easy, though."

"Oh?"

"The car's in my name. So, technically, it's mine. But it's yours, really. Does that help?"

She was smiling now; her cheeky smile. It broke my resistance.

"That's cheating."

"Yup. It is. But we're partners in everything. We share everything. I don't want this issue to gnaw away at us. My money is your money. I trust you. I know you're not going to throw it away. We can easily afford anything we want. Please help me enjoy it; don't be afraid of it. God knows, I've been afraid of it long enough."

That hit me; I hadn't seen it that way before. I'd done my bit to help her overcome her father's shadow. Now I was in danger of undoing it all.

"I'm sorry, Sal. I hadn't seen it like that." I closed my eyes and took a deep breath. "Alright. I will happily spend your money from now on."

She shook her head in resignation.

"That's good enough. Come on, have a look."

We spent ten minutes looking around the car. It was fabulous. The highest spec, with a few extras added on. And she was right; I'd always dreamed of a Range Rover.

"Want to try it?" she asked.

I looked at her; keen, eager.

"Yes."

"I'll get my purse and phone."

A few minutes later, we drove out of the garage and went for a drive. Nowhere in particular. Just drove. Stopped for tea in a country pub. Stopped for a walk by a river. Finally getting home at about five o'clock. The car was beautiful. In the end, she told me to stop saying thank you.

After we got back into the house, I pulled her to me.

"How did I ever deserve you?" I asked.

She hugged me close.

"We deserve each other. We were made for each other. Perfect fit."

I let out a long sigh, pulling her tight into me.

"Anyway, birthday boy. You're day's not over yet."

Another new tradition kicked in; we dressed for dinner. While she cooked, we flirted. She teased, I warned her of dire punishment. Her teasing went up a level. I was biding my time. She knew it.

After dinner, we moved to the living room, and she gave me another present.

"I'm not sure about this one."

I opened it. A strap-on set. I looked at her.

"For me? For you?"

"How about us? You like me using a dildo on you. I wondered if you might ..."

She looked away; then straight at me. Slightly flushed.

"I'd like to fuck you," she said.

I looked back at her; said nothing. I loved it when she was slightly nervous.

"If you'd like me to, that is."

I told her I would, and her relief was palpable.

"I got the most versatile one. We can both use it. If you use it, it's got a slot for your cock, but you can put a dildo above or below it."

My mind wandered through the possibilities. Hers did as well. We both came back at the same time.

"One final present," she said, handing it to me.

I peeled off the paper and recognised the box. One of Steph's jewellery cases. As I went to open it, she placed her hand over mine.

"This isn't for you, in a way. But it is. What I mean is, it's for us. Something we can share."

She lifted her hand away, and I removed the lid. Lying on a plush base was a velvet choker. I thought it was black at first. But it was blue; the deepest blue I'd ever seen. An inch wide, with a simple but elegant interlocking clasp at the back. But that was all nothing compared to the main feature. Set into the front of the collar was the sapphire. The setting so simple, it was almost invisible. It looked like the sapphire was floating on the velvet.

"Well?"

"It's beautiful."

"I wanted to use one of the stones just for us. Secret and private. Only you and I will ever see this. And we'll only see it when we're doing something special to both of us."

I understood what she meant; it was a wonderful thought.

"Can I pick it up?"

"Of course. It's yours."

The velvet was soft and silky. It flowed through my hands. The stone sparkled under the lights. But she was wrong, and she knew it. It wasn't mine. I turned and offered it to her.

"And now it's yours."

She took it from me.

"Thank you. Do you want to put it on me?"

I thought about it for a moment.

"No. Not tonight."

I handed her the case, and she laid the choker back in it.

"Did Steph know what it was?"

"Yes. It's not the first one she's been asked to design, apparently."

"Did you want to use it tonight?"

"I'd have been happy to, but I've got one or two other ideas."

"Oh?"

"Anything you fancy?"

I moved towards her.

"I could have phrased that better. Anything you particularly want to do?"

"What did you have in mind?"

She moved closer, putting her arm around my shoulder.

"How do you fancy dealing with a cheeky little minx? A really cheeky little minx?"

"One who's going to need taming?"

"Probably."

"Who's going to need a firm hand?"

"Definitely."

"Who needs to be spanked until she screams, and fucked until she squeals?"

She kissed me.

"Sounds perfect ..."

It was. Every minute of it. She did cheeky so well, you wondered if it was her default mode. But her cheeky was so alluring, so erotic, you forgot she was really in control. She knew what she wanted that night, but it matched my desires. I was patient enough to deny her at times, but she knew she could drive me wild with a look, a touch or a flash of her eyes.

By the end of the evening, her bum was deep red from my attention. She loved it; continually challenging me to give her more. Then taking pleasure when I offered it. The pain pushed her higher; the pleasure enabled her to take more pain. Along the way, I took my pleasure too. Using her when she dared me to. Accepting a lighter touch when she offered it. By bedtime, we were both fully satisfied. And one of us had a very sore bum.

When I woke in the morning, Sal was just stirring. I pulled the covers back and examined her bum. I always did after we'd had an impact session. It was back to its usual colour. She recovered quickly; even cane welts only lasted a few days. Particularly if we treated them properly. She lay on her front, watching me as I stroked her bum.

"Good morning. That feels good."

"Any soreness?"

She giggled.

"Not yet."

I slapped her bum hard; she squealed. I lay beside her and snuggled into her, pulling the duvet back over us. We fell asleep again.

When I woke again, I stretched. She was moving about the room.

"Are you awake?" she asked quietly.

"Mmm."

"How are you feeling?"

"Mmm. Good thanks."

She came to the side of the bed and knelt. Leaning over, she kissed me and sat back on her haunches. Bright, smiling; she looked beautiful. She held out both hands towards me, her fists closed. When they were fully stretched, she opened her fingers.

The sapphire collar sitting in her palms. I looked at it, then at her. Her eyes were slightly glazed. I recognised that look. She was already blocking the world out. Ready to spend time in her special place. I wasn't going to deny her. I sat up, taking the collar and laying it around her neck, locking the clasp.

"Comfortable, Sally?"

"Yes, thank you, sir."

I didn't take the collar off until late in the evening. We agreed after our first submission session it wouldn't be a regular thing. We did it occasionally; we wanted it to be special. It only ever lasted a few hours. She'd talked a few times about submitting for a whole day, but we'd been doubtful. We weren't sure we could sustain it for that long; the mood, the tension.

But we learned that day there didn't need to be something happening all the time. The collar altered the dynamic between us. There was a heightened connection between us, even when nothing was going on.

It was strange at first. I was aware of her altered state. Constantly alert to me, constantly focussed on me. She seemed oblivious to everything else. She almost knew what I wanted before I asked. I slowly changed too. I played with her; pushing her, guiding her. She seemed like an extension of me. Compliant to me. I alternated gentle teasing with harsh usage, allowing us to recover in between.

I took the collar off an hour before bedtime, to allow us to come down. To allow her to chill. She lay curled up on my lap, her head on my chest. She tried to tell me how it had affected her. She'd tried before, to explain about her special place. But she never managed to find the right words. I understood the theory, but I'd never been there; I couldn't hope to understand. I listened; she talked. Odd phrases, brief sentences. Before she started crying. The tension, the feelings. All flowing out of her.

It had happened after some earlier submission sessions. The first time, I was worried, but I knew now I didn't need to be. It was part of the experience. For her, it was the culmination of the process. It was only afterwards she truly came back. But this time, she cried on and off for half an hour. I held her. That was all I needed to do; hold her.

The crying stopped. I waited. She took a couple of deep breaths and lifted her head to look at me. Her face tear-stained, her eyes soft and mellow. I stroked her hair.

"Hello," I whispered.

"Hello. I'm back."

"Are you okay?"

"Never been better. Ever. Ever, ever, ever."

She threw her arms around my neck and hugged me tight.

"I love you so much it hurts."

She giggled when she realised what she'd said. She was still grinning as we went downstairs to bed. Still smiling the next morning.

Chapter 18 – Lucy

I handed Sally the letter Annie had forwarded to me. It had hit me hard. I'd come to terms with the break from my parents years ago, but it still hurt at times. When they had rejected me, I'd tried to explain; tried to help them understand. But to no avail. The things my father had said to me had been horrible. It had been his actions which had finally extinguished any faith I had left. If that was what it meant to be Christian, I wanted no part of it.

My mother had meekly gone along with him. I had seen how weak she was; servile. She had made no attempt to support me. She took direction from my father; as she had taken direction from her father, I guess. I'd had the letter a few days; re-read it umpteen times. Each reading brought a different emotion. Pain, laughter, sadness, indignation. I didn't know how to deal with it. I sat on the edge of my chair as Sally read it.

Dear Lucy,

This is a difficult letter for me to write. I know we haven't spoken for several years. But I feel I should reach out to you. Annie tells me you know about your father's illness. He suffered a major stroke and the doctors think he will not get any better. His fate is now in God's hands. I don't know if you wish to see him, but I think it would be best if you didn't. He can understand what is going on, and what we say. I think seeing you would only upset him.

The life you chose was impossible for him to accept. Since you left, he has never mentioned your name. This was hard for me, but I am his wife. I supported him, as the Lord intended. I knew you did not share our faith, and I prayed every day you might return to the fold.

But I am now questioning my life. You were lost to me many years ago. My husband is still with me in body but cruelly struck down and my other daughter and her husband have rejected our congregation. What is left for me? I am doubting everything I have believed all my life.

I don't want to lose my husband and my family. I know it comes out of the blue, but I would like to see you again. I don't know how or where. But I ask you to consider it. If you can find it in your heart to agree, please let Annie know. I will understand if you don't feel able.

Your loving mother.

Sally lowered the letter to her lap and looked at me; concern on her face.

"Did she send it to you?"

"It came via Annie. Bless her, she did warn me it might upset me."

"And has it?"

Sally was here for one of our nights together. They were precious; I looked forward to them. But I had to talk to someone about this. I knew Sally would understand.

"I've read it several times. It says different things to me every time. There's so much in it for a short letter. After fifteen years."

"You've had some contact, though."

"A few birthday or Christmas cards. Never anything so direct; so personal. I wasn't expecting it. Honestly? I thought she might blame me for Dad's stroke."

"What's this about Annie and Tim?"

"I don't know. Remember last Christmas? Them inviting me for the day? I never did work out why."

"I remember you saying they were making jokes about your parents."

"Oh, yes. I'd forgotten that. Sounds like they've pulled away from them."

"And your mother is feeling isolated. She might end up widowed with both her children estranged from her; along with her grandchildren."

"But does she mean it? What if she's being manipulative? Trying to make us all feel guilty, so she can get her own way."

"What are you going to do?"

"I don't know, Sal. I keep changing my mind. What would you do?"

"I'm not sure my opinion's worth much, Luce. It took me fifteen years to sort myself out. Remember?"

"Yea, I know. But you're the only one I can talk to about this. My other friends don't know about my family and they aren't anything like as close as you are."

Sally thought for a few moments.

"My first step would be to speak to Annie and Tim. Be honest with them. Show them the letter, if you can."

"Yes. I thought of that."

"If what your mum says about them is true, at least that bit is honest."

"Good point."

"If your mother is really questioning her faith, surely Annie or Tim would have noticed a change in her?"

"Possibly, but I don't think they see her as often as they did."

"But isn't it worth at least asking?"

It only confirmed what I'd already decided was the only option. I needed to speak to my sister. We weren't exactly close, and we'd need to be open with one another for the first time in years.

"Right. I'll go and see Annie and Tim."

"Do you want me to stay, or shall I leave you with your thoughts?"

"I've got plenty of thoughts in my head. But right now, none of them are about my family. When I get you to myself, I'm not letting you go."

As I turned into Annie's drive, my mouth was dry. I wasn't looking forward to this. She and I got on okay. We'd kept in contact over the years; largely without our parents knowing. She never mentioned my sexuality, and we tended to stick to safe topics. But the contact had increased over the last couple of years. Now I thought I might know why.

It was Tim who greeted me at the door. I'd already heard their children, Sarah and Nathan, playing in the garden. They rushed through, screamed 'hello' at me, and disappeared again. They knew who I was, but we'd had no time to connect.

I followed Tim through to the lounge, where Annie was waiting. We had a slightly awkward embrace, and they offered coffee. When we were settled, I got straight to the point and showed them the letter. They sat side by side reading it; looking up when they had finished.

"Mum did hint at what she'd written," Annie said.

"I'm sorry if it embarrasses you both. But it all came as a surprise to me. I'm not sure what to do."

Annie looked at Tim; I noticed him nod slightly.

"Lucy, I think Mum is being honest, if that's what you mean."

"I did wonder. Can you tell me how you get on with her now?"

"Well …" She was winding a lock of hair around her fingers. "We're not as close as we were."

She looked at me and sighed.

"The truth is, Lucy, we did leave their church. It was a long time coming, but we began to feel trapped. Always being told how we should behave. How to bring up the kids. It was all rules, rules, rules. The crunch came when one of the congregation who we knew well was diagnosed with cancer. The pastor persuaded him to rely on prayer rather than medicine. I don't need to tell you how that ended." She turned to Tim. "That was the last straw, wasn't it?"

"Yes. That and Stuart, I guess."

They shared another look. Tim continued.

"Stuart and I have known each other for twenty years. We worked together at the same place, and after I left, we stayed friends. There's a group of five or six of us. We go out regularly; bowling, to the movies, walking. They're the only friends I had outside the church. Then about two years ago, Stuart told me he lived with another man. I hadn't even guessed."

He looked at me a little bashfully.

"Sorry, Lucy, but I'm a bit naïve when it comes to …"

I waved him on.

"Well, it was a shock, I have to admit. If it had happened a few years before, I'd have stopped meeting. But I thought about it and talked to Annie. He was a friend. He was … well…"

He looked sheepish again.

"… just like me."

"Don't worry Tim. The rumour we all have horns is largely a myth."

"That," he said, turning to Annie, "and the cancer patient at the church, made the final decision for us, didn't it?"

"Yes," she replied. "We realised we weren't being very Christian. We stopped going. We go to the local C of E church now. It's different, much more relaxed. I think some people use it more as a social club. But everyone's friendly. We still feel we can commune with God in our own way. But he's a loving God, not the one Dad believes in."

"How did Mum and Dad react?"

"Dad went through the roof. He hasn't spoken to us much since. Mum kept in touch as best she could, but we didn't see her much."

"Until your Dad's stroke," Tim said. "Since then, she has visited a few times. She loves seeing the kids."

"So," I said. "She's scared she's lost me, now Dad, then you and her grandchildren."

"Yes," Annie replied. "I think she's frightened. I don't think she can imagine life without Dad if he … passes."

"But does she think any differently to Dad? If not, I'm not sure I want anything to do with her."

"I honestly don't know, Lucy. I've wondered about that. And as far as I can think back, I don't remember her doing anything other than copy Dad. I don't remember her being … independent. I have no idea what she thinks."

The discussion helped. I at least knew Annie and Tim's position. But I came to no conclusion about the way forward. Did I want to see my mother again after all these years?

My second visit was much more relaxed. Dinner with Sally and Marcus. It had become a regular event, normally every other week. I always went to them. I'm not sure why it happened like that, but I was more than happy. I liked my flat, but it wasn't very big. It was generally a bit of a mess. I wasn't the tidiest person, and there were always various pictures lying around unfinished. Their flat was wonderful; I loved spending time there. And they had spare rooms ready if I wanted to stay over. I always did.

Over dinner, I told them about my visit to Annie's and filled Marcus in on the things he didn't know. He didn't pry. I knew he could get information out of a stone if he tried; he'd done it at our first meeting. But he was also a sensitive man; in tune to a situation. I let him read the letter.

"Okay, Mr Analyst. Any thoughts?"

"Well, Lucy. I don't want to be rude."

"I won't be offended."

"Firstly, she talks about you choosing your life. I assume she really means choosing to be gay. You didn't choose it, it's who you are. So, she hasn't understood that. And secondly, she is scared. But I don't get the feeling from this she's changed."

"No, but the problem I have is having no contact with her for fifteen years. I have no real idea of her relationship with Dad. Was she a servile wife or was she equally rigid in her views?"

That was the crux of the problem. If she was as bigoted as my father, I saw no purpose in meeting her again. We'd have an argument, and both regret it. But if she had changed, did I have a duty to at least try? I didn't expect Sally or Marcus to give me the answer. I'd have to find that myself.

We moved to lighter topics. I asked Marcus if he'd had a good birthday. Sal had told me a little about it, but not much detail.

"Great, thanks, Luce. Your bum is already on display in our bedroom."

"Is it? I thought you'd hang it in a spare room somewhere."

"No. It's gorgeous. The picture I mean."

"Her bum's pretty good as well, darling," Sal said.

Marcus smiled at me.

"From what I've seen, I'd have to agree."

I blushed; unlike me, but it did happen occasionally.

"What else did you get?"

He showed me an oil lamp Mary had given him. It was a wonderful present. Mary seemed to understand people. I coveted the lamp myself;

it was an honest everyday object. Naïve, rustic and beautiful. He listed a few other things.

"So, what was your favourite?"

He looked slyly at Sally.

"Two things, I think. The first present Sal gave me. And the biggest."

"What were they?"

"She didn't tell you?"

"No, I don't think so."

"The biggest was a car."

"What? A model?"

"No. A real one."

I stared at her.

"You didn't tell me."

"Sorry. I didn't tell anyone."

"No, I didn't mean it like that. You didn't have to. I'm just surprised you could keep it a secret."

"Me too."

Marcus told me the story about the car. How Sally had kept it quiet until after lunch. Quite a present.

"What was the first?"

"Oh, that was much smaller."

"What was it?"

He looked at Sally with a grin.

"Why don't you show her, Sal?"

She turned to him.

"Really?"

"Yea." He took a mouthful of dessert. "Why don't you go and put it on?"

I noticed Sal flush and she almost squeaked her reply.

"What?"

"Dare you."

They sat staring at each other, defying each other to yield. Marcus was challenging Sal; I waited to see if she'd accept. After a few seconds, she put her napkin on the table. She looked at Marcus, then at me; a faint smile on her lips. Challenge accepted. Pushing her chair back, she stood and left the room, heading for the stairs.

"Am I going to be shocked?"

"I doubt it, Lucy," Marcus replied. "I suspect there's not a lot that would shock you."

He had me there.

When Sally returned, she wasn't carrying anything and was wearing the same dress she'd had on all evening. She walked over to Marcus and bent over to give him a kiss.

"Sure?"

"Mmm."

She approached me, turned her back and bent forward slightly. I wasn't sure what was happening. She put her hands behind her and lifted the hem of her dress over her waist. I let out a little squeal as I saw her bare bum with a fluffy black tail sticking out of it. Whatever I'd been expecting, it hadn't been that. She wiggled her hips and it swayed from side to side. I burst out laughing.

"Is it on a plug?" I asked.

"Yup."

"What's it made of?"

Marcus jumped in.

"Feel free to touch it, Lucy. Give it a stroke. Touch the tail as well, if you like."

"Watch it, you," Sally said to Marcus. She was grinning, though.

I reached out to touch it. The tail was a ball of fluff. It did look good against her skin. I allowed my hand to flow over one cheek as I removed it. I'd have liked to do more, but I was the guest here.

Sal lowered her dress and stood straight.

"I wonder if I can sit comfortably with it in?"

She sat down carefully.

"Mmm. Not bad."

She wriggled on her chair.

"Not bad at all."

"New experience?" I asked, wondering how much they'd give away.

"Oh, no. I wear one quite often, don't I, darling?"

"Mmm."

"What? Outside the flat?"

"I wear one to work sometimes."

"All day?"

"Yea."

She was smiling her wicked smile. A smile I was growing to love; I bet Marcus did too.

"Wow."

"I've got one with an 'M' on the end, haven't I?" She was addressing Marcus but turned to me. "I get him to put it in sometimes before I go to work."

She turned back to Marcus.

"And take it out when I get home."

His chuckle said all I needed to know.

"God," I said. "I couldn't wear one all day."

"Why's that, Luce?" Sal asked innocently.

And I knew I'd walked into her trap; I hadn't seen it coming. She was playing with me, watching me. Daring me to give the true answer; the answer she already knew. I looked straight back, matching her smile.

"Because, Sally Fletcher, my ass is very sensitive. And wearing it all day would turn me into a quivering wreck. As you well know."

Marcus laughed.

"I think that's fifteen-all."

Sally winked at me.

"Marcus wears one sometimes, as well."

"Really?"

"Yea. He's sensitive too. Aren't you darling?"

He looked at me.

"Do you get the feeling she's enjoying playing you and I against each other, Luce?"

"I think she might be."

"Okay. I'll punish her later. You punish her next time she's with you."

"Deal."

Sal put on a defiant pout.

"Promises, promises."

When we'd settled in the living room, Marcus turned to me.

"Lucy, we'd like to commission a few pieces from you."

"What of?"

"We thought we'd leave that to your imagination," Sal said.

"That's not very helpful. What of? Where are they going?"

"We've finally finished the last room," Marcus said. "We need some special pieces for it."

I still didn't have a clue. Sal looked at Marcus.

"Shall I show her?"

"Why not?"

I followed her downstairs; Marcus didn't come with us. We went into their bedroom. It's size never ceased to amaze me. They had one or two new pieces of furniture since I'd last seen it, as well as a certain picture of two bums on the wall. She led to me a door I hadn't even noticed before in the space between the bedroom and the bathroom area.

Going through it, I was confused again. I thought this would be the space opening onto the unused vaults. But I was in a panelled corridor with a heavy door at the other end. The only other door was in the left-hand wall. Sal opened it and went in; I followed. The lights went on, and I stopped in my tracks.

My mouth slowly dropped open. My mind gradually realising how much I didn't know about my best friend and her lover sitting upstairs. I'd never seen a room like it. Well, I'd seen pictures, but never dreamed I'd be in one.

It was quite large; roughly square with a double vaulted roof. The walls were panelled to waist height in dark wood. Two of the walls were bare brick; the other two plastered and painted a deep green. One had a huge green velvet curtain in the centre. On one side, a large leather chesterfield a few feet from the wall, a large TV facing it on the opposite wall. Another sumptuous large chair with a high back and buttoned upholstery sat alongside.

But that was where the conventional ended. There were various hooks and rings attached to the walls. A metal bar running across the ceiling. Another short bar hanging from a wire attached to a mechanism on the first bar. In front of me was a beautiful piece of furniture. Made of wood and padded leather, it looked like a small vaulting horse. But with a padded step either side and a lot of metal rings dotted over it. I knew what that was for.

On the wall by the door were rows of hooks. Hanging from them were various implements. A couple of leather strips, a few floggers, two canes. Some leather cuffs and collars, various ropes. Underneath this were some drawers; I wondered what was in those. Did I want to know? Yes. Yes, I really did.

I don't know how long we'd been there. Sally hadn't said a word. I hadn't even been aware of her presence while I'd been taking it all in. Now, I turned to look at her. She was standing inside the now-closed door, watching me. Her face was difficult to read. A mixture of pride and nervousness. When I didn't say anything, she did.

"Well?"

"So, this is what you two get up to. It's amazing. Just incredible."

"It was only finished last week. So apart from the horse, we haven't got much equipment yet."

I looked around.

"You seem to have quite a lot."

"Well, we already had all the bits and pieces," she pointed to all the implements. "The furniture we bought. That's mainly to relax, although it has its uses. The horse is the first piece of special furniture we've bought. We haven't put it to much use yet."

"It looks very … adaptable."

She giggled.

"We think it'll prove rewarding."

She went over to the sofa. I joined her and simply gawped. Over my initial surprise now, I took it all in. The room was beautiful in its own right. Plush but restrained. Subtle lighting; speakers around the room. Polished wooden flooring with soft rugs strewn about. A tiny kitchen area in one corner with a sink and a fridge. They seemed to have thought of everything.

Sally was letting me take my time. I asked her what the curtain was for. She went over and pulled it back revealing a huge mirror. Floor to ceiling and at least eight feet wide. She replaced the curtain and rejoined me. I thought about the room; what it meant. Tried to imagine what Sally and Marcus got up to in here. I imagined her tied over the horse. That was better left for another time. I suddenly wondered if I'd got it right. Would it be Marcus tied down? I turned to her.

"Well. This is a bit of a surprise."

She laid her hand on my leg.

"Not shocked, surely?"

"No. I guessed you two did some kinky stuff. You've dropped a few hints. But I wasn't sure how seriously to take them. Have you been into this long?"

Sally told me a bit about what had brought her and Marcus together. Some of it I knew; some I didn't. But it made sense. I began to understand why they were so happy together. They'd found their ideal partners. In everything.

"And now, we're exploring. We don't know how far we'll go."

"I guess it's not easy to find the right partner for this?"

"I didn't think I ever would. Nor did he."

"So, you started off helping each other act out your fantasies."

"Yes, and we found we matched perfectly in everything else as well."

"You're a lucky girl, Sal."

"I know." She laid her hand on my arm. "In all sorts of ways."

She leaned forward and kissed me softly. I'd learned more about my friend and lover than I expected.

"So," I said. "What do you want from me?"

She pointed around the room.

"We want some pictures for the empty spaces. Images to match the room. Whatever you want to paint. Sensual, explicit, soft, rough. Anything. No-one but the three of us will ever see them. Let your imagination run riot."

It was a tempting proposition. I'd already done some explicit works. But here, I would be unconstrained. How far did I want to go? It might be fun finding out.

We eventually returned to the living room.

"I was about to send out a search party," Marcus said. "I thought you'd tied each other up and were now stuck."

"Ha," Sally said. "You wish."

He'd topped up our glasses.

"Marcus," I said. "I see you in a whole different light. You've corrupted my best friend."

"I wouldn't be too sure, Lucy. Sal can do enough corrupting for both of us."

"Actually," I replied, "for all three of us."

"True. So, can you oblige with some pictures?"

"Yes, I'd love to. I've got some ideas already. But there is one thing."

"What's that?"

"I'm going to need a pliant model."

He looked at Sally.

"I don't think that'll be a problem."

I didn't either.

I stayed the night. Lying in bed, I thought about the room Sal had showed me. I'd never really been interested in bondage or S and M. I'd seen it on the internet, read about it. I'd had a brief fling with a girl who had dabbled with it. I had nothing against it; it just hadn't been in my view.

But as I lay there, I tried to imagine what it would be like. It wasn't an unpleasant experience. Sally and Marcus provided background noises. Moans, groans, squeals and giggles. I enjoyed the next thirty minutes. Well, as much as a girl could listening to her lover being spanked and fucked by someone else.

Chapter 19 – Sally

"Virgins or whores," Lucy said.

"Yes, there's nothing much in between."

"It's standard for the period. You rarely see women in any other guise, except a few formal portraits. The men who commissioned these paintings wanted virgins to display in their homes to show the world their devotion and piety. But they also wanted naked women to put in their private apartments. It's a lesson in hypocrisy, really."

"Nothing much changes, does it?"

We were in London. Lucy wanted to see this exhibition, so we'd made a weekend of it. Now we were sitting on a bench in one of the galleries, looking at a huge canvas. It was unattributed and had a bland title, but it was clearly allegorical. A naked woman, bathing in a woodland pool, with various wild animals arranged around the picture peering at her from the bushes. As the viewer, you were simply another voyeur.

"She's a strange shape, isn't she?" I mused. "I'm not sure any woman has ever been that shape."

"That's not the point. The emphasis was on arousal. This would have been a private picture. Seen by the owner and perhaps a few chosen friends. The breasts and particularly the hips are exaggerated." She looked around us and pointed to another work. "The same with this one over here."

She was right, the women were virtually identical; at least, their bodies were. She directed me to another work.

"Compare them with that one. Clearly religious. The woman there is fully-clothed, granted, but her shape is totally different. Her curves are ignored; hidden."

"Did these artists use models, or are these women imaginary?"

"Oh, they all used models. Artists were slightly apart from society; they were thought of as beyond the pale. Some used to charge people to watch them paint, but the viewers weren't watching the artist."

"Who were the women?"

"Anyone. Women who needed the money. A few artists had regulars and you see the same features in painting after painting. But the idea of a muse as we think of it only happened later."

I looked sideways at her.

"Like Zoe?"

"And now you."

Lucy had started work on some pictures for our playroom. As always, she created lots of pieces, only finishing the ones which worked. I'd already done some modelling for her. It was fun posing for your lover, but it could be distracting and that had slowed her progress somewhat.

I took Lucy to my meeting with Mr Wynne. I'd spoken to him during the week and arranged to sell some of the remaining stones. When we arrived, I introduced Lucy. He took us through to his office again, and I gave him the items I wanted to sell. True to his word, he was interested in them all and gave me a receipt. He'd confirm them and the prices in a few days. I showed him some pictures of the jewellery I'd had made.

"They are exquisite, Miss Fletcher. I like the conjunction between the older style stones and the modern setting. Have you worn any of these yet?"

"Well, the emerald set I've worn once so far. I can't see myself wearing it very often."

"But beautiful jewellery is always a pleasure. It will always be there for you. If you haven't worn it for a while, take it out of the case and hold it. It will give you joy."

I understood what he meant. I had even done it once or twice. I'd also worn it a couple of times for Marcus with little else, but I couldn't tell Mr Wynne that.

"The other pieces I do wear, and I gave some items as presents."

"Very generous. I hope the recipients wear them with love."

I looked at Lucy.

"They do, Mr Wynne. I'm sure of it."

As we walked away from the shop, Lucy linked my arm.

"He was nice. You could feel he loved his work."

"We picked the right person there, I think. Now, one more place to visit."

We got a taxi to the place Mary had bought Marcus's oil lamp. At first sight, it wasn't promising. A run-down warehouse in a back street. I double-checked the address; it was correct. How Mary had found it in the first place, I had no idea, but when I opened the door, we were both instantly in heaven.

It was part reclamation yard, part antiques shop, part junk shop. It seemed to go on forever. Piles of doors, fireplaces and beds. Cabinets full of brassware and fittings. Old advertising boards and figures. Elsewhere, little nooks full of interesting items. All of it good quality. And a section for antiquities. Statuettes from Egypt, Assyria, Greece. Roman glassware. Lamps from all over the ancient Mediterranean. Jewellery, keys, coins, bowls, axe heads. We spent two hours exploring the warehouse and had still only seen a small part of what was on offer.

We ended up back at the antiquities section. I'd seen something I wanted for Marcus. He had a small ushabti; an Egyptian funerary figure. He'd had it for years, and although it wasn't complete, I knew it was one of his favourite things. I selected another one to match. Lucy had looked at a Roman ring several times. When an assistant arrived to retrieve my purchase from a cabinet, I asked him to get the ring out as well.

"See if it fits, Luce."

She gave me an objecting look. I stared back. She gave in and tried it on. A little loose, but otherwise perfect. I bought it for her. She thanked me. She was learning.

We'd been to the theatre the night before, so had nothing planned for the Saturday night. When we got back to the hotel, we did a quick search for restaurants nearby. We called one or two we fancied but couldn't get a table. The third proved more fruitful. They'd had a cancellation, so we accepted it immediately.

We decided we were going to dress up, so spent the next couple of hours having baths, resting, and getting dressed. This time, it was me in the red dress, and Lucy was in blue. Both elegant and alluring; at least, we liked to think so.

Suitably attired, we walked to the restaurant. It turned out to be further than it appeared on the map app, but we arrived in plenty of time, and stood at a small bar, waiting for our table. The place turned out to be something of a conundrum. It was busy; every table booked. The tables were far enough apart to feel private. The staff were unfailingly polite; there just didn't seem to be enough of them. It proved impossible to attract their attention. Service was slow; really slow. But we were in no hurry, so chilled and went with it. The food was good, but each course was about an hour apart. We ended up drinking more than we intended.

It was ten-thirty by the time we paid the bill and left.

"Walk or taxi?" Lucy asked.

"Oh, let's walk. This seems a pretty safe area."

So, we reversed our route and set off for the hotel arm in arm. We got some complimentary comments from a group of grinning lads; well, as near to complimentary as they knew. As usual, we were torn between frowning at the sexist Neanderthals or secretly grinning at the fact we still seemed to have it. They were only around twenty after all.

As we turned the corner, Lucy let out a little squeal and stopped.

"Look. Is that a lap dancing club?"

On the other side of the street was a door guarded by two large penguins. Above the door, a discretely lit sign: 'Bowen's Gentleman's Club'.

"Looks like it."

"Let's go in."

I looked at her.

"No," she said. "That's not right, is it." She grinned at me. "I know. I dare you to take me in."

I kissed her lightly on the cheek.

"Okay, but they might not let women in. I don't think they all do."

We walked across the street, and up the steps.

"Evening, gents. Are women welcome?"

Both bouncers looked us up and down and exchanged a glance.

"Certainly ladies. Always welcome, go on in."

One opened the front door, and we found ourselves in a short hallway. At the other end, another big lad was already swinging the next door open.

"Good evening, ladies. Reception to your left."

We were now in a large lobby, similar to the one I'd encountered in the excursion with Marcus. We were greeted by a girl on the reception desk, who asked the same questions. I guess whilst women were welcome, they were the exception rather than the rule.

There were differences here though. The club had its own currency. A pre-loaded card; you put on as much as you wanted and could top it up by coming back to reception. This was used for both the drinks and the dancing. The girl had some advice for us.

"Entry is twenty pounds each, or you can take a booth. That's a hundred pounds, but it includes waitress service, so you don't need to fight your way to the bar. To be honest ladies, on a Saturday night, it might be better for you."

We guessed what she meant, and I didn't fancy having pinch marks on my bum. Not from an unwanted source, anyway. We took what was apparently the last booth and went through another door with the obligatory goon standing guard. There the similarity with the earlier club ended. This one was different. Very restrained. Dark wood and leather everywhere. No neon, no shining steel. It did look like a gentleman's club.

There was a central long bar, with sofas and chairs dotted around. Behind the bar was a stage where three or four girls were strutting their stuff. We stood for a moment to take it in. There were plenty of girls moving around in not very much. No dresses here. Only underwear; the occasional costume. Quite a few dressed as maids. I quickly worked out they were waitresses; whether they danced as well, who knew. I stopped one as she went by, and she led us to our booth.

The place was a mass of small interconnected rooms. Each one had two or three booths; most were occupied. We seemed to attract little attention, and I spotted a few other women who appeared to be customers rather than staff. Our maid took our drinks order and disappeared.

I soon realised the designers had been clever. Although there were two other booths in our room, they were angled so you couldn't easily see a girl dancing in either of them. And they were angled that way because they rotated. Normally, they faced the walkway. You could watch the world go by. But if you selected a girl, she could turn the whole thing around. The booth was self-contained. A semi-circular leather bench with a shelf behind it at arm level, the leather continuing upwards. It meant no table was needed, leaving the space in front of you free.

"Is this like the one you went to?"

"Not really. That one was very modern. Shiny metal, neon and a big open space. Everybody could see everybody else. This is much cosier."

The waitress brought our drinks and we sat watching people go by. The waitresses, the security guys, other customers. And lots of girls. Since Lucy and I had become lovers, I'd enjoyed the freedom to look at women more openly. It had never been a problem for her, and we watched them come and go. Occasionally swapping the odd comment. One or two of the girls stopped and asked us if we needed anything, but we weren't in a hurry. I wanted Lucy to choose first, anyway.

"Well," she finally said. "There's plenty of pussy here."

"Yup. I think that's the idea. Seen anyone you fancy?"

"A lot of them are pretty fit. There were one or two."

"Grab one if you see her go by."

She did. A tall blonde, very curvy, wearing a red teddy. She turned our booth and performed for us. She was good; didn't say much. Didn't need to. After she'd left, I turned to Lucy.

"Well?"

"Not bad."

"Is that it?"

She grinned and leant over to give me a soft kiss.

"It's strange, isn't it?" she said. "At another time, I might think a guy going to a strip club was a bit of a saddo, or worse. But here I am, in a strip club and loving every minute."

"Yup, that was my view before I went to one. Well, before I met Marcus, I guess."

"Had he been to them?"

"No. It was his first time, too. But I've been more open since I met him; more willing to try new things."

She looked at me grinning.

"Yes, so I saw. And heard."

"Heard?"

"Mmm."

I wasn't sure what she meant. We'd both had a bit to drink.

"I don't follow?"

"When I stay over."

It slowly dawned on me. I felt my face flush and hoped it wasn't bright enough for her to see.

"Your walls aren't as thick as you'd think."

She was smiling now, enjoying my discomfort.

"Really?"

"Mmm."

"Oh, God. Sorry, Luce."

She grinned.

"Don't apologise. I enjoyed it."

My mind raced through what Marcus and I had done when she'd last stayed over.

"Yes, but …"

She shuffled closer to me and put her arm around me.

"Last time, I enjoyed myself listening to you. Sounded a bit like spanking, and lots of moaning."

She laughed at my sharp intake of breath.

"At least, I think that's what was happening."

She was loving this.

"I could be wrong. You tell me."

"I … well …"

I thought back. A couple of weeks ago; the bunny tail. Showing her the playroom. She was right. I recovered my composure.

"I think you're right," I said. "I seem to remember getting a good spanking and a really long fuck. Hope you enjoyed it. I did."

She kissed me on the cheek.

"Touché."

As I gave her a kiss back, a man appeared at our table. Smartly dressed in a slightly dishevelled way.

"Hello, ladies. Fancy some company?"

"No, thank you. We're fine."

"I'm great company."

"I'm sure you are, but we're happy for now thanks."

He wandered off, slightly unsteadily.

"Why do we always attract them?"

"Because we're women, Luce. That's all it is. Plus, we're two women in a lap dancing club. His type will make all sorts of assumptions."

"Yea. Guess so."

We selected another girl; not as good as the earlier one. She was a bit mechanical. I understood it. They needed to look glamorous and erotic all the time. It wasn't possible and sometimes the act slipped. We ordered more drinks, and 'great company' appeared again. Sitting down, this time.

"Come on ladies, let me get you a drink."

"No thanks, we've just ordered."

"I'm Garry."

"Hello, Garry."

First rule in such situations; never give your name. Even a false one.

The waitress arrived and handed us our drinks. As she did so, Garry went to grope her. She was used to it and moved her body out of the way as if she was made of elastic.

"Great move," Lucy said.

The waitress winked at us and walked away. Fifteen seconds later, a security guy appeared.

"Everything alright, ladies?"

The waitress had obviously spoken to him. Garry took the hint, and wandered off, mumbling under his breath.

"One more dance, then are you ready to call it a day?" I asked. I was beginning to realise I'd drunk too much and I was feeling horny. The two often went together. It had got me into trouble a few times when I was younger. But now, it tended to make me mellow. Mellow, horny, and playful. Marcus loved it. Sometimes he refilled my glass a little too often. I let him. We both enjoyed the result.

"Yes, okay. Can we wait a bit, though? There was one girl I rather liked."

She described her, but I couldn't remember seeing her. I was happy to wait. Then Garry appeared again.

"Ladies, ladies. I'm sorry. I didn't mean to upset you earlier."

"You didn't."

"Then what was the bouncer doing?"

"His job, I should think."

"Ha, ha. Good. Yes."

He sat on the end of the bench. I noticed the security guy standing at the edge of the booth. I assumed he'd been watching Garry, but Garry hadn't spotted him.

"What are two beautiful girls doing here?"

"Having fun. Same as you."

"Yea. But I enjoy looking at all these beautiful women."

We both stared at him. His brain slowly whirred away. Understanding lit up his face. Followed a second or two later by a leer.

"Oh. Fancy them too, do you? Never mind. All you need is a good man to show you what you're missing."

This was the first time I'd heard a man use this line. I knew Lucy had heard it hundreds of times over the years. I still couldn't believe anyone would say it.

We looked at each other and understood what to do. We burst out laughing; fake, of course. But he was too drunk to know. His face went through a variety of expressions as his brain tried to deal with this. First confusion; then smiling as he thought he'd said something funny. Finally, a frown, as he realised we were laughing at him.

"What's so funny?"

I was about to say something when Lucy leaned towards him.

"We don't need a good man, Garry. We've already got one."

His mouth opened and closed a few times. Again, it took a while for the cogs to come to life.

"Got one?"

"Yes. At home."

The cogs were steaming now. Lucy didn't let him reach a conclusion this time. She put her arm around me.

"It's like this, Garry. We fancy each other."

She kissed me full on the mouth; long enough for me to respond. When Lucy pulled away, he was staring at us, a pathetic leer on his face.

"So, we fuck each other. Sometimes he watches. Then we fuck him."

Garry looked like his little world had exploded.

"Any questions?" Lucy asked in a hiss.

At this point, the security guard intervened.

"Come on, sir. Let's leave these two ladies to enjoy their evening, shall we?"

Gently but firmly, he stood Garry up and pushed him. Garry lumbered off.

"I don't know how much of that was true," he said. "But I want to believe it. Sorry about him. I'll keep an eye out."

"Thanks. Oh, can you do something else? Do you know a tall redhead wearing a leopard-print catsuit?"

"Yea. Sounds like Nina."

"If you see her, can you send her in our direction?"

He did. She arrived about ten minutes later. Twenty minutes later, she left having performed two of the most skilful dances I'd ever seen. One whilst removing her catsuit, the other naked. She would have given Celine a run for her money. It wasn't as personal; we were in a public space. But she had a fabulous body and moved like a cat.

"Well?" I asked Lucy.

She chuckled.

"Let's get back. Seeing that cat's made me hungry for pussy."

"Me too."

We made our way out to the exit. As we stepped out of the door, Lucy put her hand on my arm, indicating across the street. Garry. Standing by a lamppost. He looked too drunk to be a problem. But …

Lucy turned to one of the bouncers.

"Any chance of finding us a cab?"

He looked across the road.

"Him?"

"Yea. He pestered us once or twice."

"He got thrown out just now."

His face broke into a broad grin.

"Are you two ladies the ones who got the better of him?"

The story must have got around.

"We might be."

"Step back inside, and I'll let you know when I've found you a cab."

We were only waiting a few minutes. He took us to the taxi and made sure we were in safely. Bouncers may have their critics, but that night, they'd shown their professionalism too.

In the cab, Lucy ran her hand up my leg. I didn't want to stop her, but I wasn't going to give freebies to the cabbie. It was only a few minutes to the hotel. We were quite drunk and by the time we got to the room, we'd snogged in the cab, snogged in the lift, and in the corridor. We stumbled into the room, giggling.

"Miss Fletcher, you're a disgrace. Look at you. Have you been drinking?"

I tried to stand to attention.

"Yes, Miss Halstead. I cannot tell a lie. I have been drinking."

"Disgraceful. You don't see me drinking."

Saying that, she stumbled on the corner of the bed and ended up sitting on the edge. More fits of giggles. I walked towards her, and bending over, gave her a sloppy kiss. She responded. When I surfaced, I looked at her; wanted her.

"So, Miss Halstead. Do I escape punishment?"

I saw a gleam in her eye, as I realised what I'd said. I shrieked as she grabbed me and pushed me over her lap. My head and shoulders on the bed, my legs hanging in the air.

"No, Miss Fletcher, I don't think you do."

She pulled my dress to my waist, pulled my knickers down, and spanked me. She'd never done it before, and it showed. She was a bit clumsy and it was all a bit playful, but it had me shrieking and giggling in equal measure. God knows what the guests in the neighbouring rooms were thinking.

After a while, she stopped to catch her breath. I rolled off her and stripped off. Standing her up, I lifted her dress over her head and removed her underwear. Pushing her back on the bed, I climbed on after her.

We had to find somewhere for brunch the next morning; we were too late for breakfast.

Chapter 20 – Marcus

Martin the genealogist was a precise man. I'd noticed when he'd visited us the first time. The way he sat, the way he arranged his notebook. The way he searched for the right word or phrase. Sally had noticed too. I think it was one of the reasons she'd hired him. She was a researcher, after all. She recognised a fellow perfectionist. When he came back to see us, he sat in the same place and placed a folder on the table in front of him. It looked thin.

"Well, Sally. I do have something for you, I think."

We sat on the sofa opposite him. Sal was sitting on the edge, her hands resting on her knees. She wanted answers but was afraid of them.

"I have a few things to show you. I should point out I cannot currently guarantee any of them relate to the man you knew, who called himself Tony Crowther. We have too many breaks in the history at the moment."

"Okay, Martin. Show me what you've got."

"I trawled through the birth records for 1943, the year he said he was born. There was no trace of anyone with that name. However, it's worth mentioning some records were destroyed during the war, particularly in London and the Blitz cities. I went a few years either side and still found nothing.

I wondered if it was worth looking at the records of children's homes, if only because he never mentioned his parents. You suspected he came from the London area, so I started there and came across this."

He handed Sally a sheet of paper; a copy of a record.

"As you can see, it's a child, well, a baby really, called Anthony Crother. A slight difference in spelling. He went into the Balham orphanage on August the twenty-fourth, nineteen forty-four. The details are scant, as you can see."

He paused to let Sally read the document. She handed it to me. I struggled with the handwriting. Martin continued.

"It tells us he was a baby about a year old. Found in a bombed-out building the day before. Originally, I think he was marked as unknown. The name has been added by another hand, presumably when he could be identified. I don't know yet how they did that. He went through several children's homes in the following years. Mostly in London, but two in the home counties.

"The record has gaps in it, and he may have been adopted or at least fostered on a few occasions. These presumably didn't work as he returned to the system each time. At one point his name changes from Crother to Crowther. Possibly a clerical error, but all the other details match, so I'm fairly certain it's the same person."

He slid a few sheets across the table.

"Those are all the records. The last thing I have is a discharge sheet. This was completed on the day he left the care of his last children's home."

"How old was he?"

"About fourteen."

"What happened to him?"

"All it says on the sheet is 'apprenticed'. No other details."

"So, he was kicked out on his own at fourteen."

"Yes, it looks like it. It was the age at which working-class boys often went out to work. It's possible he went to live with whoever he was apprenticed to. It's a shame we don't know what he did. It might have given us a clue."

"I don't think he wanted to leave many clues, Martin."

"No, sorry. I was thinking aloud really."

"Oh, it's okay. I'm used to dead ends now. Is there anything else we can do?"

"I think it might possible to find one or both of his parents. I can look for deaths around the time he went into the orphanage. It sounds like his family may have died in a raid. I might be able to find them. I can also search the census records for the fifties and sixties to see if I can locate him."

"Okay, Martin. That would be good."

After he left, I could see Sal was a bit down. I sat by her and put my arm around her.

"Thoughts?"

She shrugged.

"It's a start, I suppose. He's an orphan. He spent years in various children's homes. I guess they weren't exactly holiday camps. At fourteen, he's on the street. No wonder he never talked about it. He wanted to forget it."

We spent some time looking through the copies Martin had given us. There wasn't much tangible information. All very bureaucratic. Nothing about the person being processed.

"I wonder if Mum ever knew about any of this?"

"Who knows? From what I've heard from you and Mary, I suspect not."

"Why's that?"

"Well ..."

"Go on."

"I get the feeling your mother wasn't the type to ask too many questions. If she got fobbed off once or twice, she'd drop it. Mary said she'd asked him a few times about his family and what he did. Never got an answer. If Mary couldn't get anything out of him, would your Mum?"

She thought for a while.

"No, I guess not." She gave a hollow laugh. "If you'd said that a year ago, I'd have rushed to her defence. But not now. I see Mum for what she was, now. A rather sad figure."

"No, Sal. Not sad. Unrealistic, perhaps. She wanted the fairy-tale marriage. You know, fair maiden marries her prince. She wasn't the first to find life's not like that."

We fell silent. Eventually, she took a deep breath, sat up, and looked at me. A brighter face now. She gave me a kiss.

"Sometimes it is, Marcus. Now, what does my prince require of his maiden tonight?"

I looked around the room.

"I've got a maiden? Where? Why didn't I know about this?"
She whacked my arm.
"Me. I'm your maiden."
"Aren't maidens supposed to be virgins?"
She gave a wicked laugh.
"Well, this one isn't."
"Thank God for that."

***

"All set?" I asked.
"Yes. Let's go."
We were taking a big step. While Matt and Yasmin had been creating our playroom, we had the chance to talk to them. They were a couple and her choker was significant. She was collared to Matt and had been for four years, but they'd known each other for a few years before that. They'd got together when their previous relationships had ended at around the same time.
Matt had been a full-time builder, and it had been Yasmin's idea to concentrate on the fetish and dungeon work. It had proved successful and they worked all over the country.
They told us about a local group they helped to run. A bunch of people into all sorts of fetishes and alternative lifestyles. Sally and I knew they existed. We'd joined two sites where we could talk to others about shared interests. It had proved useful to talk to people more experienced than us. We could ask questions and usually get sensible, helpful advice. But, like most of the members, we used pseudonyms.
Yas told us they held a public munch once a month. A few times a year, they held private events. They invited us to come along to one of the munches. We discussed it several times. Did we want to go public? What if we bumped into someone we knew? It was quite a step for two introverts. But we eventually decided we had to try it; we were intrigued.
One of the attractions was that Matt and Yas lived about twenty miles from us, so it wasn't too close to home. As we drove to the pub, we were quiet. We found it easily and turned into the car park.
"Nervous?" I asked.
She turned to me.

"Yes. You?"

"Yes. Remember, we can leave at any time."

"Okay."

She gave me a kiss.

"It's only a bunch of fetishists, sadists and masochists. How bad could it be?"

I'd texted Matt to let him know we would be attending, and he'd sent us a little list of rules for the munch. They were good, common sense things. Normal clothes, normal behaviour. And so it proved. Almost as soon as we walked in the door, Yas came over to greet us.

She spent the next ten minutes or so introducing us casually to some of the other people there. There were a couple of other first-timers as well, and Matt and another guy were looking after them. As we mingled, it was a strange feeling. Nerves, yes. But also knowing what to talk about. Everyone here presumably had interesting stories to tell. Many would be able to give us advice. But how much to say? How much to reveal?

We'd agreed to be careful about what personal information we gave. First name, job, city. But beyond that, nothing until we were more comfortable with the group. It soon transpired that was the norm. Nobody pried; nobody was nosey. We heard people discussing more intimate things, but never loudly and it was clear the participants knew each other well. People asked us what our relationship was; politely. We were happy to tell them. They always told us theirs or pointed out their partners across the room.

There were only about twenty-five attendees, but they were a wide mix. The youngest, a startlingly cute girl with blonde hair, didn't look much more than twenty. The eldest appeared to be a lively gentleman in a mobility scooter; an elderly woman who turned out to be his wife constantly trying to keep up with him.

We met gay couples, straight couples; those in between. And the majority were couples. There were a few singles, but they were in a minority. It looked like any other social gathering.

Matt came over to see us.

"Hello, Marcus, Sally. Welcome. I hope Yas made you feel welcome."

"Hi, Matt. Yes, she did thanks."

"How are you getting on?"

"Fine. It's an interesting group."

"It's the same old bunch who come along to this one. We get a lot more people at the other events. Lots of them find this one boring."

"Oh, it seems good to me," Sal said.

"It is, particularly if you're new to this. But they can be freer at the play meet; be themselves publicly but in private, if you see what I mean."

Sally stumbled as something bumped into her. It turned out to be the guy in the scooter. He'd backed into her by accident. His wife scolded him.

"You've turned your beeper off again."

"It's too noisy indoors."

He proceeded to apologise profusely, and Matt introduced us.

"Gerald, Peggy, this is Marcus, and this is Sally. Two new converts. And this is Gerald and Peggy. Two old hands."

Peggy frowned.

"Not so much of the old, Matt."

She had a twinkle in her eye. Matt bowed his head in acknowledgement and made his excuses. I pulled up a chair for Peggy, and a couple for us to sit on, so we were on the same height as Gerald.

"So, this is your first time?" he asked.

"Yes."

"Been to other events?"

"No," Sal said. "We're virgins."

Peggy laughed.

"Surely not?"

Sal flushed but giggled.

"Well, no. You know what I mean."

"You'll have to excuse her," Gerald said. "She's naughty. Always has been."

He gave her a look full of love. She returned it.

"You've been together for a long time?"

"Married for forty-eight years," Peggy replied.

"Wow."

"And doing all this …" He waved his arm towards the people milling around. "… for even longer. Haven't we?"

"Yes, dearest."

"Was it different in those days?"

"It was, and it wasn't as easy. No internet, you see. People didn't know about it, but it was there if you knew where to look."

"Which you did?" Sally asked, raising an eyebrow.

"We were part of it. Have you ever heard of Bettie Page?"

"Yes, of course."

He paused and beamed at Peggy.

"Peggy was the British Bettie Page."

We both looked at her. She smiled at us, contentedly.

"I had my moments," she replied.

"Which I photographed. We made a decent living, didn't we?"

"We did."

"We ended up in court once or twice, but we wouldn't change anything."

When they wandered off again, Peggy was still trying to keep up with Gerald.

After a couple of hours, we'd chatted with a few of the other attendees. More importantly, we relaxed. No dramas, no awkward moments. We found Yas and thanked her.

"Enjoyed it?"

"Yes, thanks. It's been good."

"Hope you'll come along next time."

"I think we might."

Several people we'd spoken to nodded or waved as we left. On the way home, we talked about the evening.

"Funny, isn't it?" Sal said. "Neither of us like social gatherings much. Yet put us in a room with thirty other kinky buggers and we're fine."

She had a point.

"Perhaps we've found our metier?"

"Perhaps."

She put some music on, and we drove in silence for a while.

"Darling?"

"Mmm."

"Have you ever taken any pictures of your cock?"

I turned to look at her quickly.

"No, I don't think so. Oh. Well, an ex and I tried to make our own porn movie once."

"How did it go?"

"Disaster, really. Mind you, this was in the days before smartphones. We were using a big old video camera. It was too unwieldy to hold it. We kept on having to stop, move the camera, start again, stop, move the camera. It was about as erotic as a pickled herring."

"Did you finish it?"

"No. Just gave up."

"So, no photos of your cock?"

"No. Why do you ask?"

"Oh, Lucy asked me."

"What?"

"It's for the pictures she's doing. After all, it's not a subject she's overly familiar with."

"They're not exactly difficult to find on the web."

"No. But she wants to do pictures of us. She's using me as a model-"

"I bet she is."

She grinned.

"-she's using me, and one or two might be of her."

"Really?"

"Yes. Interested now?"

"I'll tell you when I've seen them."

"Behave. She thought it would be good to use you, too."

"Well, if you don't mind giving her pictures of my cock."

"God, no. I don't mind showing that off at all."

"Flatterer."

"Just being honest, darling."

"Let me get this straight. For the first time in history, a woman has actually asked for a dick pic, and she's gay."

She giggled.

"That's about it. No need to worry. I can take them when we get home."

I looked at her again.

"You might have to persuade me."

Chapter 21 – Marcus

When we got home, I went to go upstairs.

"Oh, no you don't. In the bedroom; now."

I wasn't going to argue with her instruction. We both went to the loo and returned to the bedroom. She came over to me and put her arms around me.

"So, I'm going to have to persuade you, am I?"

"I don't think I thought that one through, did I?"

"Perhaps I've lost my touch."

"You don't even need to touch me."

Her eyes were sparkling. I could feel my cock stiffening already. She slipped my jacket off, untucked my shirt, unbuttoned it and it soon fell to the floor. Still looking into my eyes, she undid my belt, trouser button and zip and slowly dropped as my trousers fell. I lifted each foot and she pulled them away, removing my socks at the same time.

She put her hands on my bum and her lips closed over my cock through my trunks. I felt her teeth on it, gently squeezing it. I let out a sharp breath as she bit quite hard. I heard a chuckle from deep in her throat. Her hands slipped into the waist of my trunks and she slid them down, releasing me. She was sitting on her haunches in front of me; my cock inches from her face.

She was looking up at me, her hands now back on my bum. Holding my gaze, she stuck her tongue out and moved forward. I was waiting for that first touch. She got within a hairsbreadth before veering to one side, and slowly standing up.

"Patience, darling. Patience."

I reached out towards her, but she stepped backwards. Smiling, she lifted her top over her head and kicked her shoes off. Undoing her jeans, she turned around, bending forward, as she slid them over her bum. She giggled as she tried to take her jeans off beguilingly. But jeans aren't designed with this in mind, and she had to do some one-legged hops before they came free.

Walking towards me she disposed of her bra, leaving a pair of lacy shorts. Once again, as I was about to reach for her, she walked straight past me to the dressing table. She turned around, phone in hand.

"Remember why we're here, darling. Strictly business. Not for pleasure."

She came back and made a play of being a professional photographer. Moving around, taking pictures of my cock from umpteen angles.

"On the bed, please."

I knew her game and was desperately trying to think of ways to get my cock to deflate. But with her walking around in just her knickers, that was going to be difficult. She was still taking pictures. Me lying flat, lying with my legs open, lying with my legs held over me. God knows what Lucy would make of those pictures.

"How many photos does she want?"

"We'll need to select the best. So, we need a lot to choose from."

She was enjoying this. So was I, in truth. I loved it when she was in this mood. She lay me flat again and climbed on the bed. Kneeling by my side, she took some close-ups. She looked at me, her eyes wide and silently handed me the camera.

I took it, and before I'd even lined it up, her lips were over the head of my cock, sinking down as she took me into her mouth. Trying to take decent pictures while she was doing that was almost beyond me. I managed to take a few before she lifted off. I kept taking photos as she used her lips and tongue to tease me.

At one point, she looked at me; she knew I'd want to give in. To wallow in her skills. She dropped sharply back over me, taking nearly all of me into her mouth. I groaned, she chuckled. I put the phone down; she let me and allowed me to enjoy those wonderful sensations for a few minutes.

When she finally lifted off me, she came up and kissed me. As she did so, she slid her shorts off. Lifting herself over me, she lowered herself gently, guiding my cock inside her. When she was comfortably settled, she reached out, picked up the phone and handed it to me.

"Really?" I asked.

"Of course. I don't know what Lucy might want to do."

So, as she slid herself on and off me, I tried to take some photos of the action. It wasn't easy. She turned around, leaning forward. That view was always good. More photos. But she was struggling now. She was turned on, and I could hear her enjoyment. I thought it was my turn to play the game.

"Right," I said. "Next position. On your knees."

She looked back over her shoulder with a pleading expression.

"The photos can wait."

"No, Sal. Business, not pleasure."

She dropped sharply on my cock. I gasped.

"Are you sure?" she said. I wasn't.

"Turn around."

She spun around. I beckoned her with a finger. She bent forward, as I put the phone down. She kissed me, as I put my arms around her, and pulled her tightly to me.

"Had enough photography?" I asked.

"For now. I want something else."

"Take it."

She blew into my ear and went to sit up. I held her tight.

"No. Like this."

She chuckled and moved backwards and forwards. She couldn't move far but she was near enough not to need to. She put her hands under my shoulders and pulled herself onto me, her head buried in the pillow beside mine. This allowed me to let go and move my hands to her bum. I heard her breathing grow louder; short, shallow breaths. I squeezed her cheeks and ran a finger over her ass. She groaned as I eased the finger into her.

That was enough. Even muffled by the pillow, I heard her cry out several times as her climax came. Her hips jerking on mine, pushing her clit hard onto my pelvic bone. As she subsided, I withdrew my finger, moving one hand to caress her bum. The other stroking her back.

She lifted her head and kissed me.

"That's better. Now. Where were we?"

"I think we may have enough photos."

"You think?"

"Mmm."

"Well, what else can we do?"

She was moving up and down on my cock a tiny amount. Just enough to tease. Her face looking about as far from innocent as it's possible to be.

"Whatever you like," I said.

"Really?"

"Mmm."

"Anything?"

"Yup."

"Wait here."

She lifted off me, almost jumped off the bed and disappeared around the partition. I heard her open the door towards the playroom. What did she have in mind? I soon found out. She reappeared wearing the strap-on and holding a rechargeable wand.

"Anything?" she asked again.

She climbed onto the bed and got on her knees, with her legs spread. Unhooking the dildo, she slowly slid it into herself. Watching me, she fucked herself with it, spreading her lips, so I could see its movement. She removed it and hooked it back into the harness. It was glistening with her moisture. She moved towards me and straddled my chest, the dildo a few inches from my face.

"Suck me."

It wasn't a request. I opened my mouth as she moved forward and closed my lips around the cock. Instantly tasting her distinctive flavour. She looked down as I sucked the head, before slowly moving forward. The dildo moved into my mouth. She stopped moving and allowed me to control the depth. I slid along its length, sucking it.

It was a strange feeling; unlike anything I'd experienced before. Sal was kneeling over me while I licked her wetness from her artificial cock. It was intensely erotic. There was a hint of submission but also a feeling of giving. I understood Sally's love of giving oral a little more. This went on for a minute or two before she moved back and shifted her body down mine. Bending, she kissed me.

"Good boy."

"Thank you, ma'am."

She laughed and kissed me again; several times.

"Now, I'm going to fuck you."

I knew she wanted to. She'd bought the strap-on for my birthday, but we hadn't used it yet. I wanted it, too. She often used a dildo on me, but this would take it to a new level. She moved back until she was kneeling between my legs. She bent forward and lightly kissed and licked my cock. Her fingers running down until they reached my ass. Her fingers stroking it. She took some lube, and her fingers pressed into my hole. I spread my legs, loving the touch of her fingers; feeling them invade me. Her lips still around my cock.

She grabbed a couple of pillows and I lifted my hips as she put them under me. I spread my legs as wide as I could, my knees bent. I watched as she spread lube around my bum, and stroke some onto the dildo. She moved forward and the tip poked my ass. She watched me, gauging my reaction as she slowly pushed.

I felt that initial flash of pain as my muscles gave in to the pressure and groaned. I watched as she went deeper until her skin touched mine. She'd used dildos on me before, but this was a different league. I could feel the whole weight of her body behind the push, not just her hand. She bent down but the angle prevented her from reaching my face. She kissed her fingers and placed them on my lips.

"Okay?"

"Oh, yes."

The feeling around my ass was intense. She'd been right when she told Lucy my ass was sensitive; it was. But it had never been fucked like this. She slid in and out, slowly, gently. Watching my reaction. I nodded to her and she speeded up. Long regular strokes. I could feel the muscles around my ass rolling over the dildo as it slid in and out. Their nerves spreading heat outwards.

She was enjoying it now; fucking my ass. She put her hands on my thighs and pushed, spreading my ass wider. Allowing her to go deeper. My cock had responded. It was rigid, as hard as I could remember it for a while. My balls throbbing, seemingly in time with her thrusts. Then it got better.

She slowed and reached for the wand. Turning it on, she placed the tip lightly on my perineum. The shock went right through me as nerves and muscles fought each other. I cried out; loud and long. She pressed the wand more firmly, connecting with more and more nerves in that hyper-sensitive area. I was moaning almost continually now, my head laid back, my eyes closed. Her other hand flattened over my balls, squashing them against my cock, which, in turn, was squashed against my tummy.

Abruptly, she took the wand away, and my body relaxed. I opened my eyes to a familiar sound. She was still slowly fucking me, but the wand was now between her own legs. She was close to coming. I watched. I couldn't do anything else. I couldn't reach her.

I lay there as I watched my lover, her strap-on fucking my ass, bring herself to orgasm with the wand. She shook and wobbled as she came, her hand going onto the bed to steady herself. The movements stopped as she recovered; looking up at me. Flushed, breathing unsteady. A broad smile on her face. Neither of us said anything.

After a few deep breaths, she rearranged her position and picked up the wand again. Turning it on, she started to fuck me again. Wrapping one hand around my cock, she dropped the wand back on my perineum. The feeling was incredible. Everything from my cock to my ass was being stimulated. I couldn't separate the sensations. They all merged together in one huge sensory overload.

She moved the wand to my frenulum and touched it lightly; that made me jump violently. I knew I wouldn't last much longer. She knew too. She returned the wand to the area between my balls and ass and gripped my cock. Slowly sliding the skin, stretching it tight. Stroking my frenulum with her thumb. All the time, pressing the wand into my skin.

I almost screamed as my balls made their first contraction. She pulled the skin hard down my cock and held it there. My cock fired its first shot into the air, hitting her breasts. The second shot followed, falling back onto my tummy. Several more followed, accompanied by my cries.

I was panting now, hardly able to concentrate on what was going on. I gave in. Allowing my head to fall back, and simply feel. Feel the dildo deep in my ass, the wand between my legs. Her hand around my cock. Driving my orgasm to overdrive.

My climax was over its peak now and the sound of the wand stopped. As my cock went through its final spasms, the dildo gently slid out of me with one final flash of pain. Hands stroking my thighs. My legs slowly dropping, sliding down the bed.

I looked up. Sal was removing the harness. She pulled at the pillows and I lifted my hips so she could remove them. When I sank down, she bent over me. Kissing me.

"Are you okay?" she asked.

"Mmm. Give me a minute."

She stroked my hair, kissing my forehead. Eventually, I put my arms around her, and she sank onto me. We lay there for a few minutes.

"Wow," I finally managed.

"Did you enjoy that as much as it appeared?"

"Fuck, yes. That was intense."

"Pretty good for me too. Now you know why I like my ass fucked."

"Only fair we both get to do it."

"Another one on the repeat list?"

"Definitely."

We returned to silence before she hit the pillow with her hand.

"Damn."

"What?" I asked.

"We didn't take any photos of that."

I could reach her bum now and gave it a few hard slaps. She giggled.

"You think we've got enough?"

"Not quite," I replied. "I've thought of one more subject."

"What?"

"I'll show you tomorrow evening."

Chapter 22 – Lucy

"Hello, Lucy."

"Hello, Mum."

We were at a garden centre near Annie's home. It was the only place we could think of in the end. I'd been honest with Tim and Annie. If we'd met at their home, and it had all gone pear-shaped, it would have been unfair to them. They'd seen my point. We sat at a table outside the café. As agreed, Annie and Tim had stayed while Mum and I met, then gone to one of the other tables. To give us privacy was the explanation. I guessed it was more to rescue us if a fight broke out.

Now, looking at my mother, it seemed unlikely. She was a shadow of the woman I remembered. She was only sixty but looked ten years older. Thinking back all those years, she had always looked younger than her age. Or was that the naivety of youth?

"How are you?" she asked.

"I'm well, thanks. You?"

I knew this was going to be a stilted conversation. We hadn't seen each other for fifteen years. We'd had little contact of any sort. We had no common interests. What did we have to talk about? Catch up with all those lost years? That wasn't going to happen. I'd promised myself I wouldn't argue; wouldn't let her get to me.

"Yes. Not too bad."

"How's Dad?"

"No change really. He's trapped in a useless body. He gets very frustrated; angry. It's not like him."

I hid my amazement. Not like him? I don't remember him being anything other than angry. Or is angry the wrong word? Perhaps it is. He wasn't a violent man. He rarely used his anger against a person. No, it was zeal. He was always raving against something. Never *for* anything; always against. Alcohol, television, pop music, teenagers. Ho-mo-sex-uals, as he phrased it, stressing each syllable. Or using more damning words. When he found out I was one of them …

"Is there nothing they can do? Physio? Speech therapy?"

"They tried. He wasn't very co-operative. He thinks God will cure him."

Ha! The blind ignorance of faith. If God loved him so much, why did he have the stroke in the first place? What sin had he committed to deserve such a bolt from God? I had to ask the question that came into my mind.

"Do you?"

She looked troubled. Looked away. Looked back at me but couldn't hold my gaze.

"I don't know, Lucy. I'm not sure anymore."

"You would have been sure years ago. What's changed?"

She sat still. Not moving. I realised she was thinking about how to tell me whatever was on her mind. I might not want an argument, but I was going to be direct. She'd asked for this meeting. I wasn't going to pussyfoot around to appease her. I'd agreed to one meeting. What transpired would decide if there were any more.

"I've lost my faith."

She'd said it. I was surprised by how bluntly it had come out.

"Completely?"

"No, I guess not. I can't believe in a world without a maker."

"When did this happen?"

"It's been building up for a while. Annie and Tim left our congregation. Your father ranted about that, but I spoke to Annie. Her reasons struck home. Then he had his stroke."

"Did you talk to Dad about it?"

Her facial reaction told me the answer before she replied.

"No. I couldn't. And now I never will."

"Have you got anyone you can talk to?"

She looked sad suddenly. I realised why she looked as she did. She was a broken woman.

"No. I can't talk to anyone in our church, and I don't know anyone else."

"Annie?"

She smiled; it was the first time since we'd met.

"No. I don't want to burden her. They're working things out as well."

A sense of dread suddenly washed over me. Surely, she wasn't trying to use me as her sounding board? Her confessional?

"Besides," she continued, "I'm not sure I could discuss my feelings. I never have."

No, I thought, you haven't. My childhood wasn't bad. Dad had always provided for us. But there wasn't much love. I didn't remember much in the way of fun. Most of the things my school friends did was forbidden by my father. Mum had tried her best, but I guess her relationship with him was cold. She didn't know how to reach children.

Annie's experience must have been the same as mine. I didn't learn anything about growing up from my mother. We never had those chats every girl needs as she goes through her teenage years. I learnt everything from friends.

"Are you still attending church?"

"Not as often." She looked embarrassed. "I'm afraid I use your father as an excuse."

"Well, it's true, isn't it? He does need care."

"Yes, but I can get away when I need to. He has carers to wash him, feed him, change the bed. That sort of thing."

"Should he be in a nursing home?"

I thought she was going to cry. She sniffed a couple of times.

"I'm his wife. I should look after him."

"Mum, it's no shame. If he's that bad, he should be in the right place for him. It would be better for both of you."

"Annie keeps saying that as well. But I'd feel as if I'd failed."

"It's not a failure. It's being realistic."

"I promised Annie I'd think about it."

"Good."

I'd been wondering why she wanted to meet ever since I'd received the letter. I was no nearer finding out.

"Mum, what do you want from me? Why this meeting?"

"I'm scared, Lucy. My whole adult life has been with your father. He's always did everything. I've never had to think for myself. I've never had to work. I look at Annie and Tim. Their lives are so different from the way mine has been. Then I think of you. You've been independent for fifteen years. I can't even imagine what that's like. I know most people do it, but it scares me. I've never had my own bank account, never driven. Never had to find a plumber or mow the lawn. If your father goes, how will I cope?"

I understood her now. But I still didn't trust her motives.

"I'm sure Annie and Tim would help. They've always been there for you. You've always loved them."

The sting in my words hit home. I hadn't intended the barb; it just came out. A few tears ran down her cheeks.

"Your father was wrong. What could I do?"

"You could have supported me."

"I couldn't. Not then. I agreed with him. I disagreed with the life you'd chosen."

I had to bite my lip.

"I didn't choose it, Mum. It's who I am. Nobody chooses their sexuality any more than they choose their eye colour. It's the way I was born, and I'm proud of it. I wish my parents had been."

She was crying softly now, tears rolling down her face. I handed her a tissue and she dabbed them away.

"I didn't understand. I accepted what I was told. It was a sin against God. I still don't understand. It's my own ignorance. I don't even know what you've been up to for the last fifteen years. Annie's told me bits, but I don't know my own daughter. That hurts. Particularly now."

Yes, I thought, now you're facing being alone. But I did feel a pang of sympathy. She was right, she didn't know me. Mind you, she wouldn't have wanted to know everything I'd done. She wouldn't have understood half of it.

"But I want to," she continued. "I want another chance."

I did a quick run over everything she'd said. She seemed to be telling the truth. She seemed to want to try again. Perhaps for the wrong reasons, but I didn't think she was being manipulative. If she was, she was a better actor than I had imagined. She was simply scared of the future. Terrified.

"I'll be honest, Mum. My life is good. I'm not going to let the past hurt me." I thought of Sally. "I've seen it happen to someone close to me and I don't intend to take the risk."

She was looking at me, nervous about where I was going.

"So, I'm going to go away and think about it. Give me a week or so and I'll get in touch with Annie. I can't make any promises."

She managed a brief smile.

"Thank you, Lucy. Thank you for coming."

I passed Annie and Tim as I headed for the exit, briefly letting them know it had gone okay and I'd be in touch. I had some thinking to do.

***

"What are you going to do?"

"I'm not sure, Sal. I'm still suspicious of her motives."

"It does sound like she's doing it mainly for herself."

"Exactly. She's frightened she'll end up on her own. She never supported me before and now she wants me to support her."

"What did you feel when you met her?"

"Nothing much, to be honest. A bit sad for her, I suppose."

"If you continue with this, would it be for love of your Mum or a sense of duty?"

That was the crunch question. I'd been thinking about it since our meeting.

"Duty. I'd be lying if I said anything else."

"Do you want your family back?"

"I've lived perfectly well without them for years. Almost in spite of them. I'm not risking all that. You know all too well what families can do to you."

"Indeed I do."

"And I don't want to put myself through that. I don't think she accepts I'm gay even now."

"Let's be honest, Luce, she probably never will. She doesn't understand it and doesn't want to understand it."

"I doubt she could. I suspect sex was never a high priority for my parents."

"You never know. Lots of religious people have good sex lives."

"As long as it's in a marriage. But I doubt it. When Dad and I had our big bust-up, I remember something he said. Not the exact words but to the effect sex was about procreation, nothing else. It was a duty, not a pleasure. You know what that means?"

"What?"

"My parents had sex twice."

Sally burst out laughing but quickly stopped herself.

"Sorry, Luce, I couldn't help it."

I was smiling too.

"Don't worry, I find it funny too. Sad, but funny. Their loss, I suppose. But if they really think that, it's not surprising they don't understand gay sex, is it? No chance of procreation there, is there?"

"But relationships are about more than sex. What about love? They're Christians; they should understand that."

"Do you know many Christians? The most judgemental people I've ever met have been self-professed Christians."

"True."

"Besides, I'm not sure my parents knew the meaning of love. I never once remember them showing any signs of affection. To each other, or to Annie and me. I think their idea of marriage revolved around duty, not love."

We fell silent. Thinking our own thoughts for a few minutes.

"Sorry, Sal. I didn't mean to bring back any painful memories."

"No, Luce. I'm over that now. It gives me a thought, though. Why don't you speak to Jenny again?"

"That's a possibility. I'll mull it over. I still need to decide what to do next."

"Gut feeling?"

"I'll meet her again, see what happens. But the minute she starts draining my energy, or causing me stress …"

"Anything I can do help?"

"I don't think so at the moment. But I wouldn't mind talking occasionally. I don't have anyone else who knows about this."

"Whenever you need me."

We'd discussed this over dinner; it was one of our nights together. I knew I needed to talk to someone about it. I'd had a chat with Annie, but she was too close to the problem. I knew Sally would listen and not judge. I needed that. Speaking to Jenny might be a good idea. She'd helped me before when I'd been coming to terms with things, including my family history. She wouldn't remember the details, but I'd told her the history once; I could do it again.

"Made any progress on the pictures?" Sally asked.

"I've got dozens of sketches, but still can't decide which to work on."

"Want to show me?"

"Yeah, if you like."

I'd tidied them all away before she'd arrived. Now I got them all out again, and we went through them. I was more comfortable with this now. I'd given up my artwork years ago. I'd lost confidence; was never happy. I didn't like showing them to anybody. But two years ago, I refreshed my skills with some classes. I was rusty, but eventually, Sally had persuaded me to put a few into a local exhibition. To my surprise, they sold.

I started doing more sensual work; life drawing and nudes. They had become more explicit when I was with Zoe. I still did the normal stuff, like the portrait of Sally I did for Marcus. But I loved drawing the human body. It was fascinating looking at it with the eye of an artist. It made you think differently; see differently. It made you notice things you'd never noticed before.

I did a lot of sketches of my own body, sitting in front of a mirror. Some very intimate. I saw things I'd never noticed before, and I was very familiar with it from a sexual point of view. Sketching other people was the same. It had been with Zoe; it was with Sal.

"These are good, Luce. How are you going to decide which to use?"

"Haven't a clue. Do you want to choose?"

"Oh, no. We're leaving that to you. Who knows? Perhaps you can produce half a dozen and replace them in six months' time. There'd be a market for these, you know."

"I know. But I'm not sure about going public with some of these. I don't think the faculty would be keen."

"Use a pseudonym."
"Yea, possibly."
"Are you still selling any work?"
"The odd one, but I'm not really trying at the moment. I can't commit the time. If I do things I like, I put them to one side, and then show a few in a local gallery."
"Sorry, have we interfered with that?"
"Yes," I said with a grin. "But I'm not complaining. This is something of a challenge. I'm trying to push my imagination into areas I don't know enough about."
"You mean bondage and stuff?"
"Yes. But men's bodies as well. Did you get any photos?"
Sally grinned.
"Uh, yes."
"But?"
"Well, I went a bit overboard."
"How so?"
"I've got a hundred and thirty-seven photos."
"What? Why?"
She looked a bit bashful.
"We got a bit carried away."
I laughed; she grinned.
"They're not just of his cock."
"Oh?"
"I'm not sure you'll want to see them all."
"Show me, show me."
She got her iPad out, and we sat next to each other. She found the first picture; Marcus's cock, erect.
"I'm no expert, but that's quite impressive."
"I'm happy with it, thanks."
I zoomed in.
"It's so intricate. Lots of different colours and textures. And the veins."
"Is it? I've never noticed."
She was grinning.
"Liar."
"Guilty. I could look at it for hours."

"I'm guessing you often do."

She poked me in the ribs. We started going through the pictures. Marcus's cock from every angle imaginable.

"Do most men shave now? I thought it was mainly for porn films."

"He's the first for me. It's wonderful. All that smooth skin."

"The balls are interesting, too. I'm not used to seeing them up close."

"There's nothing else like them."

"You certainly took a lot."

"Marcus told me to select a few, but I thought I'd let you see the lot. You can choose the ones you like. I mean, need. Well, you know what I mean."

"It will be fascinating to draw. And the colours are interesting. If I go with the part coloured idea, this would be a striking focal point. The veins are fascinating too. Wow …"

The next picture caught me by surprise. Still Marcus's cock but with Sally's lips wrapped around the top.

"You may not want to see the rest."

"You can't stop now; just when it's getting interesting. Are you happy for me to see them?"

"Oh, yes."

"And Marcus?"

"Yes, but he thought you wouldn't be interested."

Curiously, I was. I slowly went through the pictures. Various amounts of cock in Sally's mouth. A few of her kissing or licking it.

"You seem to be enjoying yourself."

"I love it."

"Why?"

She thought for a moment.

"It's the heat, the texture. Hard but pliable, and super sensitive. At least, Marcus is."

I must have looked puzzled.

"He's the most sensitive guy I've ever known, particularly when it comes to his cock. I can make him squirm and moan with the tiniest flick of my tongue. He loves it. When he lies back and leaves me to it, it gives me a tremendous feeling of power. Teasing him and watching his reaction."

"Is he unusual?"

"Oh, all guys love a blowjob. But he's so responsive. It turns me on too. I can come from giving him one."

"Really?"

"Yup. It's only happened two or three times. But it's happened."

"Wow."

I swiped the photos. The subject changed again. Sally on top of him, riding his cock. I looked closely; her pussy impaled on him. Then her facing away from him. Again, his cock in her, her ass tight as she leaned away from him. I found them strangely erotic. But she was my lover too.

My eyes opened wide with shock.

"Good God, Sal. Is that … is that you?"

"Yup."

A bum filled the screen. Her bum; I knew it pretty well, and I knew the pussy and ass so clearly visible. But that wasn't what took my breath away. Not even the fact her bum was pink; flushed. No. It was the horizontal stripes across her cheeks. Livid; purple and red. The skin clearly raised at the edges.

"Are they …"

"Cane welts."

I looked at her. She had a dreamy look on her face. I looked at the photos again. Zoomed in on the welts.

"That's got to hurt."

"That's the idea. Well, part of it."

"You like this?"

"God, yes."

"Why?"

"It's simple; pain turns me on." She paused for a moment. "Actually, it's not that simple. It's also because it's Marcus. I'm not sure it would be as good with anyone else. I don't think I'd have trusted any of my exes to do this."

"Do you do this often?"

"Caning? Fairly often, but this one only comes out on special occasions. We've got another cane that's our favourite. It's thinner and whippier; stings rather than hurts. He can use it much longer on me. But we use other things as well. You may have seen them in the playroom."

"I did see a few. Yes."

"And we do a lot of spanking. You may remember hearing us ..."

"Don't know what you mean."

"... and wanking while you eavesdropped?"

"Oh, that spanking."

She gave me a gentle push. I was still engrossed in the photos. Her skin, which I knew to be so soft, marked by the hardness of a cane. Mixed emotions were going through my head. Sally clearly loved it, but it was physical pain. How would it feel? What was the turn-on? I briefly thought about how I would feel receiving such pain. I wasn't naïve, I knew people did this. I'd guessed Sally and Marcus did it. I'd seen the canes. But I was now seeing the results. That was a bit different.

"How long does it hurt? How long do they last?"

"These hurt for a few hours. Then they're a bit sore for a day or two; particularly if you forget them and sit down hard. With me, they're gone in three or four days. Depends how many he's given me. The whippier one heals much quicker."

I counted them in the picture in front of me.

"Six. Is that normal?"

"Well, we did this one specially to look good. For this cane, six is good; sometimes more. If I've been particularly cheeky. Or if I ask for them."

"You never cease to amaze me, Sal."

We came to the end of the photos.

"Which ones do you want?" she asked.

"Is it rude to ask for them all?"

"No. You can have the lot, as long as we don't find them all over the internet tomorrow."

"I promise. My own private collection."

"Will they help?"

"Yes. They've already sparked ideas in my head. The colour and veins on his cock and your caned bum in particular."

She air-dropped them onto my iPad. As they transferred, I had a thought.

"When were the caning photos taken?"

"Two nights ago. Why?"

"I want to see those marks in the flesh."

Chapter 23 – Sally

"Christmas all sorted?" Marcus asked.

"I think so. You and me Christmas day. Mary's going to Ken's family again."

"I must admit, I didn't think it would still be going by now."

"Me neither. Ken must have something."

"A big cock?"

"Marcus! I'm not sure they're even lovers."

"From what Mary's said, I think they are."

I thought about it and had to agree with him. She had dropped a few hints. Well done, Mary.

"But she's going to come over for a day in the week before New Year."

"Okey-dokey."

"Lucy's going to Tim and Annie's again. She thinks her mother might be there."

"What about her father?"

"They're looking for a nursing home for him. He may be in by Christmas."

"Ah."

"I don't think she's looking forward to it."

"I wouldn't either. Spending the day with a sister and brother-in-law she hardly knows, and a mother who sounds as much fun as a pickled herring."

"She's making an effort for the moment. But she's coming to us again on Boxing Day, if that's all right. We may need to revive her."

"Course it is."

"Thanks. So that's it."

"Same as last year."

"Yup. It was all right, wasn't it?"

He broke into a big, warm smile.

"Best Christmas ever."

"We'll have to make this one even better."

"We can only try. Now, what about your birthday?"

"Oh," I said as lightly as I could. "I hadn't thought about it."

"How about you go to Lucy's Friday night. We all go out on Saturday evening and then you're all mine on the day."

I went over and hugged him.

"It would be perfect if that's all right. I didn't want to suggest it."

My birthday was on a Sunday this year, and I wasn't sure he'd be happy with me spending time with Lucy over the weekend. I shouldn't have doubted him.

"Where are we going on Saturday?"

"Wait and see."

I'd had a busy week. I was still doing my normal job, but I was spending a couple of days a week working on stuff for the new library. The audit was taking longer than we'd expected; we'd spend a day on it and seemed to have achieved nothing. I was also attending planning meetings; they were well out of my comfort zone. But I struggled through and hoped I was contributing something worthwhile. By Friday evening, I was exhausted.

When I arrived at Lucy's I had to smile. She'd put her table in the middle of the room. Laid it very formally; flowers and candles. More candles all around the room; no other lights. She kissed me.

"Happy birthday, lover."

"Thank you. This is beautiful, Luce."

"Do you want a shower or bath first?"

That sounded like a great idea.

"Yes. It'll wash the day away."

"Go ahead and I'll finish dinner preparations."

I put my bag in the bedroom and went through to the bathroom, slightly disappointed Lucy wasn't joining me. Shedding all my clothes, I stepped under the shower and stood there with water pouring over me. I closed my eyes and let it soothe my aching muscles. Clear my mind. I always found a shower relaxing and stimulating at the same time.

I jumped as another body pressed itself to my back and arms reached around me, enclosing me. I relaxed as Lucy reached in front of me for the shower gel, poured some onto her hand and washed me. Her hands roving over my body as her nakedness rubbed against me.

I went to turn around to face her, but she stopped me, holding me close as the water washed the lather away. I was already feeling relaxed. She had laid my wet hair over one shoulder and was kissing my neck. Always a winner. Even better as her hand dropped between my legs and she brushed my clit. She knew a lot about me now; what I needed. She knew how to draw it out, and she knew how to take me there quickly.

This was one of those quick times. I wanted it; she knew. I was soon squirming on her fingers. As she pulled me close to her, kissing my neck, I had my first orgasm of the evening. Nothing intense but it took the edge off my desire.

She slowly released me, and I turned to face her. We kissed under the cascading water and I went to start on her, but she stopped me.

"No. I thought you might need that. Now you can relax. I've got plenty more planned for you tonight."

I went to object.

"It's your birthday. Let me give you a few freebies. Dinner will be ready in about twenty minutes. Let's get dry."

We got out of the shower and towelled each other dry. Cue a lot of giggles and shrieks.

"If I'd known you were going to go to this trouble, I would have brought something to dress up in."

"Why wear anything?"

So, we didn't. It was strange eating dinner naked. But I soon got used to it and it saved time later.

***

"You're back early."

"Lucy said you had something planned."

"Did she?"

"Yes. How did she know?"

"Can't imagine."

I kissed him and let it be. I knew if he didn't want to tell me, I'd have to wait and see.

"I'm going to change."

"Put on some old clothes."

It became even more curious when he got us brunch not much after eleven. We sat and chatted over some bread, cheeses and hams. Our usual weekend lunch, really. The doorbell rang; Marcus answered it and came back with Lucy.

"Hi, Sal."

"What are you two up to?"

They both tried to put on innocent looks. Neither of them was very good at it.

"Right," Lucy said. "Are you ready? We're going out."

"Do I need anything?"

"No. See you later, Marcus."

We drove a few miles out of the city, before turning down a lane. I saw a sign for an artist's collective. She parked the car and I followed her to what looked like the gallery for the centre. As we got to the door, she turned and gave me a quick kiss.

"We're going to make a pot."

I followed her through the entrance, we registered at the desk and were given directions to the potter's studio. Over the next ten minutes, two more women arrived to complete the class, just four of us. Lucy and the potter, Ellen, knew each other a little. They both used the same gallery and were on greeting terms.

Ellen welcomed us and talked briefly about what we were going to do. Throw and decorate a pot; it sounded so simple. Ellen showed us how to do it. Sitting at her wheel, she explained how to throw a basic bowl and made it look easy. She threw two or three other shapes so we could choose what we wanted to do.

"That's the demonstration," Ellen said. "I could go on, but the best way to learn is to do."

We each sat at a station. A large box with a wheel in the centre, controlled by a pedal under the right foot. In each box was a large lump of clay, and a bowl of water. Ominously, we'd all been given large aprons. Very large aprons. We soon found out we needed them. The principle of pot throwing hasn't changed for thousands of years. It's simple, effective and quick.

Unless you're a complete novice and hopelessly uncoordinated. The first few times, I didn't throw the clay on the wheel hard enough and when I set it spinning, the lump flew off. When I'd mastered that and was easing out the side of the bowl, I put my fingers through it. Bits of clay flew everywhere; spots hit my face. That was when I discovered it wasn't a good idea to wipe your face when your hands were covered in muddy water. I started laughing. The others joined in.

One of the other women wasn't faring much better than me. But the other was and Lucy was being her usual calm self. A picture of concentration, the tip of her tongue poking from the corner of her mouth. I'd seen it when she was sketching me.

"Have you done this before?" I asked her.

"Yes," she said. "But about ten years ago."

She'd already completed three simple bowls and was now building something taller. Ellen came over and gave me some guidance. Eventually, I managed to create a reasonably symmetrical open bowl. It did become easier as I got used to the speed of the wheel and the amount of pressure I needed to apply.

I made several bowls, crushing them and using the clay to make another one. I wanted to make at least one which would be good enough to decorate. I looked over to Lucy. She had several bowls of different sizes and a couple of taller pots, one with a rippled edge. Show off.

After an hour or so, Ellen asked us to finish whatever we were working on and choose two of our creations. That was easy for me; I only had two that didn't look like something from an archaeological dig. The woman who had been rivalling my incompetence also had two. We looked at each other and shrugged. Her friend had several items to choose from, as did Lucy.

We carried our chosen pots to a table, where we spent the next hour decorating them with various coloured slips. Ellen also provided us each with an item she'd made, in case ours were complete disasters. The decorating required less concentration and we all chatted. Ellen answering questions about what we were doing and about the far more complex work she did. By the end, we each had three decorated items, which would be fired and ready to collect in two weeks.

When we got back to the flat, Lucy dropped me off.

"I won't come in. Got to get cleaned up; see you later."

When he saw me, Marcus burst out laughing.

"Hello, Moley."

I looked in the mirror and grinned. I had clay on my face and a lot in my hair. I had tied my hair back, but it was still messy.

"Have fun?"

"Yes, it was great. I was useless."

"Did you make anything?"

"Yes, two bowls. They'll be ready in a couple of weeks."

"So, you weren't useless."

He always supported me, no matter what.

"Lucy was much better, but she'd done it before."

"Yes, I know. Tea?"

"Ooh, yes please."

We sat drinking it and eating eclairs.

"We'll need to get ready soon," he said. "We need to leave about five-thirty."

"That's early. Where are we going?"

He raised an eyebrow. We both smiled and, in unison, said …

"Wait and see."

"How do I know what to wear?"

"Whatever you like. You can dress up but it's not essential."

I went downstairs, put all my clay-stained clothes in the washing basket and had a shower. I struggled to get some of the clay out of my hair; it was drying out. I thought I'd managed it, but there were still a few remnants which made me wince when I drew a brush through my hair.

I thought about what to wear. Whatever it was, I wasn't going without underwear this time. It was early December and I wasn't getting frostbite between my legs for anyone. So, I chose my underwear first. I was fickle when it came to underwear. My favourite this week would be different from next. I never did work out why.

I finished my hair and make-up and chose a dress. A simple navy-blue one, but I had a long jacket that matched it perfectly for a cold night. Marcus appeared as I was finishing off.

"I've missed all the fun."

"I'll be doing it in reverse, later. Want a ticket?"

"I suspect I can't afford it."

I kissed him.

"I'll take payment in kind."

"In that case, save me a seat."

He went off to have a shower and I went upstairs to wait for him. It always amazed me how quickly men could dress. But their hair didn't take long, and Marcus wasn't one for make-up. Less than fifteen minutes later, he appeared and we set off.

We went to a restaurant we'd only visited once before. We'd been impressed, but it closed shortly afterwards in a dispute between the two owners. That had been settled and it had re-opened. It was very popular; Marcus must have booked it some time ago. I was never that organised.

We had their special pre-theatre option, so that gave me a clue for later. It was a taster menu. Small amounts of many of their offerings, placed centrally, so we could help ourselves. Mary listened as Lucy and I told her about our pottery class.

Marcus looked at his watch.

"We need to move in about ten minutes, so if anyone wants to freshen up ..."

Predictably, we all traipsed off to use the facilities. By the time we returned, Marcus had settled the bill. The theatre wasn't far away and as we turned the corner facing it, I saw the posters. I reeled slightly as memories came flooding back; many of them things I'd tried to forget for years. We were going to see a ballet; The Nutcracker. Mary and Lucy were walking in front of us. Marcus pulled me nearer.

"Is this okay?"

"Yes," I replied. "Yes, it is."

He must know something I didn't remember telling him. Mary? Possibly. I'd have to wait and see. But as I walked across the square to the theatre, I thought it was about time I faced the last taboo from the past. Marcus had reserved a box; just for us. Perfect height and a perfect view of the stage. He let me choose a seat first, then Mary and Lucy, before disappearing.

We chatted quietly for a while and he returned with some drinks, sweets and chocolates. We settled ourselves as the curtain went up for the first half. As the performance began, my mind wandered for a few minutes. I brought it sharply back to the present and concentrated on the stage.

At half time, the lights came up and we stood to stretch. We had plenty of room in the box. We all needed the loo and, fortunately, the row of boxes had their own toilets, so we didn't have to wait long. When we all retook our seats, Mary looked at me.

"Okay, darling?"

"Yes, Mary. It's fine."

She patted my leg.

"I thought it would be."

I saw her look at Marcus, and they exchanged a knowing smile.

"Have you two been plotting?"

"I saw this was on," Marcus said. "But I dimly remembered a conversation about ballet, and I thought it included Charlie, so I checked with Mary."

"We discussed it and decided you'd be okay with it now."

Lucy was looking from Marcus to Mary, clearly trying to work out what we were talking about.

"Charlie and I were both ballet mad as kids," I told her. "We went to classes. I grew too tall and too gangly to be any good and gave it up. But Charlie loved it; she was good too. Mary took us to see ballets, didn't you?"

"I did."

"But after Charlie died, I couldn't face it anymore. I haven't been to one since."

I reached over and gave Mary a hug; grabbed Marcus's hand and kissed it.

"It's about time I did."

By the time the performance came to an end, I'd cleared my mind. I'd loved it; the grace, the music, the emotion. I'd thought of Charlie while I watched; I'd seen her dancing. A few tears had come to my eyes.

But they weren't tears of despair or anger, as they would have been years ago. They were tears of love and happy memories. Another demon banished. In all honesty, the last one I was aware of.

As we came out, Marcus offered to give Lucy and Mary a lift, as he always did. They declined, as they always did, and he found them a cab. I gave Mary a big hug.

"Thanks, Mary. For everything."

"It's nothing. Happy birthday for tomorrow, darling."

I went around and gave Lucy a hug and a sneaky kiss. She squeezed my bum.

"Have a good day tomorrow."

With that, they were gone, and we walked back to our car, arms around each other. When we got home, he poured me a drink and asked me if he'd done the right thing. He knew I'd associated anything to do with Charlie with the shadow. It had hurt because I loved her; missed her.

That had all gone now. I hadn't thought about ballet. It had got lost over the years amongst the heavier baggage. But when I'd seen the front of the theatre, it had all come back. And watching it had washed it away. We lay on the sofa in each other's arms; warm, comfortable, safe. Eventually, I yawned.

"Tired?" he asked.

"It's been a busy day."

"Let's go to bed."

I kissed him.

"Let's go to the bedroom, anyway. I seem to remember I saved you a seat. Can't remember what for."

"I can."

We switched everything off and went downstairs. He laid on the bed, watching me. I had an idea and found the music for The Nutcracker on my phone; put it through the speakers.

"I haven't got a tutu, I'm afraid."

"I think I might get you one."

I slowly pulled my dress off, revealing my underwear.

"Will this do for now?"

Chapter 24 – Sally

The first thing I heard in the morning was water running and it took me a moment to work out where it was coming from. Marcus came around the partition and over to the bed. Still naked, he bent down and kissed me.

"Good morning. Happy Birthday."

"Thank you, darling."

"Your bath awaits."

He took my hand and led me to the bathroom. The bath was the centrepiece of the room; literally. It sat in the middle of the space and was easily big enough for two. This morning it was full, with masses of bubbles sitting on the water. The lights were low and a table by the bath had some bubbly and a plate of smoked salmon blinis.

He spent the next hour pampering me. Washing me, feeding me, stroking me. Eventually, he joined me. Unfortunately, you couldn't have sex in the bath, though. We'd tried. It was big enough, but as soon as you started any rhythmic movement, the water sloshed all over the place. You had to get out, then get back in when you'd finished. But the bathroom was big enough and that's exactly what we did.

When we went upstairs there were flowers everywhere. Several vases; all stunning.

"Oh, darling. They're beautiful."

"Well, I haven't gone over the top with the presents."

I looked at the table; a small pile of beautifully wrapped parcels.

"Well, a few," he said. "But mostly silly things."

I kissed him.

"That'll be perfect."

He cooked breakfast and fed me presents. He was right; silly things which made me laugh. A few things we would both get a lot of fun from.

"This is from Mary."

It looked like a picture. As I unwrapped it, he watched me with an expression I couldn't place. He seemed a little uncomfortable. I pulled the paper away and promptly burst into tears.

"You knew?" I finally managed to say.

"Yes. We talked about it. She wasn't sure and nor was I."

I looked at the framed photograph. My mother and father on their wedding day.

"I've never seen this photo."

"She thought you hadn't."

I sat there, my tears drying. It was a lovely picture and I looked at them both. My feelings were mixed. Not really love; but no anger, no fear. Merely acceptance.

"Sal?"

"I want to put this somewhere. It's part of me, after all."

"Perhaps you can let Mary know."

I rang her. We both shed a few tears and I could sense her relief. But she'd been right, I needed that picture.

"This is from Lucy."

Lucy always seemed to give us pictures, but we weren't complaining. It was large and well wrapped. I had to carefully peel the tape away before I could get into it. As I pulled the paper away, I couldn't help breaking into a broad grin. It was a day full of surprises. A portrait of Marcus.

"It's brilliant. She's got you."

"You think?"

"Don't you?"

"I don't know. You know how much I hate having my photograph taken. I wasn't keen on having my portrait done, either."

I looked at him slyly.

"How did she persuade you?"

"We made a deal."

"What kind of deal?"

He handed me another parcel; the same size as the portrait of him. I was bemused.

"This is from me."

I pulled at the paper again and squealed as I saw the subject. Lucy herself.

"Oh, Marcus."

"She wasn't keen on that either, but I insisted. If she wanted to paint me, she had to do a self-portrait."

I rested the pictures next to each other and studied them. They were both in the same style as her portrait of me. Both beautiful. I went over to him and gave him a big hug, showering him with kisses.

"They're wonderful. Thank you."

Three more presents lay on the table.

"They're all connected, so you can open all those together."

I went over and looked. Two small packets and a larger one.

"Any particular order?"

"You can leave the large one until last."

I picked up the first one, ripping it open to reveal a pair of silk stockings. I knew they were expensive. I carefully removed them from the packet and ran my arm into one. Black, with a prominent seam running down the back. A single band of dark green embroidery around the top.

I moved to the second parcel and opened it. A gorgeous pair of black low-waisted briefs, with a fine self-pattern, enhanced again with subtle green embroidery. I stretched the fabric across my hand. Almost opaque; the merest hint of skin underneath. As I undid the third package, the first thing I saw was a silky material before the whole thing was revealed. I lifted it from the paper, and he pulled it away, as I laid it on the table.

It was half-way between a basque and a corset. The material was silky, but not shiny. Delicate little details, only visible close-up. It was boned. Not heavily, but firm when I flexed it. Fully laced at the back, with suspenders. I held it up. The top section looked as if it would fit well, which a lot of basques didn't, as I wasn't a big girl. And in the middle, more of the green embroidery, linking all the items together.

"This is beautiful, darling," I said, turning to him. "Thank you. I'm going to feel so good in this. Shall I go and put it on?"

"It's not a bad idea, but perhaps not yet."

"No?"

He gave me a wry look.

"I wondered if you might like to wear it this afternoon."

I was a little disappointed he'd refused my offer. He didn't usually. Never mind, this afternoon would do. We could …

Then it hit me. I looked at him, my heart beating faster.

"We … we're going?"

"Do you want to?"

I thought for a moment; my heart now racing.

"It's your birthday," he continued. "So, it's your choice."

My heart pushed my head towards its decision.

"Yes."

"Sure?"

"Yes. But I can't go in this; I couldn't do it."

"How about you wear it with a dress over the top. You'll know you're wearing it and I'll know you're wearing it. But no one else will."

He had a point. It was a great idea. Often when we went out, our knowledge of what I was wearing underneath was enough to get both of us going. This would be the same; only ten times better. I walked over to him and hugged him.

"You're on."

We'd been to our second munch, which was even better than the first. Mainly the same people, but they welcomed us like old friends, and we had a great evening. Spending time talking to some of those we hadn't spoken to at the first. Matt had told us there was a play meet coming up, but it had turned out to be today; my birthday. So, we declined.

In truth, we were both uncertain about attending. We knew a little about what went on. Matt had given us the link to their website, and we looked at the guidelines and rules. From the short list of things which were forbidden, all sensible and obvious, it was clear it was very different from the monthly munch. It seemed that within reason, anything went; including dress.

We both wanted to go. This was a big interest for us now. But we were also reserved and private. How would we cope? We didn't fancy standing around like wallflowers or making some rookie error and embarrassing ourselves or other people.

This afternoon we were going to find out. After lunch, we showered and got ready. Marcus was going to wear black; jeans, a t-shirt and a jacket. He didn't have much to wear for our games. I mused on that and decided it was going to have to change. I had a few ideas for things I'd like to see him in.

When I put the basque on, I needed his help. It slipped on easily but tightening the lacing needed a second pair of hands. When we'd adjusted it so I felt nicely constrained but could still breathe easily, I rolled on the stockings and clipped them to the suspenders. The briefs completed the look and I went to look in the full-length mirror.

I was pleased with what I saw. It fitted me perfectly and I had been right; the upper section was just right. It even gave me a bit of cleavage.

"Well?" I asked.

He came towards me, his hands playfully making a grab for me.

"Perhaps we won't go after all."

He stopped behind me and joined me in looking in the mirror.

"It looks fabulous. It accentuates your shape."

"It does. Look, I've got some boobs."

"You've always got those."

"You know what I mean."

"How does it feel?"

"Wonderful. I can feel it shaping me, but it's comfortable. Looks good, too."

I went over to the bed and picked up the dress I was going to wear. A simple black one; clingy but not tight. It was something I always felt comfortable in. I sat at the dressing table to do my hair and make-up. Marcus sat and watched; he often did when we were getting ready. As we went through the corridor to the garage, I stopped.

"Aren't we supposed to take some food and drink?"

There was a small entrance fee to the event, and everyone brought a dish for the buffet. If you wanted alcohol, you brought your own. Marcus smiled; I should have known.

"Yes, it's in the car."

"What is?"

"Two bottles of wine and a bowl of fried chicken."

"Where did that come from?"

"I cooked it when you were covering yourself in mud yesterday."

"Did you know I'd want to go?"

"Wasn't sure. We'd just have been eating fried chicken all week."

The venue was thirty miles away and we didn't say much on the way, a mixture of fear and excitement affecting us both. It turned out to be in a small industrial estate.

"Weird place for it," I said.

"I don't know; all the neighbouring buildings are probably empty at the weekend."

So it proved. Everything looked shuttered and locked, except one unit at the end of a cul-de-sac with a few cars parked outside. We'd decided to arrive early. The event ran from two until nine, but we didn't fancy walking in when it was in full swing. It was now two-thirty. Marcus parked the car and turned to me.

"Still want to do this?"

I took a deep breath.

"Yes. You?"

"Yes. Remember we can leave at any time."

"Okay."

"And if we're not together and you need rescuing, look for me. When I see you, bunch your hair as if you're putting it in a ponytail. I'll come and help. Okay?"

"Yes. Thanks. Hope I won't need it."

He opened the door but turned back to me.

"Hold on; what if I need rescuing?"

"You're a big boy, darling. You can look after yourself."

We got the food and drink out of the boot and walked towards the unit. Some black arrows led the way around the side to an open door. A small group of people were in front of us, dressed in everyday clothes but carrying large bags. We heard another car draw up somewhere behind us. Marcus stopped outside the door and turned to me. He gave me a kiss.

"I love you."

"Love you too."

And we went in.

To be met by a friendly face; Yas, who broke into a broad grin when she saw us.

"Hello, you two. I didn't think you were coming. Isn't one of you celebrating a birthday?"

"Me," I said.

"Well, it'll certainly be a different birthday party."

"Mmm."

"Don't worry. Everyone's nervous the first time. Dave?"

She looked over to the other guy in the entrance hall.

"Yea, Yas?"

"Look after things for a few minutes, will you? Two first-timers here. I'll give them a quick tour."

"Will do."

"Come with me."

We followed Yas through a doorway on the left where she showed us a row of lockers.

"Just grab a free one. The keys are on elastic wristbands, so you can't lose them, even if you haven't got anywhere to put the key. Some people don't wear enough to have pockets. Leave as much as you can here; it's a pain carrying stuff around. Those two doors are changing rooms; one for the girls, one of the guys. Some people prefer to come in civvies and change. Gimp suits aren't always welcome on the bus. The toilets are over there as well."

She led us back to the entrance and straight through open double doors into a large space. It looked like what it was; a small warehouse. But the walls were painted and there were large hangings everywhere. Some depicting various activities relevant to the event. They were also being used as dividers, breaking up the rather barren space. There were a few people milling about.

"This is the main socialising space. You can pop the food and drink over there."

She led us to the buffet table, already well-stocked with food.

"You can keep the alcohol for yourselves or add it to the pool."

We added it to the pool.

"This area is for meeting and chatting, no performance or activities here. They happen through here."

We followed her through a gap in the hangings, into an area with something akin to a boxing ring, but larger. A square raised area with a single rope all around it. Around the outside of the space, there were masses of cushions, beanbags, fabric cubes and a few sofas.

"This is where the performances and demonstrations take place, and that corridor leads to the private rooms."

She quickly went through the main rules. We'd already read them, but it was clear they weren't tolerant of rule-breakers.

"That's about it. Any questions, ask one of the team. We all wear these badges somewhere on us."

"Thanks, Yas."

"You're welcome. Have fun."

With that, she was gone; we were on our own.

"Fancy a drink?" Marcus asked.

"Yes, please."

As we walked back to the table with the alcohol on, I looked around for anyone I recognised but drew a blank. This was the worst bit. My stomach was churning, and I felt a bit light-headed. I needed to find someone to talk to; I'd be fine then.

"Hello, Marcus."

A deep, husky voice, coming from a man in tight leather shorts, leather braces and Doc Martins.

"Hello," Marcus replied. "Adrian, isn't it?"

"That's right."

"Sorry, I don't think it's going to be easy recognising people."

"So true. When you've seen someone in civvies, you might not recognise them in their gear, but you'll soon get used to it. And you're … no, don't tell me … Sally, isn't it?"

"Yes. Hello, Adrian."

"Sorry, Sally. I tend to remember the men better than the women."

I smiled at his frank remark and we chatted about the event. He told us to watch out for the demonstrations.

"There will be about a dozen through the afternoon. You're bound to find one or two that'll interest you."

"How do we know what's happening?"

"There's a list somewhere, normally pinned up in the demo area. Be careful of the listed times, though. Things tend to go awry."

A second guy appeared in a leather skirt and waistcoat. He put his hand on Adrian's shoulder.

"Ah, Sally and Marcus, this is my partner, Guy. Guy, meet Sally and Marcus. Two new recruits."

Guy turned out to be as friendly as Adrian. It became a feature of the afternoon. We didn't meet anyone who didn't have the time to stop and chat and we soon began to relax. When Adrian and Guy left us, we went into the playroom to find the schedule. Looking at it, there were a few items which sounded interesting. One wasn't going to be until much later and we'd agreed we wouldn't be staying the whole day. But the others almost followed each other, so would be fine.

"See the roping one?" Marcus asked.

"Yes. Didn't know you were interested."

"I'm not, I don't think. But have you seen who's doing it?"

"Wow. Gerald and Peggy."

"Yea. That could be interesting."

Matt came into the room.

"Marcus. Sally. Welcome. I'd heard you were here. Everything okay?"

"Hi, Matt. Yes, thanks. Just seeing what we might enjoy."

"Something for everyone, I hope."

"Matt," I said. "Can I ask you something?"

"Fire away."

"What's the etiquette about looking at people or complimenting them. Is it rude to say someone looks good?"

"Oh, no. Most people here will have an exhibitionist streak. They're here to be seen amongst people they trust. They'll love an admiring glance or a compliment. Just use common sense. Nothing too personal. You know, love your bra rather than love your tits."

"Thanks, Matt."

"Enjoy yourselves. I believe it's a happy birthday as well, Sally?"

"Yes, thank you."

We went back to the main area which was filling up. We grabbed something to nibble on and stood surveying the other attendees. I wasn't sure where to start. Again, all ages, although most people were between thirty and fifty. All shapes and sizes. As for the clothing, well. Several people like us in normal clothes, but the rest put us to shame. There were some fabulous outfits; leather, lace, rubber, PVC. From complete bodysuits to virtually nothing. Some loose and baggy, others so tight I couldn't work out how they put them on.

There were some amazing bodies on view; male and female. A few guys were muscled and toned to perfection and they knew it. I'd already seen a couple wearing tight rubber shorts, and I couldn't help noticing the way the material outlined everything underneath.

In my newly liberated state, I could freely look at the women as well. On the whole, the women made far more effort than the men and there were some gorgeous views.

"Enjoying the sights?" I asked Marcus.

"As much as you."

"Interesting, isn't it?"

"Yup. It's amazing how it feels surreal and normal at the same time."

Someone tapped a glass, and everyone went quiet as Matt stood on a chair.

"Hello, all. Welcome."

A range of mumbled replies; some light-hearted heckles. Matt did a quick introduction, reminded everyone of the more important rules and went to get off the chair. But he stopped himself.

"Oh, one more thing. We have a few first-time kinksters today. Please make them feel welcome. One in particular …"

He looked around the room.

"Sally? Where are you?"

I felt myself flush heavily as he spotted me.

"Ah, there you are. Sally's here for the first time with her partner, Marcus. It's also her birthday …"

Everybody in the room was now looking at me. I wanted the floor to open up.

"… so, make sure you wish her happy birthday if you see her."

There were lots of shouted happy birthdays from around the room. I noticed most people were smiling and happy, but I was so embarrassed. I managed to smile and mouth my thanks. Matt finished and the murmur of conversation grew.

"Am I pink?" I asked Marcus. "I feel hot all of a sudden."

"A bit."

"A lot?"

He kissed my cheek.

"Quite rosy. And quite lovely."

I'd always flushed when I was nervous. The confidence I'd gained since I'd been with Marcus meant it didn't happen as much as it did. He loved it, anyway. It often happened when I came as well. I could feel the colour on my skin. He put his arm around me. I knew it would fade quickly.

The public birthday wishes turned out to be a real benefit. It meant most people already knew who I was; I didn't have to constantly introduce myself. It made the rest of the afternoon much easier, and I could introduce Marcus. Everybody we talked to wished me a happy birthday; it was an icebreaker.

After we had been there a couple of hours, I was relaxed and enjoying myself. I watched a girl walk by in a virtually transparent playsuit. She looked stunning, but what struck me was her nonchalance. As if it was the most normal thing in the world. I wondered if I could find that courage.

Chapter 25 – Marcus

I was pleased it was going so well. Neither of us had been sure. We'd wanted to come but were incredibly nervous. But, like the munch, there was no need. Everyone was friendly and chatty. At first, it had been difficult to know where to look. Many of the outfits were stunning and demanded attention. I soon realised Matt had been right; as long as you didn't look like an old letch, people were happy to see your admiration.

I was talking to a couple I'd seen at the munch but not had time to meet. Rosie and Luke. Rosie was wearing a beautiful full-length latex dress, with a flared hem. Luke was wearing a latex pouch and a collar; the lead in Rosie's hand. But they shared the talking, Luke always ceding if they spoke at the same time. They were telling me about their relationship.

Sally had needed the loo and had excused herself. Rosie was telling me how they'd met when Sal appeared in the doorway. My breath caught in my throat. Rosie must have noticed and turned to follow my gaze. We watched as Sally strode confidently towards us in the basque, stockings and knickers, her eyes fixed firmly on me. A look on her face that said so much. Perhaps wrongly, I felt incredible pride in this beautiful woman.

"That's better," she said, as she re-joined us.

"More comfortable now?" Rosie asked.

"I didn't think I'd have the courage."

Rosie looked Sally up and down.

"You look fab. One thing I've learnt from all this is it sends your confidence through the roof. It doesn't matter what you're into, it makes you feel so good."

Sally looked at me.

"We're coming to understand that, aren't we?"

When we left Rosie and Luke, I put one arm around her and pulled her to me.

"You look gorgeous."

"Thank you."

"How do you feel?"

"A bit nervous, but it's liberating."

"Best girl here."

"Liar. Have you seen some of them?"

"Well …yes."

"There's a few I'd go to bed with."

"All right, you're the best girl here I'm going to bed with later on."

She gave me a wicked look.

"Only if you're a good boy."

With that, she wandered off towards the play area. It sounded like it was going to be a good night. She stopped, turned, and waited until I caught her up. On the way, we bumped into Yas. She stopped and looked at Sally.

"Wow, girl. You were hiding that? You look good."

"Thanks, Yas. You're not so bad, either."

She wasn't. She was now wearing a lace top, with a PVC skaters skirt; very short.

"Well, you've got to flaunt it sometimes, haven't you?"

She left us as we went through the gap into the play area. There were lots of people sitting and a few wandering around the stage. It was empty; one of the rope sides laying on the floor. They were preparing it for the next item. We spotted Gerald and Peggy on the far side, along with a youngish couple talking to them. The girl was wearing a silk robe. We found space on some cube seats.

The couple went into the ring and Gerald started speaking.

"Good afternoon. Most of you know who I am. A daft old codger who should have given all this up years ago."

The laughter indicated the audience did indeed know Gerald, and rather loved him.

"I'm too damned infirm to do this myself now …"

He looked at Peggy.

"… well, outside the house, anyway."

Peggy swatted him with her hand, and everyone laughed again.

"So, I'm going to work through these two lovely people. Richie and Bev. They're young and stupid …"

Richie and Bev smiled.

"… but they follow instructions."

What followed was fascinating. Neither of us were particularly interested in roping. We'd looked at a few videos and although remarkable to watch, it didn't do anything for either of us. But watching Richie gradually bind the naked Bev in various positions under Gerald's guidance, the skill was obvious. And Gerald's commentary, interspersed with Peggy's asides, was often hilarious.

At one point, Sal turned to me.

"She can't move at all, can she?"

"Apart from her fingers and toes, it doesn't look like it."

"I wonder what it feels like? When you tie me up, I can still move about."

"Imagine being tied like that, and utterly vulnerable."

Bev was indeed helpless. On her back; her legs and arms trussed together, tied wide apart. Completely exposed. Sal chuckled.

"It might have its advantages."

Gerald drew to a close and Richie removed all the ropes. Bev stood, stretched her numb body, and they all got a round of applause. As we waited for the next demonstration, Gerald drove past us. When he saw us, he came over.

"Marcus, Sally. Good to see you."

"That was wonderful, Gerald," Sal said.

"Thank you, Sally."

He looked at her with a keen eye.

"You look as if you're having fun. Enjoying it?"

"Yes. It's great. More relaxed than I expected."

"Well, don't get too relaxed or I might carry you away on my mighty steed."

Peggy, who had now caught up with him, shook her head.

"Leave her alone, you old fool. What would you do with her once you'd got her?"

He grinned.

"I'd think of something. See you later."

They were gone. Sal leant into me and we looked around at the others.

"Now there's one I'd go home with," she said.

I followed her gaze. Walking around the ring was the girl we'd seen at both munches but not had the chance to talk to. She looked in her early twenties, with shoulder-length blonde hair. Her beautiful face had an elven quality to it; that beguiling combination of naivety and gravity.

She had a gorgeous figure; she wasn't tall, but her curves were in perfect proportion. Shown off today by a dusky pink skin-tight latex dress. It was semi-transparent and didn't venture far down her thighs. The only accessory was a fine choker; she'd worn it at both socials. I watched as she walked toward us, occasionally acknowledging someone she knew.

"Well?" Sally asked.

"I'd come with you."

"I might let you watch."

"I think that would be enough."

"She's very cute, isn't she?"

As she went past us, she looked towards us and smiled. I smiled back. I was betting Sal did too.

The next demonstration was short but one we were interested in. All about canes. The woman talking, who introduced herself as Sophia, was obviously an expert and we learnt a few things about the differences between materials and lengths. It gave us some ideas.

The next thing we wanted to see was in about an hour's time, so we mingled again. Both now confident to approach the other attendees and introduce ourselves. People were still wishing Sally a happy birthday. I looked at her occasionally. She was magnificent now, confident with how she looked and what she was wearing.

An hour later, we wandered back into the play area. Sal nipped off to the loo for about the third time.

"Are you okay?" I asked when she returned.

"Yes. Why?"

"You keep going to the loo."

She leaned into me and whispered her reply.

"I'm walking about in my knickers. I can't let them get too damp."

I laughed; she gave me a look partway between a grin and a scowl. I'd guessed that was the problem.

The stage was being set again; a long chain hanging from the rafters. We found a spare spot, right next to the elven blonde.

"Okay to sit here?" Sal asked.

Elven girl broke into a winning smile.

"Of course, help yourself."

"Thanks."

We settled ourselves and waited for the action.

"It's your birthday, isn't it?"

Sal turned to the girl.

"Yes, it is."

"Happy birthday. And your first time here?"

"Thank you. Yes."

"Some party. I'm Penny, by the way."

"Hi, Penny, I'm Sally, this is Marcus."

"Hi, Marcus."

"Hello, Penny."

"I saw you both at the social, but I don't like to push myself forward there. I tend to stick to people I know."

"We wouldn't bite."

"No, I know. But I'm a bit shy."

Sally must have gestured to what Penny was wearing. She'd turned to face us as we talked and the view I was getting was almost indecent. Penny's face broke into an alluring smile.

"Oh, it's different here. This is a world I'm comfortable in. I'm not shy here."

It was an interesting comment and one we'd heard it a few times during the afternoon.

"May I ask if the choker is significant?" Sally asked.

Penny fingered it lightly.

"It's my day collar."

"I hope you don't mind me asking."

"No, it's fine. I'm proud of it."

"Marcus and I are only players; we don't have that dynamic."

"Whatever works for you. That's what it's all about."

We stopped talking to watch the demonstration; whips. We used all sorts of implements; floggers, straps, crops and canes. But we'd never tried a whip. When we investigated it, one thing struck us. The whip, any whip, could do serious damage in the wrong hands. Trial and error wasn't an option.

Sophia walked into the stage area again, followed by the two hunks we'd seen earlier in the tight latex shorts. Except this time, the shorts were missing. One clipped the wrists of the other to the chain hanging from the rafters and left the ring. The chain rose until the guy was suspended with his toes just touching the floor.

Sophia told us what she was going to do; introduce us to different types of whip, before concentrating on two. The snake tail, apparently good for beginners and the bullwhip, which wasn't. She gave a running commentary as she held up six different types, explaining their advantages and disadvantages.

When she'd finished, she picked up the snake tail and began a training session. How to hold it, the best position for the recipient, depending on what you were trying to achieve, where to stand for different effects. Each time, she swung the whip to show her meaning. The guy took the punishment easily. I listened as she went through the process; showing the variety of strokes, different effects and a warning or two.

She switched to the bullwhip. This time, it was mostly warnings. She showed how the whip flew through the air, whipping it well away from the guy. The noise it made was astonishing; echoing around the cavernous space. I saw Sally flinch at the first crack. I noticed Penny watching intently.

Sophia started using it on her subject. She was highly skilled. The bullwhip wrapped itself around his body until it got to the end. It was the end that caused the noise, the pain and the potential damage. If you didn't know what you were doing, you had no idea where the final impact would be.

With each stroke, she told us where the hit would be and she hit it every time. The guy gasped at every stroke. The marks on his body gradually increasing. After several strokes, Sophia stopped.

"Enough talk," she said. "Now it's time for a proper demonstration. Paul's a bit of a wimp. We need a pain junkie. Jed?"

The second guy, obviously Jed, came back in and released Paul, who returned the favour and tied Jed in the same position.

Sally turned to Penny.

"He may not be the pain junkie, but he seems to have enjoyed it."

Now he was free to turn around, Paul's erect cock was visible to all.

"They're both Sophia's subbies," Penny said. "Fit, aren't they?"

Sally looked at me and winked.

"Yes. They're definitely fit."

Sophia was now using the snake tail on Jed. Slowly at first, building until she was whipping him hard. His reactions were interesting to watch. As the whip hit, there was a momentary pause until his body reacted. It jerked away from the site of the hit; a muted cry coming from his mouth.

When she moved to the bullwhip, she showed what a different animal it was. No building up now, the snake had done that. She let fly with the whip eliciting a loud cry with each strike. She let him recover between each one. His body soon acquired many livid lines. Again, she was amazingly accurate, grouping them in safer places. Jed was panting and moaning now.

"One final strike," Sophia said. "Right where it hurts most."

The whip snaked around his middle. The crack came, followed by a savage shriek. Paul came back on stage and unhooked Jed. Jed was shaking slightly but as he turned around, we saw his cock was rigid in front of him. Even from where we were, we could see a vivid red line running across it. Sally turned to me.

"Crossing your legs, darling?"

"Certainly made me wince."

Penny laughed.

"You're either into pain or you're not."

"That's what I tell Marcus," Sal said.

"You are?"

"Yes, but he's sometimes a bit troubled by it."

"That's no bad thing, particularly in the beginning."

Penny turned to me.

"Do you like giving it?"

Sally was watching me.

"Yes," I answered simply.

"Then do it," Penny said. "Don't try to understand it. Just do it. If she's anything like me, she'll be yours forever."

Sally reached over to kiss me.

"I already am."

After another brief chat, we decided it was a good time to leave.

"You're not staying to the end?" Penny asked.

"It's her birthday, Penny," I said. "I've thought of one or two other presents I can give her."

Sally whacked my arm and Penny smiled as we stood.

"By the way, Sally. Where did you get that basque? It's beautiful."

"I don't know, Penny. It was a present from this man this morning."

Penny looked at me, then back at Sally.

"Lovely choice. If you want any more, my mistress is a corsetiere. A good one. I'm sure she'd happily take you on as a customer."

"Ooh, that sounds useful. Thanks, Penny. Can I ask you a question?"

"Of course."

"Is your mistress here today?"

"No, she rarely attends events anymore."

"So how- "

"How come she lets me attend?"

"Yes, sorry. It's a rude question."

"No. It's a good question. It's part of our agreement. She knows I love these things and she trusts me. And when I get home …"

Her face took on a dreamy look. We got the idea.

"Enjoy the rest of the evening," Sally said. "And when you get home."

"Same for you two. See you next time?"

We looked at each other.

"I expect so," Sal said.

After we'd found Yas to say our thanks and goodbyes, I waited while Sally went to put her dress back on. We walked back to the car, my arm around her, moving to her bum. When we were inside, she looked at me.

"Well?" she asked, grinning from ear to ear.

"That was brilliant. You?"

The volume of her reply caught me by surprise.

"FUCKING FANTASTIC!"

I grinned as I turned the car and we headed home.

"There's only one problem," Sal said.

"What?"

"I'm horny as hell. I have been most of the afternoon. I wanted you umpteen times."

"We could have used one of the rooms."

"I know, but I didn't feel comfortable with that. Not on our first time. To be honest, I'm not sure the idea of shared rooms appeals."

"I know what you mean."

"I do have a confession."

"Oh yes?" I guessed what was coming.

"I did deal with it once in the toilets."

"Did you indeed?"

"Yea. I had to. I thought about asking you to help. There seemed to be some of that going on quietly in the play area."

"Yes, I noticed."

"But taking my dress off was enough for today. I wasn't brave enough to do anything else."

"Still horny?"

"God, yes. You?"

"My balls are aching."

She laughed.

"We'll just have to wait half an hour," I said.

She put her hand firmly on my cock and gripped it.

"You might have to, darling. You're driving. But I'm not."

She lowered the back of her seat and pulled her dress to her waist. Pulling her knickers to one side, she started to play with herself. Luckily, the roads were quiet, so I could look over quite often as she rapidly brought herself to a noisy orgasm.

"Better?" I asked.

"It'll do for now."

"For now?"
"It's my birthday, isn't it?"
"Certainly is."
"So, I get what I want today?"
"Anything."
"Good. When we get home, I want you in the playroom. I'm going to have some fun with you tonight. If you're a very good boy, I might let you have some fun, too."

Chapter 26 – Marcus

Five minutes after we got home, I was kneeling on the floor naked. Looking up at Sally standing in front of me, looking magnificent. Sexy, confident and beautiful. She often took control in the bedroom, but rarely here. If we played the D/S dynamic, it was normally me in the dom role.

Tonight was going to be different and in this position, I got another inkling of the anticipation and nervous excitement Sally loved when the positions were reversed. She had a glass of wine in her hand and was smiling.

"Now," she said. "What shall I do with you?"

She tapped her lips a few times, as if thinking. I knew she'd decided exactly what she was going to do. I just had to wait and find out. She leaned forward and kissed me.

"No talking, no touching, unless you need to stop. Understand?"

One of those games. I silently nodded assent.

"Good boy."

She put her glass on the table and walked towards me slowly. Keeping going until her feet were either side of me and her crotch pushed into my face. I could smell her; her knickers wet with her moisture. She moved her hips, grinding herself on my face; I didn't need telling.

I covered her with my mouth; the knickers were tight, and I could feel her contours beneath them. The material meant I couldn't be delicate; I pushed my lips onto her firmly and moved my tongue about, hoping I was hitting one or two right spots. This continued for a minute or two before she pulled back slightly.

"Pull them down."

I raised my hands and putting them into the waist, slid her knickers down her legs. With a bit of jiggling, we disposed of them. She moved forward again; her glistening pussy approaching my face again. But this time, she kept going. It hit my face and pushed it backwards. I had to lean back and put my hands on the floor behind me to support myself. Her legs went beyond my shoulders and came together around my neck. My head was now locked between her legs. My mouth covering her pussy.

Placing my lips around her sex, I explored her with my tongue. Her familiar scent filled my nostrils as my tongue recognised the taste of my lover's arousal. She towered over me, gripping me with her stockinged thighs. All this spurred me on, but it wasn't enough for her. Her hand grabbed the back of my head and she pulled me into her. Hard against her. I couldn't see what I was doing now; I was too close. I closed my eyes and relied on what my lips and tongue could feel. The soft folds of her sex yielding to my actions. I could feel her clit under my top lip.

She was moaning now; pulling my head and forcing herself onto me. She gave a cry as she came; her thighs trembling against my neck; her hand slowly releasing my head. Her legs released their grip and I saw she was steadying herself with one hand resting on the horse.

As she recovered, she looked at me; her face flushed. She moved forward, releasing me from her grip, and turned around. Squatting, she bent down and licked her own wetness from my face, before kissing me.

"Stand."

I obeyed. She circled around me, smiling that wicked smile. Behind me, she squeezed my bum hard, almost to the point of pain. Going to the front, she stroked my balls with her fingers.

"Still aching?"

I nodded. She chuckled.

"On the horse."

She moved it so as I put my knees on the side-steps and laid on it, I was facing the mirror. She came into view, with the double-ended strap-on I'd given her this morning. Looking at me in the mirror, I watched as she inserted one end into herself, and tied the straps.

My bum was slightly over the end of the horse, my cock lying flat under my body. She made me rise slightly and pulled my cock back, so it was hanging against the side. Picking up the lube, she slapped some on my ass and covered the dildo. I waited for that first pressure.

Instead, she grabbed my cock, slowly stroking it with her hand. My balls were exposed, and she massaged those too. They were tender now and every movement resulted in exquisite pain. Her finger circled my ass, pushing at it gently until it slowly slipped inside. A second followed; stretching me. She was watching me in the mirror. A faint smile on her lips and a determined look in her eyes.

Her fingers eased out and the dildo pushed against my muscle ring. She put one hand on my hips and grabbed my cock with the other. I gave a gasp as the dildo broke through, and she slid it all the way in, sending shivers over my tummy and down my thighs. Irregular spasms shooting through my groin.

She grinned at me in the mirror as she adjusted her stance. Releasing my cock, she held my hips with both hands and started to fuck me. Slowly pulling out each time, before forcefully driving back in. Occasionally slapping my bum. Gradually speeding up. By now, I was grunting with each stroke. I looked at her and recognised the glazed look on her face.

The dildo embedded in her was doing its work, too. She stopped looking at me; concentrating on fucking me in such a way to give herself the best angle. With a couple of loud groans, she came again. The dildo pausing in me as she went through each wave. Still breathing heavily, she again looked in the mirror and gave a wicked smile. Her hand going to my cock again.

"Need to come, darling?"

I nodded vigorously. I did. My cock was so rigid, it hurt; my balls throbbing. She chuckled.

"Not yet. Be patient."

She slowly withdrew the dildo for my ass. I saw her undo the straps and remove the harness.

"Come here."

I stood, and she put the strap-on on the table. Turning back to me she was holding one of the other things I'd given her this morning; a face dildo. I opened my mouth as she put the short end between my teeth. She went around my back and fastened the strap. We'd not used one before, and it was uncomfortable at first. Quite restricting when it was in place.

"Lie down."

I settled on the rug and she knelt by my side. Stroking my cock, she lowered her mouth over it and started to suck. I needed to come but knew it wasn't going to happen yet; she wasn't going to let me. She lifted off and gave me a delicious smile. There was no chance of response now. It was difficult enough to remember to breathe properly with the dildo fastened in my mouth.

She lifted a leg to straddle me, facing over my head and reached for the dildo. I moved my head as she lowered herself onto it. Watching her pussy spreading as an artificial cock slid in a few inches from my face. I could smell her; see the beautiful details, wet, swollen. But couldn't touch them; just watch.

She slid up and down the dildo, her pussy landing on my face with each stroke. I so wanted to reach up; to stroke and squeeze her bum. But I was under orders; no touching. She carried on doing this for a while. Long enough for me to feel her moisture on my face; on my cheeks, my lips, my chin. Her bud rubbing my nose with each stroke.

She slowly lifted off and turned around. As she lowered herself this time, it was almost too much to bear. Her legs spread over my face, her pussy swallowing the dildo again, and her gorgeous bum a few inches above me. I watched as her pussy stretched with every stroke. The muscles around her ass contracted in unison.

Occasionally, she'd pause when fully down, and rock. Her clit rubbing itself on my chin. I could hear she was enjoying this. So was I; but the frustration was overwhelming, and she knew it.

After a while, she dropped forward and teased me again. Her hand held my cock as she licked and sucked it. Only the head at first, but slowly taking more into her mouth. The sensations were driving me crazy. The dildo was preventing me from making any loud noises and I was moaning and groaning deep in my throat. I couldn't move my head from side to side either.

She sat back up and with one hand slapped her own bum. Taunting me. I watched as she rode the dildo harder. Seeing the delicate flesh moulding itself around it each time, her moisture now seeping down, and running over my face. I could feel it on my neck.

She was breathing faster now, clearly building again. She leaned forward and her mouth enclosed my cock, fucking herself on the dildo at the same time. No slow blowjob this time. She was trying to make us come at the same time. The view, the feelings, the situation were all mind-blowing. I knew I was going to come soon. I tried to hold it; tried to wait for her orgasm and succeeded; just.

I heard a muffled cry from her, as her body froze halfway up the dildo. At the same moment, my balls tightened before exploding. Painfully and hard. I could feel my cum forced from them and racing up my cock. This produced another muffled sound from Sal; a splutter. She shook as she came hard, but kept her lips clamped over my cock, as it pumped out several hours-worth of pent up cum.

Thinking I could risk it now, I reached out and stroked her bum. She didn't object. We lay there for several minutes; silent. She stroked my thighs, my balls and my satisfied cock. I could feel her head laying on my hip.

I felt a tickle in the back of my throat; I tapped her bum three times. She lifted herself off the dildo and turning, I saw a look of concern. I shook my head and pointed to the dildo. She undid the strap and removed it from my mouth.

"You okay?"

I coughed several times.

"Yes. Some of you dripped onto the back of my throat. It was starting to catch."

She handed me her glass of wine. I sat up, took a few sips and it settled. She put her arms around my shoulders.

"How was that?"

"Fabulous. And bloody frustrating."

"No touching?"

"Mmm."

"I must admit, there were times when I'd have loved your hands all over me. But I think both these presents pass muster. Thank you. Are you all right with the one in the mouth?"

"Yes. It's a bit strange, but I'll get used to it. It's really hard not to reach up."

"I might let you next time."

"And perhaps a vibe or a dildo in your ass?"

She looked away as she considered the possibilities.

"How about both?"

"You little harlot."

"Have I passed grade three?"

"Not quite. Still a few finishing touches."

We moved over to the sofa. I sat, she laid along it on her back, with her head on my lap. We talked about the day; her birthday, the meet and what we'd done this evening.

"Okay," she said. "You've got to pick one person at the meet to go to bed with."

"Well, there were a few candidates."

"Only one."

There was a challenging look on her face. I think she knew who I was going to say.

"It would have to be Penny."

She chuckled.

"Good choice."

"You?"

"Male or female?"

"Yea, that's not fair. All right, you can have one of each."

"Well, I did see a girl in a transparent playsuit."

"Long black hair in a plait?"

"Mmm."

"I noticed her, too."

"But I'd have to go for Penny, too."

"And your guy?"

She was pensive for a few moments.

"Paul or Jed. Either would do."

"From what I saw, Jed was bigger."

"He sure was."

Realising the speed of her response, she giggled.

"Oops. Did I say that out loud?"

"How about both?"

She looked up at me. I saw her mind considering the offer.

"Well, we are only fantasising. So why not?"

It was getting late, and Sally had to work the following day.

"Are we done for the day?" I asked.

She looked at me.

"Not quite."

"No?"

"I can't have a birthday without some nice fresh marks, can I?"

"What would you like?"

She sat up and kissed me. I watched as she went over to the racks of implements. She ran her fingers over them until her hand settled on one. She lifted it off and coming back, handed it to me.

"This one, please."

Our longest cane. Supple, swishy, with a wonderful sound and a breath-taking touch.

"On the horse?" she asked.

"No," I replied. "On the bed."

The more the buttocks were stretched the more an implement hurt and marked. That was particularly true of the cane. Bent over, it was at its worst, but lying flat, it was less painful. I wanted to enjoy this; take my time. We put all the things we'd used in one place to clean the next day and went through to the bedroom. She touched the basque.

"Off?"

"Oh, yes. I want you naked."

I helped her remove it and sat watching her roll off the stockings. She came over and kissed me, climbed onto the bed, and lay on her front. I placed a pillow under her hips to raise her slightly and stood by the bed. Over the next twenty minutes, I gave her the marks she wanted. Light tapping touches, stinging strikes and firmer strokes.

Nothing harsh; no hard welts. But masses of delicate pink lines. Mostly on her bum but a few on her thighs. By the end, she was quivering. Her hands gripping the pillows tight as she revelled in the ecstasy of pain. When I finished, I placed the cane on the bed beside her to let her know it was over. Her eyes had a slightly gazed, dreamy look; her smile spread over her whole face.

Caning her had had its usual effect on me. I was hard again. She saw it and let out a long low moan. I climbed onto the bed beside her.

Running my hand down her back, I let my finger slide between her cheeks to her pussy. Wet, swollen again. She gasped as I reached it and reached out to grab my cock.

"I want that."

"You're going to get it."

Her eyes widened which made my cock twitch.

"Am I? How?"

"Right where you are."

I straddled her thighs and guided my cock into her willing pussy. She moaned as I slid it firmly in and fucked her. Deep, regular strokes. My hands pulling her cheeks apart so I could watch my cock entering her. I maintained the rhythm as she came, gripping the pillows again.

I pulled her hips bringing her to her knees and continued to fuck her. Harder, pulling her back onto me with each stroke. Pushing my thumb into her ass, stretching it. Her shoulders were on the bed now. She'd surrendered to her body; letting it accept the sensations. She drifted into another orgasm as I reached my peak and my climax came. Her body was almost limp now. I pulled her back towards me as my cock jerked several times, before gently lowering us both to the bed. Still speared together.

We lay for a few minutes. I hugged her as best as I could; kissing her neck and shoulders. She gave little giggles and shudders as I did so and gradually came back to reality. Eventually, she went to turn over and I lifted myself to let her, sinking back onto her again. She put her arms around me and pulled me tightly to her. My head sank onto the pillow by her side. She kissed my ear and whispered.

"Best birthday ever."

Chapter 27 – Lucy

Was this the worst Christmas Day ever? It was trying hard to be. I was sitting in Annie's living room with Tim, while Sarah and Nathan played with some of their presents. The day hadn't been easy. Conversation had been stilted, even between Mum and Annie. She had hardly said a word to me, other than the obligatory pleasantries. Annie had now taken Mum to see Dad. We'd told her there wasn't any point, but she saw it as her duty, and it had given the rest of us a break.

Dad had gone into a nursing home and had another stroke shortly afterwards. Only a minor one but now he didn't seem aware of what was going on. It appeared he no longer recognised anyone. He probably didn't know it was Christmas and Mum could have had the day with her family.

We'd met twice since that first reunion. Both meetings had been short. Nothing untoward had happened but our conversations were stilted. We had nothing to talk about. She avoided anything to do with my private life and we had no shared interests. It was hard work.

She asked me about my job, and I described the arc of my career and what I did. But her version of Christianity saw most art as blasphemous. Even traditional religious art was seen as idolatry. She had no liking for art; no appreciation of it. Probably couldn't understand why anyone would study it.

I had thought we could talk about Annie and Tim and the kids. But I soon realised there wasn't much scope there, either. She and Annie talked quite often, but there was no close connection. The third meeting had been at Annie's with the kids running around.

I was immediately struck by the lack of connection between Mum and her grandchildren. They knew who she was, they were polite. But they didn't share any fun with her; there were no games or silliness. I realised there wouldn't be. Annie and I hadn't had any fun with our parents; why would she be any different with her grandchildren? It struck me as sad.

"Does Mum ever play with Sarah and Nathan, Tim?"

He looked at me and I realised he was a bit embarrassed.

"Not really, Lucy. She doesn't seem to … understand children."

"No, you're right there. I just need to think back to my childhood."

"Annie says the same."

"It's such a shame. What do they think of her?"

He shrugged.

"They know her as Grandma; she gives them presents for Christmas and Birthdays. That's about it. They were both scared of her, I think. But not now they're getting older."

"How is she coping?"

"Better than we thought she would. We've helped her open a bank account and transfer all the bills into her name. Annie takes her shopping. She didn't even know how to do that, which surprised us. But she's picked it all up well. No confidence and the slightest thing sends her into a panic, but she's getting there."

"How can we get her to meet people? It might help."

"I know. We were thinking about that. She doesn't go to her church anymore, so we've suggested several times she comes with us. She's coming around to the idea. There are a lot of older women there; they organise lots of activities. If we can get her to join in, it might help."

"Sounds promising."

"We'll have to see."

"What time are you taking Mum home?"

"About six."

"I'll leave at the same time. At least you'll have some of Christmas Day to yourselves without the killjoys getting in the way."

"You're not a killjoy, Lucy."

"You know what I mean."

I was so relieved when I got home. The day had been a chore, not a pleasure. I lazed in a bath and lounged around watching an old Christmas movie. But the whole Christmas thing got too much and I went to bed early.

Sally and I hadn't spent a night together since her birthday weekend. Both of us had had Christmas parties to attend, and other things had conspired to prevent us from finding a night when we were both free. We'd agreed at the beginning we wouldn't meet on a Saturday or Sunday night; it was unfair on Marcus. He was being wonderful about our arrangement and I didn't want to try his patience. I lay there thinking about my life. It had definitely improved, but that night, I was lonely. Tomorrow would be better.

"Hi, Luce. Come in."

Sal met me at the door, and I stepped into the hallway. She enveloped me in a big, friendly hug.

"Happy Christmas."

"Thanks."

"You sound a bit down."

"Sorry, I'm okay."

I followed her into the living room. Marcus was nowhere to be seen.

"Marcus?" Sally called out.

"In the kitchen."

"Lucy's here."

He came into view, walked over to me and I got my second warm hug of the morning. It struck me there hadn't been one hug the day before. All handshakes and awkward air kisses.

"Hi, Luce. Drink?"

"Isn't it a bit early?"

"Sal's already started."

"Oh. All right then."

Sally poured me a glass of wine and I sat next to her. There were still some presents under the tree.

"Wasn't Christmas yesterday?" I asked.

"It was, but we left some for today for you to join in. I had a suspicion yesterday might not have been exactly fun-filled."

"You can say that again."

I briefly recounted the details. They listened, didn't judge; didn't try to make light of it.

"Right," Sally said when I'd finished. "As bad as we thought. So today is Christmas Day round two. We'll have a second Christmas dinner, open some presents and have some fun. How does that sound?"

"I don't know what to say. Thank you."

"Hold the thanks 'til later," Marcus said. "It might be worse than yesterday."

I suddenly thought of something.

"Ooh, I've brought some more presents. Can you give me a hand with them?"

Sally followed me out and I opened the boot.

"Are these what I think they are?" she said.

"Might be."

We carried them back indoors and stood them against the wall by the tree. Sally was taking care of lunch but seemed to have it all under control. Marcus handed out some presents. I wasn't expecting anything; I'd forgotten they'd done something similar the year before. I was glad I'd brought something, but I noticed they had left the other presents I'd given them until today.

We spent the next hour slowly opening presents. They were mainly little things; funny books, toys, things to eat or drink. The pile got smaller and smaller until there were three left, apart from my six parcels.

"Right, last ones here," Marcus said, handing one to me and two to Sally. She looked quizzically at hers.

"Why have I got two?"

"Because you're greedy," Marcus replied.

I undid the paper and burst out laughing. A box of chocolate vulvas. Quite detailed. Sally laughed as she opened the same thing. We both guessed what was in the other box. Sure enough, a box of chocolate dicks. Again, more detail than you'd expect. Sally took one out and sucked it, with exaggerated moans and groans.

"I'm just getting in some practice, darling."

"You don't need any practice, Sal," Marcus said.

I smiled as I saw her flush. She poked her tongue out at him and bit the dick in half.

"Okay," I said, taking a deep breath. "You'd better open mine."

"Any order, Luce?"

"Nope; however you want. I hope – "

"Luce …"

"Sorry."

I was always nervous when I showed my work; particularly if it was a commission. This was, although I had no intention of charging them. Sally carried two over to Marcus and they unwrapped them. When they'd cleared the paper and had them up the right way, I waited for the reaction. They looked at each other and both broke into a broad grin.

"Wow, Luce," Sal said.

I didn't know which ones they'd opened, so went over to sit by Sal. She had the caned bum; simple pastels, the cane resting between the cheeks. The deep welts across them the only bold colour. Marcus was holding the one of Sal riding him. They opened the other four and lined them up against the wall.

"They are fabulous."

"They're gorgeous."

"Are you sure?"

Sal put her arm around me.

"Luce, come on. They're amazing. Which is your favourite?"

I hadn't thought about it. I ran my eye along the six.

"It may sound strange, but the oral one."

It was a picture of Marcus's cock. In all its detail and vivid colour. Everything else was unfinished; except for a sketched face. Clearly Sal's. But the only colour was her green eyes and the bright red lips resting on the tip of his cock.

"I did three versions of it. I couldn't work out how much to leave uncoloured. But I think this one's about right."

"I think you may have used a little artistic exaggeration, Luce," Marcus said.

"She had the pictures, remember?"

"In that case, she may need glasses."

"Shall I make it smaller?" I asked.

He smiled at me.

"No, I can live with it."

"Which is your favourite, Sal?"

She thought for a moment.

"It's so difficult to choose one. I love the oral one, too, but I guess if you forced me, it would be the caned bum. I can almost feel those stripes."

"You did. Remember?"

"So I did." I noticed her flush and look lovingly at Marcus. "But I've had more since, haven't I?"

"Yes, you have, haven't you?"

"Before you two get carried away," I said. "What about you, Marcus?"

He studied them for a moment.

"That's difficult, they're all beautiful. I love Sal in the submissive position, staring out at us. But it's got to be one of those with two girls. I like the two bending over …"

"It's only a reworking of the one you've got."

"Yes," said Sal. "But a whole lot more explicit."

"But," Marcus continued, "I'd have to plump for the girl straddling Sal's face. It's fantastic."

Sal grinned at me.

"That's Luce. Drawn from life, too."

"In that case, I'd better not comment," Marcus said.

Sal was in a playful mood.

"Oh, go on, darling. Lucy's drawn herself very accurately."

"Behave."

"See much difference between us?"

He turned to her, smiling.

"I'm sure Lucy can do without a man's assessment of her genitalia."

"You must have thought something."

He considered for a moment.

"She's very … neat."

I felt myself blush a little.

Sal put her arm on Marcus's shoulder.

"Oh, she is, darling. Very neat indeed."

Lunch was so good. Not turkey; they'd cooked pheasant instead, with all the usual trimmings. There were crackers, wine, little place presents. I forgot the actual day had passed and enjoyed a proper Christmas Day.

As they cleared the table between courses, refusing to let me help, Sally put her hands on my shoulders.

"Feeling brighter?"

I put my hand on hers.

"Oh, Sal. It's brilliant. Thank you."

Marcus brought in a large platter of goodies; mince pies, a bowl of soft fruit, cream, profiteroles. We helped ourselves. Sal looked at me thoughtfully.

"Do you remember the Christmas after my Dad was killed?"

My hand paused over the platter. I wondered where she was going with this.

"Yes."

"Remember how terrible it was?"

"How could I forget? I thought about it yesterday."

Sally turned to Marcus, who was watching us quietly, picking at the fruit.

"Have I told you about that?"

"No."

"Can I, Luce?"

"Of course. It's mainly your story."

"Well, the car crash was at the end of October. I'd lost my father and Charlie. I had no real home and no family, except Mary. Mary and this one here ..."

She gestured to me.

"... had picked me up and dusted me down. But I still felt awful. Then I found out Lucy had been disowned by her family. Mary insisted we spent Christmas with her. We didn't want anything to do with Christmas, did we?"

I thought back to that time.

"No. I just wanted to hide."

"So did I. But Mary insisted; wouldn't take no for an answer. We must have been the worst guests ever. But she did everything as normal. Presents, lunch, crackers, cake, mince pies. It helped, didn't it?"

"By Boxing Day, we were at least able to laugh."

"Perhaps the alcohol had helped."

"Perhaps."

"I'm not saying this to bring back bad memories, but to show how far we've come. Almost full circle. It's taken a long time, but I can talk about Dad and Charlie, and you're in contact with your family again. If we could deal with that awful Christmas, we'll cope with anything."

She was right. I wasn't going to let one miserable day with my mother spoil anything.

"To families," Marcus said, raising his glass. "May they all bugger off."

We all raised our glasses.

"Except Mary, obviously," he added, and we raised a glass to her too. She'd been a saviour to Sal, but she'd helped me out over the years as well. We were quiet for a few moments, each with our own thoughts.

"Right," Sal said. "What shall we do this afternoon?"

We played silly games. Charades, pass the parcel, twenty questions. It was daft and wonderful. Sal and I had switched to soft drinks, realising we had perhaps started on the wine too early. By late afternoon, we had to take a nap. When we woke, Marcus had tea ready for us; lots of lovely little cakes and mince pies. We watched the second half of White Christmas on TV and chilled out.

"Anyone ready for supper?" Sally asked.

Marcus and I groaned.

"Supper?" I said. "I don't think I could eat a thing."

"How about if I put a load of picky things on the table and we help ourselves when we feel like it?"

That's what she did. It's surprising how the availability of food gives you an appetite.

"How about a good old-fashioned game?" Sal asked.

"What did you have in mind?"

"Monopoly."

"Yes," I said. "I haven't played in years."

Marcus got the game from a cupboard; an old set. Wooden houses, cardboard pieces in little wooden blocks. He set it all up. He chose the warship; I was the racing car and Sal chose the top hat.

"This could go on for hours," Marcus warned.

"Well, let's set a time limit."

We agreed on two hours. The food was still on the table, so we picked at it as we went along. Sally and I were on the wine again. We weren't taking it too seriously and chatted about the past.

Marcus had played lots of games with his parents as a kid. Even Sal had, after Mary had become her replacement mum. I never had; my parents wouldn't even understand the concept. I'd played them when I'd visited friends, but I kept it quiet.

"This looks like an old set."

"It belonged to my father," Marcus said. "I suspect it came down to him. No idea of its age, really."

"Are all the cards and values the same as they are now?"

"I guess so. Couldn't be sure."

"Haven't the values gone up over the years?"

"No idea. I did change things a bit once."

Sally looked at Marcus.

"How?" she asked.

"I changed the Chance and Community Chest cards."

"To what?"

"Something a little more interesting."

He was grinning.

"Such as?" I asked.

"Oh, dares, IOUs, sexual favours. You know, that sort of thing."

"And rent could be paid in kind, I suppose?"

"Of course."

"Did it work?"

"Well, yes and no."

"How so?"

"It worked as a concept, but we never reached the end of the game."

"Too busy collecting the rent?"

"Something like that."

We'd cheated from the start, giving ourselves twice the allocation of money. So, we all bought every property we landed on and built houses and hotels. The rents soon mounted up. Sally had a bit of a competitive streak and was taking it more seriously than Marcus and me. Strangely, she was faring worst. When she landed on Bond Street with a hotel, she couldn't pay the rent to Marcus, who owned it.

"I'll have to sell some property," she said.

"I might accept something else."

"Such as?"

"Make me an offer."

She was grinning and went to speak but Marcus held up his hand.

"As Lucy's here, I think these things should be private. Let's write them down." Sally found a pad of stickies and a pen. She came back, thought for a moment, wrote something and gave it to him.

"I think that's fair. Rent paid."

We carried on and fortunes changed. Sally acquired more money and Marcus struggled. When he landed on one of my properties, he couldn't afford the rent.

"Make me an offer, Marcus."

He thought for a moment.

"That's difficult. Sal's got it easy. She can offer us both all sorts of things. We can offer her stuff, but you and I?"

Suddenly he smiled and started writing. He passed me the sticky note. *'Use of the playroom for a session with Sally'*. I laughed.

"Not sure that's wholly yours to give, is it?"

"True, but I'm pretty sure the other party will prove more than willing."

I showed it to Sally. She grinned and looked at Marcus.

"Pimping me again, darling?"

"Any objections?"

"Absolutely none."

I accepted the rent and we continued the game. It had taken on a slightly different mood now. It was as if we all wanted to lose. I wondered what I'd offer Marcus if I needed to. He was right, he and I were restricted. Sally hit a run of bad luck again and Marcus and I ended up with a wad of IOUs. This was fun; images of what Sally had offered ran through my head.

Again, Sally recovered and now it was my turn to suffer. I landed on one of Sal's properties and we easily dealt with that. But then I landed on one of Marcus's. I spent a couple of minutes thinking about what I could offer. I could sell a property, but this was much more fun. I had an idea. *'An explicit picture of me in any pose you want'*. I handed it to him. He read it and looked at me.

"Are you sure?"

"I wouldn't have offered."

"Accepted."

"What was it?" Sal asked, looking from me to Marcus and back.

Marcus tapped the side of his nose a few times.

"Secret, darling."

She pouted beautifully but he continued the game. We were over an hour into the game and it was working well. Sometimes, Monopoly can become boring. One person wins everything. But this one was a rollercoaster. The fortune moving around the table quickly. Sal was struggling again; I suspected she was doing it deliberately. She was wicked enough. She landed on Mayfair; Marcus owned it.

"Oh, bugger," she stated eloquently. "This is going to cost me, isn't it?"

Marcus had a sly smile on his face.

"It might ..."

"Or?" she asked.

He handed her one of her earlier offers. She read it and looked at him, frowning.

"What about it?" she asked.

"Do it now. Rent paid."

I saw her flush.

"Seriously?"

"Up to you."

She looked at the note again, looked at me, then back at Marcus. I saw her face take on a determined expression. She handed him the note and pushed her chair back. She headed to the hallway door and disappeared.

"She'll be a few minutes. Comfort break, I think." Marcus said.

He headed to the loo and I followed when he returned. He topped up our glasses and picked at the food again.

"What's she doing?" I asked.

"Wait and see. I think you'll like it."

Chapter 28 – Lucy

I heard heels crossing the wooden floor in the hallway and turned to the door as Sally came through. Smiling and confident. Wearing a French maid's outfit; largely made of PVC. A tight, laced bodice, giving her a nice cleavage and a short flaring skirt. Very short; ending well above the tops of her black hold-ups. Finished with black heels and a little black and white lace bow holding her ponytail in place high on her head. She walked over to the table and did a twirl.

"Well?" she asked.

"Luce? What do you think?" Marcus asked.

Sal looked at me. I was grinning.

"You're right, Marcus. I do like it."

Sally looked at Marcus.

"I don't need to ask you, do I?"

He chuckled.

"No, you don't. I'll warn you, Luce, she tends to be a very cheeky maid. Don't you, darling?"

"Me? I'm a good girl."

The time was nearly up on our game. One or two more IOUs changed hands and eventually, I was declared the winner. I'm not sure I was, but I wasn't going to argue.

"What do I win?" I asked.

"We'll think of something," Sal said.

"I bet you will," Marcus added.

Sal winked at me. That made me feel good.

"Top-up?" she asked.

"I'd love some coffee."

"Okay."

I watched as she rose and walked from the dining room into the kitchen. Perfectly poised, her bare thighs visible between stockings and skirt. I regretted the skirt was long enough to cover her bum. I mused on what knickers she was wearing. I smiled to myself as I wondered if she was wearing any at all.

Marcus packed up the game and put it back in the cupboard. We moved to the sofas. Sal returned with the coffee. I saw Marcus was right. She was loving her role; walking in a slightly exaggerated way, her hips swinging that bit further than normal. She was teasing us. It was working well enough for me; God knows what it was doing for Marcus.

I never thought about dressing up. I didn't have any costumes or outfits and had never done it for a lover in the past. I knew men saw things a bit differently. Sally had told me she often dressed up and she enjoyed it as much as he did.

I began to see the attraction. She looked hot; she looked up for anything. She handed me the coffee and instead of sitting with Marcus, she went to sit on the third sofa. Again, she was teasing. She sat slightly sideways and crossed her legs, ensuring both Marcus and I got a good view of her bare thigh.

"Told you, Luce. She'll be flashing us in a bit."

Sal smiled but said nothing. We talked about anything. Reminiscences of past Christmases; the better ones. The ones we'd enjoyed. The funny things that had happened. Presents we'd received.

"What's the most inappropriate present you've ever received?" Marcus asked.

I thought for a moment. Before I could answer, Sal replied.

"A pair of knickers."

We both looked at her.

"Doesn't seem inappropriate for you," Marcus said.

"Behave. They were from a guy I worked with. I hardly knew him. Wasn't in any sort of relationship with him. He handed me the present on the last working day before Christmas without a word."

"When did you open it?"

"Luckily, not on Christmas day."

"Just a pair of knickers?"

"Yup. A cheap scratchy pair. Crotchless, too."

"Ugh. That's gross. What was he thinking?"

"Whatever it was, I didn't want to know."

"I don't know how you let that one slip through your fingers."

"I avoided him like the plague. I was only temping at the time, so wasn't there long. What about you?"

I did remember one Christmas present I could have done without.

"My worst was from a girl I was with at the time. A year's membership for Weight Watchers."

"Was she trying to tell you something?"

"Well, that's how it looked."

"You've always been about the size you are now," Sal said.

"Yea. She must have wanted a beanpole."

"Was she thin?"

"Thinner than me."

"What happened?"

"I found someone else in time for New Year's Eve."

"What about you, Marcus?"

"Nothing springs to mind. Except perhaps some of the things my mother bought in her later years. She had no imagination; she always had to ask for a list. She saw us giving jokey things to each other and decided to join in. But she had no sense of humour either, so she bought things that had no meaning at all. We kept them until she went home, then ditched them."

I couldn't help watching Sally, so completely at ease. No embarrassment; no awkwardness. And she wasn't trying to hide anything. Every so often, she changed position. At one point, facing me, with her legs crossed a little too high. I could see a tiny patch of black material between her legs; she was certainly wearing knickers.

And flashing them at me. I realised she'd been flashing them at Marcus too. I wondered if it was time for me to make my exit and leave them to it. I checked the time; only about ten.

"Can I leave my car here? I'm going to need to get a taxi."

"Oh, you're staying, surely?" Sal said. "You don't need to go home."

"If you're sure. I don't want to get in the way."

I made a vague gesture to what Sal was wearing.

"Oh, don't worry. You're fine. And we'll try to keep the noise down later."

I felt myself blush.

"Honestly, Luce," Marcus said. "Stay. If you want to move bedrooms, you can."

"No... I ..."

"Don't worry, darling," Sally said with a mischievous grin. "She likes listening to us. Turns her on. Doesn't it, Luce?"

I was blushing now.

"I ..."

"Behave, you," Marcus said, wagging a finger at her.

"Or what, darling?"

"Or someone might get their bottom spanked."

"Not in front of Lucy, I won't. You wouldn't dare."

Her face was full of life; challenging him.

"No. I wouldn't want to embarrass your friend. But just you wait."

Sally blew him a kiss.

"I fancy another glass of wine," she said. "Luce?"

The coffee had sobered me up.

"Yes, please."

She found the bottle on the table empty, so got up to fetch a new one. As she walked past Marcus, he moved like lightning. She squealed as he grabbed her hand and pulled her down. She fell exactly where he wanted her. Over his lap, with her body lying on the sofa on one side; her legs hanging down on the other.

"Marcus!" she managed, in between giggles.

"So, I wouldn't dare, eh?"

He was running his hand over the skirt. It was so short, I could see the curve from her thighs to her bum now, and a hint of black material.

"Marcus ..."

She was still laughing. I noticed she was struggling, but only playfully. She made no attempt to cover herself. I watched; intrigued as to how far they would go. Would he spank her in front of me? Did I want him to?

"So, I wouldn't do it in front of Lucy?"

He was running his hand over her thigh. His fingers exploring under her skirt.

"Darling. No."
"Why not?"
"I … well … I don't want to embarrass Lucy."
Marcus looked at me and raised an eyebrow. I looked at Sal; she was protesting. But her whole manner was joyful; bubbly.
"Oh, I won't be embarrassed. I fancy watching a cheeky girl get punished."
"Lucy!" The cry was somewhere between a gasp and a giggle.
And Marcus's hand came down on her bum. Still over her skirt, but she squealed and giggled. She was still making a feeble attempt to escape, but Marcus had his arm across her back. He spanked her lightly over the skirt, running his hand over her thigh each time. He moved her to a better position; she stopped protesting and let him. He looked across at me.
"If you move to the other sofa, you'll get a better view, Luce."
"Marcus …" Sal's protestation was only a token. I took up his invitation.
"Right," he said. "This is in the way."
He pulled the short skirt over her back and tried to tuck it under his other arm, but it was a bit short. Eventually, he gripped it. I took in the view in front of me. My lover in a very revealing outfit, lying over Marcus's lap. Her skirt lifted, exposing her bum in a pair of sheer black knickers. It was exciting. I'd never watched anything like this before; not in the real world, anyway. It wasn't sex, but it was hot as hell.
Marcus began to lightly spank her. His hand coming down on each cheek, occasionally dropping to her thighs. She had ceased any struggle. He kept going, sometimes slowly, then speeding up. Sally letting out little noises and occasionally raising a leg after a rapid series of blows. I've no idea how long this went on. The skirt fell back over her a couple of times; he pulled it back. The third time it happened, he stopped.
"Sal, are you going to be a good girl?"
I heard her chuckle.
"Possibly."
"Good enough to take this off and get back on my lap?"
"I'll be naked."
"No, you won't. Not yet."

He released her and she slid back over him to her knees. Looking up at him, she undid the lacing on the front and pulled the dress off. All she was wearing now were her knickers and stockings.

"Resume the position, please."

"Yes, sir," she teased. But she did. Laying over his lap again.

He stroked her bum again, running his hands over her cheeks and her thighs. I saw her legs open. I could see she was wet.

"Legs together."

She snapped them shut and giggled. He started spanking her again, going back to the same routine as before. After a particularly long series of strokes, he stopped. Pulling her knickers down, he slid them off and threw them on the floor. If I thought he'd been spanking her already, I was wrong.

He now set to it with some style. Regular strikes, alternating cheeks, changing the site of impact. I realised I was really turned on. I could feel myself swelling. She was whimpering occasionally under the heavier strokes. But also raising her hips at times to meet his hand. She'd told me she enjoyed this; I was seeing it for myself. She was.

Marcus shifted position again and split her legs. Putting one up on the sofa, the other still hanging towards the floor. Her pussy exposed now between her spread legs. I smiled as I saw how wet she was. He set to work on her bum again. Quite hard now. Her bum had gone pink and was now taking on a red hue.

Her whimpering had increased; a little exclamation with each stroke. He gave her a heavy prolonged series of strikes, before stopping. Stroking her burning cheeks with his hand. I heard her breathing heavily. I copied their example and stayed silent for a while.

Eventually, Marcus looked at me.

"I think that's enough for now. I'd normally give her some pleasure after the pain. But not today."

I heard a frustrated moan from Sal.

"I don't mind, Marcus," I said. I was staring at the moisture glistening on her thigh. "It looks like she needs something."

"Sure?"

"Yea."

He let the hand wandering over her bum slowly creep between her legs. When his fingers hit her perineum, she gasped. When they reached her pussy, she jumped, and I heard a loud groan. They continued over her pussy until his fingers touched her clit. She almost screamed, raising her hips to give him better access. I wished for a moment that fingers were playing between my legs; I would have welcomed them.

"Well, darling. Lucy thinks you should be allowed to come. What do you think?"

"Yes, yes. Please."

"Promise you'll find a way to thank her?"

"I promise."

Before she'd finished the words, two of his fingers invaded her forcefully. She cried out and began to pant almost at once. No gentle teasing here; she didn't want that. I guessed if I hadn't been here, he'd be fucking her now. I watched as he fucked her with his fingers instead, a third running over her clit with each stroke. She was near now.

I drew an involuntary breath as his thumb pushed its way into her ass. She cried out; that seemed to be the final push. He had her impaled on his hand, and her back slowly arched as her climax came. A loud cry piercing the air, her body arching, before jerking several times. Her breath ragged, panting as she slowly sank onto him. I saw he'd removed his hand as she peaked and was now gently stroking her bum.

We sat there as she recovered. I was so worked up. I wanted to deal with it but would have to wait. After a few minutes, she chuckled and slowly slid back over his lap and dropped onto her haunches. Marcus was looking down at her. Leaning over, he kissed her.

At that moment, I felt like an intruder; I sat still. She put her arms around his neck and kissed him back passionately. They separated and she turned to me.

"Now you know what might happen if you're cheeky to Marcus."

She reached for her knickers. The dress had ended up near me and I offered it to her.

"I'm not going to put it back on, but I think I need these."

She stood up. Again, I was struck by how comfortable she was naked in front of us. Yes, she was a lover to us both, but this was the first time we'd seen her like this together. It didn't seem to bother her at all. She bent down to kiss him again.

"I need to clean up a bit."

Her wetness was still visible on her thighs.

"I need to clean my hands," said Marcus.

They headed for the loo. I sat there thinking about what I'd witnessed. Before I had time to reach any conclusions, Sal came back.

"Well?" she asked me.

"I don't know what to say."

"Did you enjoy it?"

She was watching me closely.

"Yes," I admitted. "Yes, I did. Did you two set that up?"

She shook her head.

"No. To be honest, even when I teased him, I didn't think he'd do it in front of you."

"You were wrong."

She giggled.

"I was, wasn't I?"

Marcus came back and sat by her.

"Lucy enjoyed that, darling," she said.

I blushed again; this was getting to be a habit.

"Good. Did you?"

"Couldn't you tell?"

"Of course. But was it better with Lucy watching?"

Sal looked at me for a moment.

"Yes. It was."

"You're becoming quite the exhibitionist, aren't you?"

Sally flushed.

"Something you haven't told me, Sal?"

She looked at Marcus and they shared a secret moment.

"I might tell you sometime."

He smiled and kissed her. We went back to friendly conversation. I found it difficult. I was feeling horny now and my lover was sitting virtually naked a few feet away. I did the best I could. Luckily, it was soon time for bed. After the last time, I'd come prepared. I'd brought my little quiet vibe. I knew Marcus would be worked up too. They'd be at it as soon as went to bed. I'd have to enjoy myself listening to their activities.

When they'd tidied up, we went downstairs, and they wished me a good night as we went to our rooms. I undressed and got into bed, my vibe on the side table. I heard a few muffled voices, followed by some giggles, then it went quiet. I didn't need to wait for them, I was already well on the way. I threw the duvet off, made myself comfortable and started enjoying my own body. Using the vibe on my nipples, slowly stroking my thighs.

My breath caught as the door opened. It was right in front of my open legs. Sally was standing in the doorway, naked. A wand in her hand. A big smile on her face.

"Like some help?"

"Sal …"

She closed the door and got onto the bottom of the bed, crawling towards me on her hands and knees. She knelt between my legs and put her hands on the pillow either side of my head. Hovering over me, she bent and kissed me.

"But … Marcus?" I said. "Does he …?"

"He's willing to share. I've promised I'll be back in an hour or he can punish me again." She gave me a sly grin. "So, we've got an hour and one minute."

As she kissed me again and her free hand caressed my body, I realised what she'd said.

"Sal, you're a little devil."

"Mmm. Now, what can this little devil do for her lover?"

What couldn't she do? The next hour was a flurry of fingers, tongues, vibes and orgasms. We were both beyond the need for foreplay and by the end were hot and breathless. My long build-up made my eventual orgasm one of the best I'd had for a long time. We lay for a short while in each other's arms; coming down.

"Got to go."

"How long has it been?"

She checked the clock.

"One hour and five minutes."

"So, another spanking?"

"Something a little harder, I hope."

"Sal, you really are wicked."

"Yup. I know. We'll try and keep the noise down."

"Don't worry, I don't mind. But you can leave the wand. Just in case."

The sounds coming through the wall were different from the spanking. He was using something on her; I didn't know what. But the sound it made as it struck her skin, her cries, her giggles, all fascinated me. I was soon using the wand on myself again. By the time I heard them fucking, I was ready for another orgasm. I came again at the same time I heard Sal climax.

As I was recovering, Marcus reached his orgasm too. A few giggles and chuckles followed; then it went quiet. I lay there; satisfied, happy. The day had been so good but had taken a turn I hadn't been expecting. I fell asleep wondering what I'd got myself into.

Epilogue – Sally

When the festivities were over and the decorations packed away, life returned to normal. If our life could be described as normal. After I'd been back at work for a week, I got a call from Martin. He had some new information to share with me. He agreed to visit the house the following Wednesday evening. I wasn't sure I wanted to continue the search. I'd see what Martin had found but it might be best to let it go. My father was a mystery man. I'd finally accepted it. Perhaps that was how I should leave it.

"I don't have much," Martin said after the pleasantries were over. "But I do have something intriguing."

"Fire away, Martin."

"The first thing is a death certificate. One Agnes Crother. Killed in a V2 attack on August the twenty-third, nineteen forty-four. It gives her address, so I checked the Census taken at the beginning of the war. Sure enough, she's resident at the address, where she's a lodger, listed as a single shop-girl."

"Any luck in earlier censuses?" Marcus asked.

"No. The nineteen thirty-one census was destroyed in an air-raid and she wasn't there in nineteen twenty-one. I've tried to find her birth certificate but no luck so far."

"Sounds like another dead end," I said.

"Possibly. But I had a thought. I took a closer look at the other two identities your father used. I have a colleague who specialises in old documents, so I took them to show him."

"Don't tell me, they're all forgeries."

"Unfortunately, he thinks they are. Well, some of them. Probably the birth certificates and possibly the passports. He did say they were very good; professional. He could have used those to get the other things legitimately."

"Brendan Mahoney and Paul Doyle are fictional?" Marcus asked.

"Fake identities are often based on a little truth. Such men possibly existed but he probably wasn't either."

Marcus and I looked at one another. We were getting nowhere.

"I'm not sure it's worth continuing this, Martin. We seem to be getting more questions than answers."

"It's not unusual, I'm afraid. But I did find something else."

"What's that?"

"I noticed the Brendan Mahoney passport had regular stamps from Nice airport. It was the most frequent place he visited by far. Why?"

"Do you know?"

"Possibly, but again, it's a little tenuous."

"Go on."

"I tried the censuses for the Nice area for the seventies, eighties and nineties. The French carry out a census every five years. From the late seventies onwards, a Brendan Mahoney is listed living under a residency permit at an address in Beaulieu-sur-Mer."

I thought quickly, trying to work out what this meant.

"He had a house in France?"

"It would seem so."

I couldn't help marvelling at my father's nerve. This meant he had a home and family in England and now, it appeared, a home in France. It seemed possible; after all, he'd kept so many secrets from us, what was one more? Martin broke my thoughts.

"There is one more thing," he said.

"Go on."

"There are other residents at that address."

My heart missed a beat.

"Genevieve Mahoney, listed as his wife ..."

"Oh, God."

"… and from the late eighties, a son, Jacques Mahoney."

Author's Note

I would like to thank all those involved in helping me bring this story to the page. You know who you are, and I will be eternally grateful.

The adventures of Sally, Marcus and Lucy will continue in the third book in the Kinky Companions series. I hope you'll join them.

To keep in touch with my writing, you can visit my website, where you can subscribe to my newsletter or blog, or follow me on social media.

Website: www.alexmarkson.com
Twitter: @amarksonerotica
Facebook: Alex Markson
Goodreads: Alex Markson

Alex Markson
February 2020

Printed in Great Britain
by Amazon